How can I be falling in love with this man? I barely know him. I must remember he's a Yankee!

Rob took her hand in his. Julia inhaled sharply at the touch of his warm skin, but did not pull out of his grasp.

"Ahh," he murmured as he caressed the back of her hand. "I see that they are still cold. I will remedy the situation."

He gently released her, then he reached inside his coat and withdrew a small package.

She quickly untied the ribbon and pulled away the paper. "Gloves!" she exclaimed, fondling the thick fleece-lined suede.

"But these are quite expensive," she whispered. "It would be wicked of me to accept them."

"It would be *very* wicked of you to reject them," he murmured.

His seductive voice sent a delicious chill down her spine.

"True, Major," she replied, pulling on the gloves with satisfaction. "I *do* try to avoid wickedness whenever possible."

* * *

Beloved Enemy
Harlequin Historical #701—April 2004

Praise for Mary Schaller writing as Tori Phillips

"Phillips is a new star on the historical romance horizon:
she's literate, witty and tells a good story."
—*Publishers Weekly*

The Dark Knight
"Filled with the turbulent details of religious intolerance
in England, this carefully crafted romance…proves that
love is the most powerful emotion when it resides in the
hearts of strong men and women."
—*Romantic Times*

One Knight in Venice
"Intense and soul searching, *One Night in Venice* swings
from the dark side of human nature through the
treacherous inquisition to the admirable characters
willing to face suffering or even death to save others."
—*Affaire de Coeur*

Lady of the Knight
"In this fun tale, Ms. Phillips weaves an
adventurous story of chase and budding love
and puts in some lessons along the way."
—*Romantic Times*

BELOVED ENEMY

MARY SCHALLER

HARLEQUIN®

TORONTO • NEW YORK • LONDON
AMSTERDAM • PARIS • SYDNEY • HAMBURG
STOCKHOLM • ATHENS • TOKYO • MILAN • MADRID
PRAGUE • WARSAW • BUDAPEST • AUCKLAND

ISBN 0-373-29301-1

BELOVED ENEMY

Copyright © 2004 by Mary W. Schaller

This edition published by arrangement with Harlequin Books S.A.

® and TM are trademarks of the publisher. Trademarks indicated with ® are registered in the United States Patent and Trademark Office, the Canadian Trade Marks Office and in other countries.

Visit us at www.eHarlequin.com

Printed in U.S.A.

Please address questions and book requests to:
Harlequin Reader Service
U.S.: 3010 Walden Ave., P.O. Box 1325, Buffalo, NY 14269
Canadian: P.O. Box 609, Fort Erie, Ont. L2A 5X3

At my birth, the front of heaven was full of fiery shapes.
—William Shakespeare
King Henry IV, Part I

This book is dedicated with lots of love to our first granddaughter, Shelby Washburne Williams, who was born on July 29, 2002—the hottest day of the year.

Chapter One

"My name, dear saint, is hateful to myself, because it is an enemy to thee."

—*Romeo and Juliet*
William Shakespeare

Alexandria, Virginia
December 1863

"I do declare, Carolyn, this is your most harebrained scheme ever."

Looking up from the cream-colored invitation in her hand, Julia Chandler fixed a properly reproving glare on her younger sister. At least, Julia hoped her expression looked stern, though she had to admit she was secretly as excited as Carolyn. The last time Julia had held such a coveted invitation as this one was two years ago. "How did you get this?"

Her sister fiddled with a broad band of green satin ribbon that circled the skirt of her day dress. Though she studied her fingers, the two bright patches of pink in Carolyn's cheeks betrayed the girl's feelings.

Julia silently reread the words written in elegant copperplate script:

The pleasure of your company is requested at a Masked Ball upon the evening of the thirty-first of December at nine o'clock, given at the home of Mr. George Winstead for the pleasure of his family and friends.

She breathed deeply to calm the butterflies that skittered in her stomach.

"I did not realize that we had resumed our friendship with the Winsteads," she continued aloud in a feigned arch tone. "I am sure that it has not slipped Mrs. Winstead's mind that our family is still very much in sympathy with the Confederate cause."

Shrugging her shoulders, Carolyn scraped her slipper over the polished floorboards of the girls' upstairs bedroom. A sly smile crept across her lips. "Wouldn't it just make that old Melinda Winstead itch if she knew we attended her grand party?"

Julia could picture the pique of the disagreeable Winstead daughter. Such boldness on the Chandlers' part would definitely twist the nose of that jumped-up Yankee chit. Melinda deserved a tweaking after all the hateful things she had said about the Chandlers, especially after Frank Shaffer's death at Manassas. Clearing her throat, Julia fanned herself with the invitation to the premier social event of the Christmas season.

"Tell me, Carolyn. How did you come by this? I don't believe for a minute that it was delivered to our doorstep."

Carolyn's grin broadened. "Found it," she replied. Her hazel eyes sparkled with unsuppressed mischief.

Julia sighed. Carolyn was notorious for "finding" all sorts of opportune items. "Where exactly?"

Her sister smoothed the dress ribbon that she had worried into a wrinkle. "On the paving stones by Dr. Brown's carriage step. A big ole envelope was just lying there in the mud. I had to save it, you know. It could have been something *very* important," she added with the innocent air of a canary-fed cat.

Julia narrowed her green eyes at her little sister. "And how is it that you happened to be walking past the Browns' when their home isn't anywhere near Market Square, where you were *supposed* to be shopping?"

Licking her lower lip, Carolyn finally looked directly at Julia. "'Cause I saw the Winsteads' butler drive by in the family carriage holding a basketful of these envelopes."

"And you followed him like a common beggar," Julia concluded, picturing the shameless scene in her mind.

Carolyn nodded without an ounce of regret. "It didn't take the brain of a jaybird to know what he had under his arm. He sat on that carriage box with such an important look on his face. Lordy, Julia, no one in Alexandria can think of anything else except that party."

Julia hated to agree. Northern-born George Winstead, part owner of the new railroad line into the Federal City, had become very rich during the past two years. He demonstrated his Yankee-bred manners in the lavish way he spent his war-fed wealth. His New Year's Ball had been the talk of the town both in the streets and behind fans at Sunday church services, even among the most secessionist of families like the Chandlers. Julia admitted to herself that she would love to attend, but since the Winsteads were firmly Yankees, her parents had not spoken to them since April 1861. She looked down at the card again.

"You know we can't possibly go." Julia sighed with

honest regret. After mourning for her sweetheart for the past two years, she was ready to wear a pretty silken gown again and to dance until dawn as she had done briefly in those far-off days before the wretched war had ended all gaiety and laughter—at least in the Chandler household.

Carolyn pursed her lips. "Speak for yourself, Julia. You can stay at home and think of Frank Shaffer, but I do not intend to miss this chance—not when I have an invitation in my hand. I've never been to a ball like you have. And the way that horrid Mr. Lincoln is going on and on with this war, I highly doubt that I shall ever go to a party before I am old and gray. Sit by the fire, if you want, but I intend to waltz till I die." She stuck out her chin.

Julia lifted one of her auburn brows. "You know there will be nothing but Unionists at the Winsteads' party. I thought you would sooner die than be caught near a Yankee."

Yankees! The very word was bitter on Julia's tongue. She couldn't imagine herself dancing with one of those people who had killed so many fine young Southern boys—like Frank, who had kissed Julia once on the cheek and quickened her heart to love.

Carolyn wiggled her nose. "I don't intend to talk with them—just dance with them." She giggled. "And I do intend to stuff myself silly with sweets. See if I don't. Mmm! Think of it! The Winsteads are bound to serve jelly cake and macaroons from Shuman's Bakery. And there will be nougats, frozen charlottes, gingerbread—and caramels." She rolled the delicious word around in her mouth. "Don't *you* miss eating caramels?"

Julia's mouth watered. Caramels were her special downfall. Ever since the Federal Army had marched into Alexandria in 1861, Mother refused to allow her daughters to patronize Randolph's Confectionery Shop just because of a political disagreement with the owner. As if eating a simple caramel was a treasonous act against the Confederacy!

Julia gave herself a shake. She must remain firm on the side of propriety for Carolyn's sake, as well as loyal to Frank's hallowed memory. "You'll be caught before you've put both feet inside the Winsteads' door. Think of the scandal," she added, though she knew that her sister didn't give a fig for any commotion she might stir up.

"Pooh!" Carolyn blew a blond wisp of a curl out of her face. "Has your eyesight grown so dim?" She pointed to the invitation. "It says it's a *masked* ball. We could go in disguise. We'll wear hoods and look divinely mysterious. No one will recognize us, and all the handsomest boys will want to dance with us. They won't resist!" She hugged herself at the prospect.

The more Carolyn talked, the more Julia's resolve weakened. The lively music of a Virginia reel played in her mind. Her toes tapped inside her slippers. She could almost taste those caramels. And laughter! When was the last time she had really laughed out loud? Not for two years, since she received word that Frank had died in a Virginia farmer's field.

"You've read too many of Mr. Dickens's novels, Carolyn. Your logic is chopped like turnips."

Instead of being repentant for her flighty taste in literature, Carolyn slid off her footstool and knelt at Julia's feet. She gave her sister a triumphant smile. "You *know* you want to go, too. I can see it in your eyes, Julia. Don't you want to have at least *one* adventure in your life, instead of just reading about them? No one will ever know."

Julia fired her last desperate argument for common sense. "That's where you are wrong. We'll have to tell Perkins," she said, referring to the Chandlers' serving man, who acted as the family's butler, coachman and occasional gardener. "We cannot possibly go gallivanting around Alexandria in the dark without an escort. The streets aren't safe, even with the provost guards out. Perkins won't approve at all, and he'll tell Papa, sure as you're born."

Carolyn twirled one of her side curls around her forefinger. "Leave Perkins to me. I'll promise him a bagful of macaroons, or something just as nice. And we'll leave the ball before midnight. Please, Julia. Say you'll go with me. There won't be another party like this one in a year of Sundays. Don't let those horrid Yankees steal away our gaiety. Kick up your heels—just once. I *dare* you."

Carolyn's challenge struck home. Julia was tired of living behind curtains drawn against the prying eyes of the insolent Yankee soldiers who daily sauntered past the Chandlers' house on Prince Street. She was tired of the plain fare that nightly graced the family's supper table because Mother refused to patronize vendors who courted the Yankee trade—and most of Alexandria's merchants did.

Julia was sick of wearing dark clothes in perpetual mourning for distant relatives who had been killed at Fredericksburg, Winchester and Gettysburg. She touched the locket that hung from a black ribbon around her neck. Most of all, wanted to heal the wound in her heart left by Frank's death. The curl of his brown hair inside the silver heart was all that remained of the charming boy with poetry on his lips and a song in his heart. Frank had taught her how to polka and encouraged her dreams of becoming a teacher.

But that was back in 1861. A lifetime ago. The guilty truth was that Julia could barely recall what Frank Shaffer looked like, even though she had promised to be his sweetheart when he marched off to join the 17th Virginia Infantry. Carolyn was right. Julia had allowed the Yankees to steal the joy of living from her soul. Enough was enough!

She looked down at the sixteen-year-old's upturned face and smiled. "All right, lady-bird, you have won me over with your Jezebel tongue. I'll go to this ball, but *only* to keep you out of trouble. I have no intention to touch a Yankee, much less dance with one."

Leaping to her feet with a flurry of petticoats, Carolyn gave her sister a loud, wet kiss on the cheek. "Pooh! You're going for the music and the caramels; I knew they would turn your head. I can read you like a book."

She certainly hoped not, Julia thought with an inward sigh. Carolyn would be shocked if she knew of the passionate dreams that Julia locked within her imagination.

"Begging the major's pardon, but may I take the liberty of asking what are the major's plans for celebrating the turning of the year?" Behind his clipped brown mustache, Lieutenant Benjamin Johnson grinned down at his somber first cousin.

Robert Montgomery, condemned to a desk job in the Office of Military Intelligence since his return from medical leave, looked up from the sheaf of field reports that he held. His irrepressible relative snapped a salute. Rob was not amused.

"You take too many liberties, Lieutenant," Rob muttered, hoping this mild reprimand would send the youngster scurrying back to his own paper-littered desktop. Ben exercised far too much familiarity during working hours.

His cousin only grinned wider. "Indeed, so I was often told when we attended dear old Yale. But the question still remains. Are you planning to visit the family or stay in Washington to ring in the New Year?''

Rob shuddered inside his blue uniform frock coat. His last trip home to Rhinebeck, New York, following his release from the hospital, had been an unmitigated disaster. Mama had done nothing but stare with open pity at his smashed right hand, while sighing with melodramatic fervor and moaning over her "poor baby boy." Meanwhile his father had used Rob's every waking moment to harangue his recuperating son into switching from the army to politics. "There's a new wind blowing through this great land," Jubel Montgomery had reiterated ad nauseam. "And the Republican Party will lead the way."

"No," Rob snapped at Ben. "I shall remain in Washington." Where it would be peaceful. He pretended to return to his papers.

Instead of retreating, Ben leaned closer. "As I thought. Therefore, would the major care to join a company of bright young bloods on December the thirty-first?" He patted his breast pocket with satisfaction. "In here, I hold the key to a night of music and frivolity among the prettiest flowers that grow in Alexandria. That's Virginia, sir. Virginia, where the girls are sweet as cream—and...and as pure as wholesome milk," he added swiftly when Rob glared at him.

Rob narrowed his brown eyes. "Need I remind you that we are, at this precise moment, on the soil of Virginia, fighting those damned Virginians? Are you suggesting that we feast with our enemies? I find that idea a highly—" he groped for the right word "—treasonable notion. We are speaking of Southerners, Lieutenant, a breed of pigheaded, uncouth Rebels. I detest them all."

Ben's maddening good humor only increased. "You speak the truth in general, but these *particular* Virginian posies are fine, true and loyal to the Union. They are the delightful daughters and sisters of many of our fellow soldiers. They come from families who had the good sense to ignore the rabble cry of states' rights—whatever *that* notion may be. Now they give aid and succor to us poor, homesick fellows.'' His brown eyes twinkled. ''Lord knows, we *do* need aid and succor from these most delightful ladies.''

''Join their company then, and may they give you—'' Rob paused, banished the lusty thought that rose unbidden in his love-starved brain, then continued ''—*some* of what you desire. I intend to stay in my rooms at Ebbitt's and read something edifying. I am no fit company for ladies.'' He covered over his paralyzed hand with his good one, then turned back to decipher the hen-scratching written by a female undercover agent operating in St. Louis.

Ben had the audacity to remain in front of Rob's desk. Leaning over the stacks of reports, he said in a low voice, ''Not all women are like your recent fiancée. You would find the truth of that, Rob, if you would deign to return to civilized society once again. You were once a lion among the ladies in New Haven. Word of your former exploits among the petticoats has preceded you here, sir.'' His voice sank to a whisper. ''It was your arm the Rebels shot up, *not* your charm.''

Rob gritted his teeth. He had a good mind to plant his polished boot squarely in his cousin's backside. He dropped his mangled hand below the level of the desktop, and thrust it into his coat pocket. Out of sight, out of mind. How dare this upstart puppy speak on the one subject that Rob never mentioned in public? Lucy Van Tassel's scathing ''I will not marry half a man'' screamed in Rob's nightmares and reverberated down the black tunnels of his memory.

He sneered at Ben. "You have no idea of women, Lieutenant. Underneath all those pretty smiles and lilting words, they are vicious, selfish creatures, vain and greedy. They are interested in a man only if he is young, handsome, wealthy—and whole."

Ben opened his mouth to protest but another voice cut him off. Colonel James Lawrence strode out of the doorway that led to his inner office. "Nor, it seems, do *you* know women, Major Montgomery."

Rob rose to his feet in the presence of his commanding officer. The colonel regarded him from under white bushy eyebrows. He blew through his large walrus mustache. "Lieutenant Johnson may be wet behind his ears, Major, but in this case, he makes a good point. You have stayed away from society for too long. It's high time you stopped feeling sorry for yourself, and start living among your fellow human beings again."

Hot blood rose up Rob's neck. A vein throbbed in his temple, though he held his anger in check. "I will take the colonel's opinion under advisement, sir."

Lawrence tapped the side of his nose. "Indeed, you shall, and sooner than you think. On the thirty-first of December, you will accompany the lieutenant and whomever else goes with him to this…this… Where is it you are going, Johnson?"

Ben suppressed his grin. "A ball, sir. A masked ball, given at the gracious home of Mr. George Winstead."

The colonel cocked his head. "Winstead? The railroad man?"

Ben nodded. "I do believe the gentleman is active in that particular business venture, sir."

The colonel returned his attention to the fuming Rob. "Very good, then. Major, you *will* attend this ball with the lieutenant. Do you understand me, sir?"

Rob clenched his good hand at his side. "Is the colonel giving me a direct order, sir?"

Lawrence flashed a brief half smile. "I am indeed, Major. You will dress in your best; you will act like a gentleman to all and you will remain at this ball for no less than three hours. Do I make myself clear?"

"Perfectly, sir," Rob said between tight lips.

"Good! Lieutenant Johnson, I will want a full report of the major's behavior on January first." The colonel turned back toward his office.

Ben snapped another salute. "Yes, sir!"

"And enjoy yourselves, gentlemen," the colonel added over his shoulder. "That is an order." He shut the door behind him. One of the civilian clerks snickered behind his ledger book.

Rob shot a filthy look at his cousin. "I presume you are satisfied now that you have made me look the fool, Lieutenant?"

Ben refused to shake his good spirits even in the face of Rob's anger. "Perfectly, Major." In a lower tone, he added. "Cheer up, Rob. It's only a dance, not a battlefield."

Rob returned to his seat and shuffled his papers into a jumble. "I may be ordered to go to this ball, Lieutenant, but I'll be damned if I'll dance."

Ben touched two fingers to his forehead. "See you in hell, Rob Montgomery," he replied, giving him the soldiers' traditional salute.

Chapter Two

Clara Lightfoot Chandler couldn't concentrate on her embroidery hoop, not when she had such an important matter on her mind. Yet she knew she had to reveal the subject carefully, or else her husband might not agree with her wonderful plan.

She sighed audibly, then stole a quick glance at the distinguished man seated across the parlor. Dr. Jonah Chandler continued to read his *Alexandria Gazette* without so much as lifting a brow in her direction. Clara drummed her bitten nails against the rosewood arm of her cushioned chair. She sighed again, this time a little louder. Jonah turned a page and continued his reading. Unable to bear her husband's obvious refusal to give her his attention, Clara pulled her handkerchief from her sleeve and sniffed into it.

Without looking up from the newspaper, Jonah asked, "Did you want your laudanum bottle, my dear?"

Clara slammed her hoop into her sewing basket that sat on the crowded marble-topped table beside her chair. Her assorted knickknacks rattled. "No, indeed, Dr. Chandler, but I do require your immediate and undivided attention, if you please," she snapped.

He lowered the *Gazette,* then neatly folded it before he said, "Very well, my dear, what crisis do we face now? Is there another drunken soldier on our doorstep, or is it merely burned bread in the kitchen?"

Clara clenched her teeth. The man could be so exasperating. Her temple throbbed; another headache would plague her all afternoon. "This is a serious problem. What are we going to do about Julia?"

At this, the doctor did raise his bushy brows. "Whatever in the world has Julia done? It's Carolyn that usually puts you into such a pet."

Clara allowed this remark to slide over her just as she had done for the past twenty-three years of her marriage. "Julia's birthday will come round next month," she began.

The doctor smiled. "Is that a fact? And how does she want to celebrate the event? We could afford a small party, I suppose. Nothing lavish, mind you."

Now both her temples pounded against Clara's skull. Was it any wonder that she was forced to rely on the solace of opium to keep her mind clear? She glared at Jonah. "Don't talk to me of such frippery, Dr. Chandler. I am not at all interested in Julia's birthday, but her *wedding.* She is almost twenty-one and *still* a spinster."

Jonah folded his hands over his stomach and twiddled his thumbs. "I believe she is still mourning for young Shaffer."

Clara pinched the bridge of her nose in an effort to cut off the rising pain behind her eyes. "That is *exactly* my point. Frank has been cold in the ground for two years. She's wept over that boy for long enough. Thanks to this horrible war, Julia has been unable to go out into society to meet any eligible men especially now that the streets of Alexandria are simply crawling with hordes of Yankees.

She should have been wed a year ago, at least. I was barely seventeen when I married you.''

A sad smile crossed the doctor's face. "That young, were you? I had quite forgotten," he murmured softly.

Clara pursed her lips. "There are a number of things you have forgotten over the years, Jonah, but leave that be." She withdrew a folded piece of writing paper from her skirt pocket. "Thankfully, I have given the matter a great deal of thought, and I have found the solution. Cousin Payton can marry Julia." She held out his letter to her husband.

With a sigh, Jonah reached across the wine-red oriental carpet for it. He wiped his spectacles with his pocket handkerchief before reading Payton Norwood's brief message informing them that he had assumed complete charge of Belmont-on-the-James, the family tobacco plantation, following probate of his late father's will.

Clara leaned against the tufted chair back. Dear Payton was a definite cut above that feckless Shaffer boy. A second cousin on her mother's side of the family, he had the blood of Virginia's first families running through his veins. Suspecting that he was now able to support a wife, Clara had written to him the minute Payton was out of formal mourning.

"He and Julia are nearly the same age and they have known each other since they were children. Payton will be a perfect match for her," she concluded with a satisfied smile.

Jonah put down the letter and looked across at his wife. "What does Julia think of this idea?"

Clara took a deep breath, then assumed her brightest expression. "She doesn't know it yet, of course. How could I have possibly asked her if she wanted to marry

Payton until I had sounded out the boy's ability to provide for her?''

A small frown line deepened between Jonah's tired gray eyes. ''It seems to me that we should give Julia's feelings some consideration. After all, she's the one who would have to live with him for the rest of her life.''

Clara smiled with fondness. ''She couldn't possibly feel anything but sheer joy. Dear Payton is a fine, handsome man, his home is a jewel and his lineage is impeccable. Julia will be treated like a queen by Richmond's society.'' Clara already envisioned long visits to Belmont and all the delightful parties she could enjoy in the Confederacy's capital. ''Julia won't be a virtual prisoner in her home there as she is here,'' she added with an arch look at her husband.

Jonah rang the silver handbell that sat on his reading table. ''Let us see what Julia has to say.''

Hettie Perkins, the family's cook and now housekeeper since the war had forced the Chandlers to economize, slipped through the parlor door. ''Yes, sir?'' she asked.

As if she doesn't already know what we want, Clara thought. She was sure Hettie had her ear pressed against the keyhole ever since she opened her mouth. Aloud, Clara asked, ''Where is Julia?''

Hettie folded her long fingers over her apron. ''I expect she's in her room, reading a book. That's what she does most days about this time.''

Clara made a face. Julia read entirely too much when she should be plying her needle or practicing her music. What good did such serious tomes like Nott's *Indigenous Races of the Earth* or the plays of Shakespeare do for her but weaken her eyesight? She should have turned her quick mind to more practical studies like the *Accomplished Gentlewoman's Companion*, written by Mr. William Parks.

That bible of cookery had served hundreds of Virginia brides for over a century. Clara swore by her own dog-eared copy. Why couldn't Julia read that, instead of filling her head with obtuse rubbish?

It was all that Shaffer boy's fault. He had encouraged Julia's book mania.

Leaning forward in his chair, Jonah told Hettie, "Please ask Julia to come down here—now."

"And don't dilly-dally along the way, Hettie," Clara added. She felt that Hettie acted far too independent for her position. It was up to Clara to always remind Hettie who she was, even if Jonah had given freedom to all their servants last January. What a foolish thing that Lincoln had done when he issued his Emancipation Proclamation! It was like letting snakes out of Pandora's box. Now there was no chance of putting things back into their proper order.

Hettie smiled. "A terrapin walks fast enough to go visiting," she murmured one of her annoying maxims as she disappeared into the hall.

A heavy silence descended upon the Chandler parlor while the doctor and his wife awaited the arrival of their elder daughter. The grandfather clock, standing in the corner, ticked away each minute with solemn steadiness. Outside, a horse-drawn carriage creaked past their house. The heavy burgundy window drapes in the parlor muffled most of Alexandria's noise in the late morning. Twiddling his thumbs, Jonah stared up at the ceiling. It was too bad that her husband's medical practice had decreased since the start of the war. Many of his former patients said they preferred to be treated by Yankee doctors. The family should have moved to Richmond two years ago.

The rattle of the door latch announced Julia's arrival. Her reading glasses were perched on the end of her nose.

"Papa? Mother?" She looked from one silent parent to the other. "You wanted to see me?"

Jonah beckoned her into the room. "Come, child. Close the door, Hettie, before the drafts kill us all."

Clara noticed that the cook remained inside the parlor once the door was firmly shut. And who was minding their dinner, she wondered.

The doctor cleared his throat. "Your mother and I were discussing your future, Julia," he began.

Clara rolled her blue eyes. At this rate, Jonah would blather on for a half hour before he got to the point. When he paused, she took command of the conversation. "The long and short of it is that we plan to arrange a marriage for you."

Julia sank down on the ottoman. "Marriage?" she repeated. Her green eyes turned a jade color—a clear sign that she was deeply moved.

"Surely you have gotten over Frank by now," her father suggested.

Touching her silver locket, Julia moistened her lips. "Yes, I suppose I have," she answered, "but I thought there would be plenty of time for courtship once the war was over."

Clara shook her head at this notion. "That event could be years from now, unless the Yankees come to their senses and give up, which I highly doubt, or else that nasty Lincoln gets himself defeated in the next election, which I sincerely pray for. In the meantime, all our boys are dying like flies in the autumn from bullets and fevers and I don't know what all." She dabbed her hankie to her eyelids for effect. "Leaving you to wither on the vine until it is too late. I declare, it is more than a body can stand!"

Biting her lips, Julia rose and went to Clara's side. She massaged her temples, as she had done for many years.

"There, there, Mother, don't take on so. It will make you sick again."

Closing her eyes, Clara allowed her shoulders to relax under Julia's gentle ministrations. Why couldn't Carolyn have the same light touch? What was Clara going to do once Julia was married and living down in southern Virginia?

Through her lowered lashes, Clara saw that her husband gave her a quick professional look before he returned to the subject at hand. "You should be married, Julia. We—that is, your mother has found a solution, we think," he ended in a mutter.

Opening her eyes, Clara patted Julia's hand. "A *husband,* Jonah. You make him sound like a prescription." She smiled up at her daughter. "I have just received word from your cousin Payton that he has come into his daddy's inheritance. Belmont Plantation! Isn't that just grand news?"

Julia blinked, looked quickly at her father, then back to her mother. "You want me to marry Payton Norwood?" She backed away until a footstool stopped her. She dropped down on it with an unladylike "thump".

Clara frowned. Julia could be so tiresome at times. "Of course I mean Payton. He's a delightful boy and, more to the point, he can support you. You can't ask for much more than that these days."

Julia continued to goggle at her mother like a frog out of the pond. "But *why* must I get married now? I am more than willing to wait for happier times. There is no rush." She touched her locket again.

Clara narrowed her eyes. Julia was usually tractable, not like Carolyn. Clara was not used to this daughter arguing a point. "If you wait until those politicians down in Richmond do something more than chew tobacco and whittle wood, it will be doomsday, and you will be too old to attract a decent husband. No, missy, it is high time that you were the mistress of your own house and had a few babies to tend.''

Julia coughed. ''With Payton? But he's so…so…stupid. Nothing like Frank at all.''

What had gotten into Julia? Clara thought. She was always so easy to manage. ''Payton received the very best education at the College of William and Mary. He will be the *perfect* husband for you.''

Julia drew herself up. ''Mother, Payton Norwood is a fool. Always has been. He thinks of nothing except horses, card-playing and heaven only knows what other amusements. I highly doubt he has the skills to run that tobacco farm of his. If he loses his overseer, he'll be ruined within a year. Why isn't he in the army, like…like Frank, and all the other boys? He talks of Southern independence and how any Southerner worth his salt can lick three Yankees before supper. So why hasn't *he* joined up and proven himself?''

Clara shook her head. ''Don't be such a ninny, Julia. Payton has a large landholding and over a hundred slaves to manage. Of course, he is exempt from military duty. His work on the plantation is as good a service to the Confederacy as joining the army. Why, he could get shot or captured. Payton's too fine a man for that sort of treatment!''

Julia's eyes turned even greener. ''But Frank Shaffer wasn't good enough except as cannon fodder? Is that what you mean, Mother? As I recall from our last visit to Belmont four years ago, Payton was a bully and a coward. I doubt that he has changed much since then. No, Mother, I will not marry Payton.''

Julia's defiance struck Clara like a lightning bolt. She

clutched her bosom. "Julia! How dare you call your cousin such hurtful things! Lies! You just don't know what's good for you. If you spent less time with your nose in those books, and more on family matters, you would understand. Oh, Jonah, I think I'm having palpitations of the heart. I truly do. Hettie, help me to my room. Julia, now do you see what you have done to me? Oh, truly I might die and then how would you feel? So ungrateful for all I have done for you. Jonah, talk some sense to this child."

Clara grabbed Hettie's arm for support. Dr. Chandler took her other arm. Over his shoulder, he said to Julia, "You know your mother can't take this excitement. I'm surprised at you. We will invite Payton to visit here at his earliest convenience. Then you will see how he has matured. There, there, Clara. You will not die before dinner, I promise you."

Though she truly felt faint, Clara smiled inwardly. Once again, she had triumphed over her family. Sending for Payton was a *brilliant* idea. Julia could be married before she turned twenty-one and came into Grandmother Lightfoot's legacy.

Julia slammed into her bedroom. Carolyn looked up from the alterations of her sister's old ball gown. "What was the buzz in the parlor this time?" she asked, threading her needle with care. "Usually I am the one on the griddle fire."

Julia stared out the window at the winter-shrouded garden below. Mother's pink rosebushes stretched up their stark thorny limbs to catch the feeble rays of the midwinter sun. *My soul is as dead as those roses.* "Mother has got it in her head to marry me off."

"Oh?" Carolyn picked up her thimble. "So who is the lucky fellow?"

Julia made a face at the windowpane. "Payton." His name tasted like ashes in her mouth.

Carolyn gasped. Her thimble dropped from her lap and rolled across the floorboards. "She's not serious!"

Julia faced her shocked little sister. She folded her arms across her bosom as if that action would protect her from her odious cousin. "She is, and dear Papa was in agreement, as he always is when she works herself into a state."

Carolyn looked truly stricken. "What will you do?"

"I told her no." Julia should have told her that she wanted to be a teacher, but she'd never stand for that any more than Payton would.

Carolyn's mouth dropped open. "You said 'no' to Mother? I can hardly believe it. You've never crossed her before."

Julia sank down on the pink satin daybed. "I know, but not this time. It's too important a decision. When she told me her wonderful plans, I just blurted out 'no.' Mother is not accustomed to hearing the other side of any argument, much less conceding to it. My refusal staggered her."

Rolling her eyes, Carolyn shivered under her shawl. "I can imagine."

Julia gave her a twisted smile. "Both Papa and Hettie had to help her upstairs to bed. I expect she's dosed up with laudanum by now. I suspect that she has already sent a letter to Payton telling him to run up here and make me his wife."

"Perhaps he's changed," Carolyn suggested, though the wrinkle of her nose indicated that she thought otherwise.

"As much as a fish can turn into a bird." Julia shook her head. "Payton was nasty when he was a little boy, and he was even more disagreeable when we last saw him."

"You can't marry Payton! You'll die of boredom—or worse."

Julia curled her hands into fists. "I know that, but Mother is set like a stone."

Out of nowhere, a wicked idea flashed through her mind. Without allowing a moment of consideration, Julia grabbed on to it like a rope out of quicksand.

She narrowed her eyes. "You know, lady-bird, I am so very, very glad that you 'found' that invitation to the ball. I intend to have the best time of my life there." She would see to it that Payton Norwood would never marry her.

Carolyn's mouth quivered. "Julia, you aren't planning to…I mean you can't…you wouldn't…"

A sly smile played across her lips. "What won't I do?"

Her sister's gaze searched Julia's face. "You wouldn't—" her voice sank into a whisper "—ruin yourself with a man at the ball so you didn't have to marry Payton, would you?"

Julia had little notion exactly what polite society meant by being "ruined by a man," though she knew from her reading that the experience was enough to blacken a girl's name forever. Whatever it was, she would find some nice Yankee boy—there had to be at least one there—to do it to her. *That* would knock Mother's loathsome plan into a cocked hat.

She barked a harsh laugh. "I have no idea what you mean, Carolyn."

Chapter Three

Christmas Day 1863 was observed by the Chandler family with the same rituals that they had followed every other Christmas: services at St. Paul's Church; a Christmas turkey stuffed with the traditional cornbread and oysters, and a crystal bowl full of cranberry sauce; gifts from Papa; eggnog and favorite carols sung around the piano with a few friends, whose political sympathies were in agreement with the Chandlers' Confederate ones.

On the morning of the Winstead ball, Julia and Carolyn pleaded joint headaches. "Too much Christmas frivolity," Julia whispered to Mother when she came to inquire after their health. In reality, the girls were in a fever of excitement, while they attempted to rest up and prepare their clothes for the evening's prohibited adventure. The daytime hours crept by at a snail's pace.

Hettie, by necessity, knew their plans since she had to let them in the back door upon their return from the party. Nevertheless, she gave the sisters a stern look when she brought up their suppers on a tray.

"You are asking for trouble," she scolded them in a low voice while she watched them wolf down cold turkey, buttered bread and pickles.

"Yes," replied Carolyn with glee in her eyes. "We are very wicked. Isn't it grand?"

Hettie examined the two black velvet half-masks that Julia had created from an old muff. "You be sure to act respectable, no matter what the devil tells you to do. That Winstead house will be full of no-good Yankees. I've heard stories about those men that would make your blood run cold."

Carolyn glanced up from her supper. "Oh, do tell one!"

Julia didn't want to know anything more about the Yankees. One of those men was going to "ruin" her tonight, and that was all she could stand to think about. She nudged Carolyn. "Not now. We have enough on our minds as it is. You can tell us the gruesome horrors when we get back, Hettie."

The cook picked up a silver-backed brush and began to rearrange Carolyn's hair. With quick, expert fingers she wound her blond curls into fashionable corkscrews on each side of her face. "Neither of you has a lick of sense in your heads. I feel it in my bones that tonight's foolishness will come to a bad end. You have no business going where you're not invited. Virginia girls mixing with Northern trash is just like washing good china in a mud puddle. Like my mama always said: crows and corn can't grow in the same field."

Julia's skin felt dry and scratchy. She didn't want to think about those Northern boys and their reputed evil ways—not yet. She placed her hand on top of Hettie's. "Please don't spoil our fun tonight. I haven't been to a party since Christmas of 1860, and Carolyn has never gone to one at all." She crossed her fingers behind her back before saying, "I promise that we will be as good as gold and twice as nice, won't we, Carolyn?" she added in a warning note to her rambunctious little sister.

Carolyn only nodded as she stared at herself in the looking glass. "First time I have ever had my hair put up. Oh, Hettie, you are a wonder worker."

Lively music and golden candlelight spilled out of the Winstead windows and flowed down the curving brick steps. Julia and Carolyn quickly handed over their velvet, fur-collared cloaks to the waiting maid in the side chamber that had been reserved for the ladies' use. With suppressed giggles, they slipped on their low satin pumps and hurried into the wide central hallway of the Winstead mansion. Julia stretched her mouth into a false smile while her stomach roiled at the prospect of meeting a live Yankee soldier face-to-face.

Great swatches of berry-rich holly looped up the carved wooden balustrade of the main staircase. Grave-faced servers passed among the revelers balancing silver trays of champagne glasses on white-gloved hands. Carolyn snatched one of the brimming crystal flutes before Julia could stop her.

"Oh, it tickles my nose!" Carolyn giggled. She took a second sip.

"Only one glass, mind you," Julia cautioned her with faint trepidation. "You promised to behave. Remember, we must not draw any attention to ourselves or we will be caught. Tonight, you will have to be invisible—and don't forget, we are supposed to be Yankees."

Carolyn made a face under her half mask. "Don't be such a wet dish rag, Julia. I'll be so good, you won't recognize me."

With that, Carolyn slipped through the throng and disappeared from view before Julia could also remind her sister that they must leave by eleven-thirty so that Hettie and Perkins, who was warming his feet in the Winstead servants' hall, could get the sleep they needed for the following day's chores. With trembling fingers, Julia tightened the ribbons that held her mask in place. Holding up her glass of champagne to the light, she stared at it as if it were medicine, then drank it down in one gulp. Thus fortified to meet the enemy, she made her way into the double-wide reception rooms that had been cleared of heavy furniture and now served as a ballroom.

A myriad of silver candelabra held a wealth of lighted tapers; their beeswax perfumed the air. The happy sounds of fiddles and banjos caught her like a sudden breeze on a sultry day. Her feet tapping to the lively music, Julia swept her gaze around the crowded room.

Half of Alexandria must have been present tonight, but Julia had no intention of mingling with them. Everyone knew that the Chandlers were firmly Confederates, and therefore social outcasts among the Northern-leaning members of the citizenry. Julia told herself that she didn't give a fig what other people thought of her. Tonight she was here to dance and laugh—and to be "ruined". She lifted another glass of champagne from a passing tray. The bubbly spirits cheered her soul and tickled her brains.

How deliciously wicked I feel! Clara Chandler would have fainted on the spot if she knew that her gently-bred daughters were drinking. Already the effervescence lessened her trepidation; her spirits felt giddy. She should not become too relaxed or she would start singing "Dixie" and that would be a disaster here.

Up on the dais at the far end of the room, Alexandria's renowned fiddle master, old Joe Jackson, led the small string ensemble in a never-ending parade of melodies; many of them were new to Julia. Most of the younger male guests wore coats of military blue, but she resolved to look only at their faces while she considered which one she would encourage. Her blood quickened with the excitement that permeated the ballroom. The war seemed a million miles away.

Then she spied what she had fervently hoped would be there. A true smile of pleasure lit up her face as she wove through the dancers toward the buffet table in the adjoining dining room. A glistening mound of tan-colored caramels coated with powdered sugar beckoned to her from their silver dish.

Rob Montgomery ran his gloved finger around the collar of his freshly starched shirt. When he had been in the field, he considered himself fortunate to have a clean shirt; starching could go to the devil. He preferred it that way. He rubbed his neck where his collar had irritated his skin. Then he fumbled for his pocket watch, snapped open the lid and squinted at the time. Quarter past ten. From his vantage point on the sidelines, he had spent the past hour watching his cousin and friends sweep laughing belles around the dance floor.

The music was very good, he admitted to himself. Before the war, he would have taken the nearest pretty young thing out to the center and whirled her into giddiness. But now—He glanced down at his right coat pocket that hid his useless hand. Even though he had pulled a glove over the lifeless fingers, he knew in his heart that no young lady would want to touch such a dead thing as his smashed hand. *Damn those Rebs!*

For want of something better to do than drinking too much of Winstead's good whiskey, Rob picked his way around the dancers and wandered back into the dining room. To kill the first hour, he had already sampled enough of the sweet delights that graced the snowy expanse of the damask-covered table. Crystallized fruits, sugar cookies and gingerbread in artful piles, savory cheese sticks and anchovy paste spread on wafer-thin crackers, pecan tartlets, flavored gelatins and frozen charlottes, sliced jelly cake, chocolate-dipped lady fingers, glossy cherries in syrup—the bounty was not only endless, but overwhelming. What Rob really wanted was a good cup of strong coffee. Even more, he longed to be back in his own bed.

Reaching for a sugared walnut, his attention was drawn to the stunning auburn-haired miss on the other side of the table. It was not her wasp-narrow waist circled with the golden ribbon or her grass-green taffeta gown that had caught his eye, nor her creamy white arms that moved with the grace of a willow in a breeze. Nor did he pause too long to regard her incredible green eyes made more intriguing by the frame of her black mask. Nor did his gaze linger too long on her moist pink lips that promised passion. Instead it was what she was doing with those lips that had piqued his interest.

First, she slipped a caramel into her mouth. Then she surreptitiously glanced over each bare shoulder. Very provocative, Rob thought, though she was obviously not playing the coquette with an unseen admirer. No, her look was definitely furtive.

Rob stepped behind a large potted palm where, unseen, he could observe her at closer quarters. Once the young woman assured herself of her privacy, she opened her reticule that hung from her wrist. It looked to be a little larger than the usual size worn at a ball. With another glance around, she dropped several caramels into her bag and pulled it shut.

Rob smothered his laughter behind his good hand. He had done that same trick himself at a Fourth of July picnic many years ago at his grandmother's home in Rhinebeck. Thinking of that reminded him once again of this year's much different Independence Day. Instead of shooting off a string of squibs among a seated flock of his assorted aunts, a Rebel's bullet, the size and shape of a marble, had torn into his hand, splintered most of his bones, and severed the main nerve.

This Fourth of July, Rob had lain outside one of the temporary field hospitals in Gettysburg, Pennsylvania, enduring both the heat of the sun and the drenching rain that followed while he waited his turn on the surgeons' butcher table. It was nearly three days before someone looked at his wound. The harried doctor had wanted to take his hand off, even had his knife out, but Rob's vanity made him object to amputation. How could Miss Lucy possibly marry him with only one hand to hold her?

Muttering "gangrene" and "touched in the head," the doctor wrapped up Rob's stiffened hand and left the healing to Providence. The Lord had allowed Rob to recover without infection since the bullet had gone clean through, but divine generosity had stopped there. Since that day, Rob had not been able to move his fingers nor experience feeling below his wrist. The worst injury was not his hand but his heart when Miss Lucy walked away from him in disgust. Ever since, Rob's passionate nature had turned stone cold.

A soft gasp from the pretty pilferer brought Rob out of his dark reverie. To his consternation, and her delight, she had spied another dish of caramels a little nearer to his hiding place. Feeling like a burglar in his narrow silken mask, Rob flattened himself against the ivy-patterned wallpaper and waited to see what would happen next. Surely she had packed away enough booty to last her until February.

But no, it appeared that the lady still had sugared larceny on her mind. Once again, she glanced behind her.

Rob, too, looked over her bright hair that was crowned with glossy green sprigs of holly. Most of the room's attention was centered around the far table where cups of very potent eggnog were ladled out to the noisy guests. He glanced back at the lady just in time to witness several more caramels dumped into her expanding bag. She pulled the ties shut with a sleek, self-satisfied smile on her lovely lips. Then she turned her back to the table, snapped open her white silk fan and cooled the pink glow on her cheeks.

Rob noticed that a third dish sat near to him, hidden from her view by a large arrangement of purple hothouse grapes. He wondered what she would do if she spied that one. Propelled by his curiosity and a small spurt of mischief, Rob stepped out from the screen of palm fronds, took the dish in his good hand and circled to the other side of the table. He had meant to place the tempting candy within her reach and withdraw before she turned around, but she must have heard him. The auburn beauty glanced over her shoulder at him, then at the full silver plate in his hand.

His breath caught in his throat. A sliver of his once-legendary charm awakened. On a sudden impulse, he bowed his head and offered her the candy dish. ''I believe you missed these,'' he murmured. One corner of his mouth twitched upward. The startled expression on her face made her look even more alluring in the golden candlelight.

She blushed a little, but did not turn away shamefaced as he had expected her to do. Instead, she beamed a radiant smile. ''How silly of me to have misplaced those little rascals, and how clever of you to find them for me! Thank you so very much.''

Without a moment's hesitation, she shut her fan, then pried open her bag and swept a few more caramels on top of the others. The entire operation took less than a minute.

She sucked the powdered sugar evidence from her fingers. Her pink tongue curled around her thumb in the most innocently provocative manner. Rob swallowed hard. She smiled at him again. Her smiles, like pure sunshine, warmed his stony soul.

Julia's vision swam. She blinked to pull it back into focus. Her heart had nearly jumped out of her mouth when the stranger spoke to her. The handsome man's sudden appearance so surprised her that she nearly lost her composure. Then he smiled.

He was extraordinarily handsome. His Federal uniform concealed his body from neck to boots, yet Julia sensed a strong physical power that lay coiled deep within him. Though the supper room was crowded, his presence compelled her attention, despite the faint air of isolation he wore about his tall figure. Beneath his thin silken mask, his bronze skin pulled taut over his cheekbones. His near-black hair gleamed in the golden light; one rogue lock fell across his forehead.

Julia snapped open her fan and tried to calm her racing heart. She was sure it was only because he caught her red-handed that she felt as though she had a fever. Best to put a good face on the embarrassing situation, and pray that this Yankee possessed manners to go with his good looks.

She started to say "I do declare," but remembered in time that her colloquialism might give herself away as a Confederate. Instead, she opened with, "I fear that I am plagued with an insatiable sweet tooth, and the only remedy I know is a surfeit of caramels. I hope you will forgive me and overlook my boldness, sir." She fanned herself a little harder. He had the most enticing dark eyes she had ever seen.

The masked officer chuckled, his voice rich and smooth

like hot fudge. "Your secret is safe with me, provided that you leave whatever more there may be for the rest of us poor mortals to enjoy." His lips twitched into a half-smile.

Julia couldn't breathe. Heavens! She must have eaten too much or her corset had grown too tight. She willed herself to remain unruffled, all the while fanning herself harder. She gave him a sidelong glance out of the corner of her eye. My, but he was tall, much taller than most of the men she knew. They must grow them big wherever he came from.

"Where do you come from?" she blurted out, to cover her discomfort.

He blinked behind his mask. Were his eyes black or merely dark brown? "From New York, miss," he replied. "And you?"

I can't possibly say Virginia. She smoothed her mask. Of course! At a masked ball, everyone pretended to be someone else. So would she.

"Over hill, over dale, through bush, through brier," she answered, quoting lines from the First Fairy's speech in *A Midsummer Night's Dream*. "Over park, over pale, through flood, through fire I do wander everywhere, swifter than the moon's sphere, and I serve the fairy queen."

Her companion cocked his head, then grinned, displaying a perfect set of even white teeth. In her champagne-befuddled state, Julia found this very attractive.

"Thou speakest aright. I, too, am a merry wanderer of the night," he replied from the same play, though he changed Puck's words slightly. Even his grin took on the impish quality of Shakespeare's "merry sprite."

Julia widened her eyes. Hardly a soul she knew could quote Shakespeare off the top of their heads, especially out of context. Only Frank did, but that was long ago. Perhaps there was more to this Yankee than brass buttons and polished boots—and those beautiful teeth. Perhaps this was the Yankee she would allow to "ruin" her.

Julia smiled up at him. "Either I mistake your shape and making quite, or else you are that—" here Julia dropped the next word, "rude", and continued "—that knavish sprite called Robin Goodfellow. Are you not he?"

Again he looked as if she had surprised him. This time his smile was warmer. He made a mock bow to her. "You have truly found me out, Fairy Princess. Which one are you? Peaseblossom, Cobweb, Moth or Mustardseed?" he asked, naming the four fairy handmaidens from the play.

Delighted to continue this unexpected literary wordplay, Julia tapped her fan against the side of her cheek while she pretended to give the matter serious consideration. She felt very light and airy. "Cobweb, because I weave many webs of intrigue," she answered with more than a grain of truth. If she continued to hold his interest, maybe she could lure him into a dark corner where her books said that men ruined young ladies. Unfortunately, her references had not described the details.

Just then, three more young officers in blue surrounded them; all of them held crystal cups overflowing with creamy eggnog.

"There you are, Rob!" cried the most inebriated member of the group. "It cheers me to the very soul to see that you are having a good time."

The other two men raised their cups and shouted "Hear, hear" before draining their contents.

Leaning close to Julia's ear, Rob whispered, "Pay them no mind. It's only my cousin and some of his friends."

His warm breath tickled her skin in the most amazing and thoroughly delightful manner. She shivered inwardly with excitement. Behind her fan, she replied, "I, too, am infected with cousins, though mine are much less pleasant than yours.'' She grimaced as she thought of Payton. She must implement her plan soon before she lost her courage or the effects of the champagne wore off.

"These merry souls are Flute and Snout," Rob said, pointing to his cousin's friends, naming two more characters from Shakespeare's romantic comedy. Looking surprised, the officers toasted the couple again, then they drained their cups. "My cousin is deservedly known as Bottom, for he is always found at the bottom of the heap."

The cousin looked from Rob to Julia. He grinned. "Alas, I see once more that I am to play the fool for Rob. If he is disturbing you, miss, you can call on me for assistance. I am Ben, that is, Benjamin Johnson, at your humble service." He hiccuped.

Rob glared at the high-spirited young man.

Julia took her companion's displeasure as a compliment. Behind her fan, she observed to Rob, "I do believe he is nearing the bottom of his cup now." She smiled to let him know that she was jesting.

Ben saluted them with his now-empty glass. "I can tell when I have been given my pass to leave, and so I shall. I am your obedient servant, miss. Go dance with her, Rob!" he added as he stumbled off to rejoin his friends at the flowing eggnog bowl.

Rob stiffened. Without looking directly at him, Julia sensed a chill curtain had suddenly crashed down between them. He must not know how to dance, she surmised. To put him back at ease, she smiled.

"I fear that I cannot dance, Major Robin Goodfellow." Holding up her bulging reticule, she giggled. "I would lose all my newfound wealth if I attempted to twirl around the floor. As you well know, I have gone to great pains to gather these confections."

He relaxed a fraction. "Then we shall not dance. I would hate to have to crawl across the ballroom trying to retrieve your…um…possessions."

Aloud, she continued, "But we could watch the others cavort and discuss the merits of their style."

He nodded, though he did not smile as broadly as he had done before his cousin's intrusion. Julia was sorry for that. This Robin Goodfellow had the most wonderful smile she had ever seen. Don't be such a green goose, her common sense scolded her as Rob led her into the ballroom. The only reason she found him so charming was due to lack of male company for the past two years.

Following behind him, she noticed that he kept his right hand deep in the pocket of his coat. She wondered if he knew that it was rude for a gentleman to put his hands in his pockets while in polite company, but since he was so charming otherwise—and because she knew that she would never see him again after tonight—she decided to ignore this breach of manners. After all, he was from New York and probably didn't know any better.

For the next half hour, Julia and the major traded witty remarks about their fellow guests. Julia drank another glass of champagne to steady her resolve. The music swelled louder and the dancing became more abandoned. The room grew more stuffy. She never knew that candles could put out so much heat. Julia fanned more rapidly. The colors of the ladies' gowns melded together in a swirling rainbow. Julia pressed her hand to her temple. It occurred to her that she had perhaps overimbibed.

The major leaned over her. "Are you unwell, Mistress Cobweb?"

Julia licked her dry lips. "I fear that I require some fresh air. If you would be so kind as to escort me to a window?"

She swallowed hard. Now was the perfect time to initiate her plan, if only her head didn't feel so wobbly.

"Of course," the Yankee muttered. His slipped his left arm around her waist and gently guided her toward an alcove at the far end of the supper room. "Are you feeling faint?"

She felt faint and terrified, excited and nervous. But Julia shook her head. Her holly wreath slipped a little over her right ear. Its stiff leaves pricked her skin, prodding her more awake.

Rob held back the brocaded curtain so that Julia could pass under it. The tiny space between the drapes and the window seemed very dark after the brilliance of the supper room. *Good,* she thought, as she watched him fumble with the window's latch. *He won't see how frightened I am.* As he raised the sash, she gulped in the bracing cold air. Payton's face suddenly rose in her mind. She shuddered. *Do it now!*

Julia had to explain to him exactly what she wanted in no uncertain terms. There could be no mistake on his part. She wished her books had been more specific. She touched the major's arm.

"Sir, I wonder if you could do me one more tiny favor?" she asked. Her heart thudded against her whalebone stays.

"I am your humble servant, Fairy Princess," he replied. His white teeth shone in the semidarkness as he smiled at her. "Name it."

Julia wet her lips, then looked up into his wonderful eyes. "Major, would you be so kind as to have…to have your dastardly way with me?"

Chapter Four

Rob gaped at the young woman. Had he completely misread her character? She swayed slightly and hiccuped. Steadying her on her feet, he realized that she probably did not have the slightest idea what she had just asked him. Glancing through the gap in the curtains, he was relieved to see that no one was nearby. Best to sober up the Fairy Princess, then deposit her on one of the side chairs that lined the dance floor. Rob could not remember ever being caught in such a ticklish situation as this one. The lady hiccuped again.

"Oh, dear," she murmured, more to herself than to him. "I do believe that I have made a splendid hash of this."

Rob had no idea what she meant. "It's the champagne," he soothed her. "It has a way of robbing our good sense. Those naughty little bubbles make us say the strangest things." He glanced between the curtains again to make sure that no one had wandered in range.

Her fingers tightened around his good arm. He prayed that she wouldn't faint on him—not in this secluded spot.

"No, Major," she said in a soft slur, "I did mean exactly what I asked. I must be ruined, whatever that is. I am desperate. Can you do it?"

Rob groaned inwardly. It was like asking him if he knew how to breathe. His loins awoke with a start. His mouth went dry. He cleared his throat. "Pardon my hesitation, miss, but do you have any idea what you are asking me to do?"

"Of course!" She nodded vigorously. Her holly wreath threatened to slide off her head. "That is, no," she countered. "I fear I do not have a precise definition of 'ruination.' My books failed me in that respect. I had presumed that you, being a man and a Yankee, would know what to do."

The way she said "Yankee" gave Rob some pause. Was he in the company of a Confederate spy? Was this a ruse to blackmail him into revealing government secrets? Before he could take action, she fell against him. Her eyes flashed with unfeigned shock.

"Oh, my! This is not what I had planned at all. Do forgive me, Major. I've never had more than one glass of wine before. I had no idea how fluffy it makes one feel. Will my intoxicated condition present a problem for you? Can you ruin me anyway?" Her beautiful eyes focused into a look of pure desperation. "Please, sir," she whispered. "You are my only hope."

Rob ignored his distaste for Rebels—at least for the moment. Confederate or not, his Fairy Princess was clearly a lady in real distress. He turned her toward the open window. "Hold on to my arm and keep your eyes open. Breathe deeply."

She gripped him as she leaned over the jet of cold air that blew inside. When he felt her steady herself, Rob continued, "Now, please explain to me why you wish to have me…ah…ruin you. Before I do anything, I must understand the particulars." Despite the cold air on his face, perspiration dampened his hair.

The auburn beauty nodded. "My parents want me to marry my cousin down in Richmond." She paused for breath. "He's a toad." She stopped again, as if to gather her strength. "So I thought that if I were well and truly ruined by another man—a total stranger—" She breathed in again. "Payton would refuse to have me, and my parents would not object to me becoming a schoolteacher," she finished in a rush of words.

Rob grunted. She was beginning to sound more reasonable. He gave her a weak smile. "You want to teach children?"

She looked up at him as if he had offered her the world on a silver tray. Her askew holly leaves and her fetching black mask made her even more like Shakespeare's fairy queen. Rob recalled that Titania had also done some silly things while under the influence of a flower's potent juice.

"Very much," she replied softly. "Little girls and perhaps even some of the black children, now that they are free. But my parents would be dead set against that idea. Proper ladies do not teach school."

"So you decided to be improper—with me?"

"Exactly so," she confessed, looking away from him. "Just a little bit. As you have discovered, I have no idea how to do it. My apologies, sir, for embarrassing you." She straightened her smooth shoulders and pulled up her fringed shawl over her ivory flesh. "I feel like such a fool. But you can have no idea…" She sighed.

Don't get involved. She's a Reb.

Rob's skin prickled. He moved closer to her until there was no space between them. Her violet scent filled his nostrils. Her lips, moist with her outrageous request, were less than twelve inches from his yearning mouth. He knew they should return to the ballroom before someone missed them. Miss Cobweb did not have any idea of the true cost of a ruined reputation, but Rob knew. Even if she were a Confederate, he did not want to be the one to debauch her. He wanted revenge for his injury, but not at the expense of this innocent. What she needed was a good fright to put some sense back into that pretty head.

The cold moonlight shining through the windowpane glinted in her jade-green eyes. Staring into their depths, Rob tried to ignore their magnetic pull on his senses.

"To ruin a young lady means to take her virtue," he began in his best attempt to remain impervious to her attractions.

"Oh!" gasped the Fairy Princess. Her eyes grew wider.

Rob continued in a hurry. "A kiss on your lips by a stranger like myself would be enough to ruin a respectable young woman such as yourself." How he wanted to do it right away!

Puzzlement filled her green orbs. "But I have been kissed already. Frank did that before he went off to fight the…to war," she finished.

Rob thought of his cold bed back in his hotel. "Why don't you marry Frank then, instead of this cousin? It would save you a great deal of grief."

The lady looked down at the floor. "He was killed at Manassas," she whispered. She touched a silver locket that she wore around her neck. "And he only kissed me once— on the cheek."

Rob was tempted to take her in his arms for comfort's sake, but that would defeat the point he was trying to make. "I am sorry for your loss," he said through stiff lips. "But to return to your present…um…problem." His loins stiffened. He hoped it wasn't noticeable. "If I took improper liberties with you—"

She looked up with warm expectation. "Yes?" she breathed.

Rob groaned as his manhood throbbed under his frock coat. How did he get himself into this hell? He had to end this nonsense quickly before he did something that he would surely regret—later. *I must be cruel to be kind.*

"To ruin you," he growled, "my kiss would be *hard*. It would bruise you." He tore his gaze away from her lush mouth. "And…and I would not stop with just one kiss. Oh, no, I would kiss you many times…in many places." Sweat rolled down the back of his neck.

The tip of her pink tongue darted between her lips. "Fascinating!"

Rob squeezed shut his eyes. A sane man could only withstand so much temptation. Miss Cobweb had no idea how warm she had made him. He had to conclude the little lecture now.

"It is quite unpleasant, miss. I doubt you would like it at all—and neither would I," he ended with a profound lie.

Rob backed away from her and lifted the drape. Fortunately, their corner was still deserted. "It's high time that we rejoined the party," he muttered, every nerve in his body aflame.

She gave him a soulful look. "So you will not ruin me after all?"

He pushed her into the supper room. "That remains to be seen."

Though her plan had failed miserably, Julia felt relieved. Who would have ever guessed that she would happen to find the one and only true gentleman in this roomful of churlish Yankees? She looked up at him and caught his sidelong glance. Though his mask covered half his face, she could tell that she had made him uncomfortable.

To ease the tension, she whispered behind her fan, "I

thank you for protecting my reputation, sir, but, at least, could you say that you had your way with me? I mean, if anyone happened to ask you.''

He looked stricken. His mouth thinned, then he replied, ''I pray that there will be no inquiries. I have no intention of eating buckshot for breakfast.''

Just then, Joe Jackson announced a polka. Couples at the refreshment table pushed past Julia and her major to claim a spot on the dance floor.

As the music began, Julia saw her sister for the first time that evening. Carolyn was in the center of the room in the arms of an officer wearing bright red Turkish trousers. The man was practically galloping her down the length of the dance floor.

Leaning down, Rob observed, ''Now *there* is a pretty minx who will leave many a broken heart in her wake.'' He nodded toward Carolyn. ''She's a candidate for ruination.''

Julia gulped. ''I fear you are right. That's my sister.''

Rob groaned. Then he turned to her with apology in his chocolate-brown eyes. ''Forgive me again, Mistress Cobweb. It is the knavish spirit within me. Is your sister named Peaseblossom for the color of her gown?'' he added in a rush.

Julia knew her mother would swoon if she saw Carolyn just now. To the major's anxious look, she remarked, ''No, we left Peaseblossom at home to grow some more. That is Mustardseed, so called because she will indeed add a great deal of spice to life.''

Finally, Rob smiled at her just as he had done earlier in the supper room. Hoping that their awkward episode was behind them, Julia returned his smile. Then she glanced back at the dance floor.

''Hellfire!'' she gasped with horror under her breath.

As Carolyn's partner whirled her faster, her sister's mask slipped down to her neck, revealing her identity for all the world to see!

Chapter Five

Across the room, Melinda Winstead stared at the petite blonde in the blue gown who had skittered to a stop in the middle of the dance floor. Within the blink of an eye, the girl pulled up her mask again, but it was too late. Melinda had gotten a good enough look to know that the lively flirt in the arms of a New York Zouave was none other than that brat, Carolyn Chandler.

"What a brazen little hussy!" Melinda hissed, as she watched Carolyn attract all sorts of admiring glances from half the men in the room. She couldn't have come here alone.

Melinda scanned the other dancers, then her gaze roved over the crowd on the sidelines. She paused when she saw a slim woman in a green gown with that unmistakable auburn hair—and wearing an exact copy of Carolyn's mask. Melinda snorted through her nose. Julia Chandler! How dare those Secessionists presume to come to her ball! Melinda's outrage grew even more livid when she noticed that Julia was in the company of an absolutely gorgeous major—easily the handsomest man at the party.

Turning on her heel, Melinda dashed through her guests and crossed the hall to the library where she knew her father entertained some of the older men with bourbon and risqué stories. As she hoped, George Winstead stood at ease with his back to the crackling fire in the center of the book-lined room. Cigar smoke tinted the air blue.

Barely acknowledging the surprised stares of her father's cronies, Melinda demanded the attention of her frowning parent. She paid no mind to his understandable displeasure at her intrusion into his male sanctum.

"Papa, you must come quickly!" She grabbed him by his arm.

George put down his whiskey glass on the blotter of his polished mahogany desktop. "Here now, young lady. What has happened? Is there a row brewing?" Though his tone was mild, his words held a sharp bite.

Melinda gave him another tug. "Not yet, but there soon will be. Papa, you must come *now*."

Giving his hasty apologies to his surprised friends, George allowed her to drag him across to the reception room. His frown deepened when he saw nothing to warrant Melinda's ill manners. She wanted to stamp her foot with frustration at his obtuseness.

She pointed to Carolyn who had finished romping on the dance floor and now fanned herself on the sidelines to the pleasure of her grinning partner. "Over there, Papa! See her? That's Carolyn Chandler. She had the brass to come to our house uninvited, and unwanted, too."

Then she directed her father's attention to Julia, who crossed the room to join her sister. That too-handsome major followed her like a puppy dog. Disgusting! "And there's that horrid Julia Chandler. I'm surprised that she could bear to leave her precious books. Their presence insults our family, Papa. Evict them at once!"

George merely patted his daughter's arm, and shushed her as if she were a four-year-old crying for more ice cream. "Hush up, Melinda," he said in her ear. "I will do no such thing. How they got in here, I cannot imagine, but since they are under our roof, I will not be inhospitable."

Melinda gasped as if her father had just doused her with cold water. "Those Chandlers are nothing but trashy Confederates. How can you—?"

George squeezed her arm in a viselike grip. "See here, missy! Dr. Chandler did me the good service of bringing you into this world eighteen years ago. I don't hold with his sentiments, but he's a good man at heart, despite his shrew of a wife. Don't forget that his daughters were once your playmates when you children were in short frocks."

Melinda pulled herself away from him and rubbed her arm where her skin bore the red imprints of his fingers. "Julia is so puffed up with her book-learning that it makes me want to scream, and her little sister is a brat, plain and simple. They are wrecking our lovely party." Several nearby guests stopped their conversations and stared at the father and daughter, but Melinda didn't care.

George whispered in her ear. "Lower your voice or I will send you to your room for the rest of the evening, Miss Winstead. I will not have you cause a scene, especially when none is necessary. The Chandler girls are behaving themselves much better than you, and I see no harm in allowing them a little fun in their lives. Julia hasn't been out in society since Frank Shaffer died, and little Carolyn not at all."

He chuckled. "Though I can see that Carolyn has done some growing since the war began. Behave yourself, Melinda, and pay them no mind. They will be gone soon enough, I expect, and there will be an end to the matter. I have paid a great deal of money so that you could enjoy the company of your friends tonight. Now do it and leave me in peace with mine.'' With that, he returned to the library.

Melinda's cheeks burned under her father's admonishment. He had no right to speak to her that way. Mama would have understood her feelings completely. She certainly wouldn't want any Confederates under her roof, even if they were former friends. Melinda realized that she had miscalculated which parent she should have approached. She knew without looking, that Papa was speaking to Mama even now, telling her about their uninvited guests and his decision to let them be.

Very well, Melinda decided. She wouldn't attempt to throw out the Chandlers herself, but that didn't mean she had to overlook their atrocious lapse in manners. Pasting on her best smile, she swept her way over to Julia and her escort. By the time she reached them, Carolyn had returned to the dance floor with yet another swain. Melinda burned with jealousy. These chits would pay, she vowed.

''Good evening, Julia,'' she purred, coming up behind the older girl. It gave her satisfaction to see Julia jump at her name.

The young woman slowly turned around as did the man beside her. Seeing him at closer quarters, Melinda was momentarily distracted from her mission. He had the most beautiful dark brown hair with a curl that dropped over his forehead in an appealing way. Strong jaw, high cheekbones and very, very seductive eyes behind that mask. He was too delicious by a country mile.

Giving herself a shake, Melinda returned to Julia. ''What a surprise to see you here—in our house!'' she continued in sugar-sweet tones. ''I can't imagine how *you* got invited, can you, Julia?'' She cast a quick smile at the silent man. "Tell me, Major, did *you* come to our party tonight without a proper invitation?"

He cleared his throat, then replied, "I must confess that I did not receive an invitation from your parents, Miss Winstead, but I came at the request of my cousin, Ben Johnson, who claims that he did. If I am remiss, I will not hesitate to leave." He drew himself up, which only served to accentuate his height.

Knotting her brows behind her butterfly mask, Melinda swore at herself. She had overstepped some invisible boundary and offended him, when she had only intended to make Julia squirm. Melinda smiled and tried to slip her hand under his right elbow. To her alarm, he pulled back from her the minute she touched him. Confused by his prickliness, she plunged on.

"Lieutenant Johnson has visited us on occasion, Major, and I especially asked that he bring some of his friends this time. I am so delighted that he chose to bring you. On the other hand, Miss Chandler here will find herself in a world of trouble if she keeps inviting herself, and her little sister, to respectable people's parties." It gratified Melinda to observe a dark red blush creep over the lower part of Julia's face.

Melinda locked the major in her gaze, forcing him, out of politeness' sake, to look at her instead of at the interloper. "Of course, what else could you possibly expect from a *Confederate* but bad manners?" she continued, savoring Julia's sudden intake of breath. "I suppose that you know, much better than I do, what these Rebels are like, Major. Nothing but low-bred ruffians."

Julia gripped her reticule tighter. Her giddiness from the champagne had completely evaporated. She didn't dare look at Rob's face. She could guess what his opinion was, now that Melinda had so cruelly explained the situation. First, her scandalous request, now this. Obviously, the ball was over for her, but she would leave with as much grace and dignity as she could muster.

At least, she had had a very lovely time, quite the nicest she had experienced in over two years—even those embarrassing moments spent in the alcove. The music had been excellent and she had enjoyed surveying the new fashions in ball gowns. She still had the caramels in her bag that she could savor over the next few weeks. She prayed that Rob would be chivalrous enough not to betray her secret proposition. She cast him a sidelong glance. He returned hers with a cool expression behind his mask. At least, he did not publicly rebuke her, nor claim her ruination. Now that she was literally unmasked, Julia realized that she would have died on the spot if he said anything.

Gathering the remnants of her composure, she replied to Melinda, "Just look at the time! I had no idea how late it had grown. I must find my sister immediately. Please make our adieus to your parents, Melinda." She turned to Rob. "Please forgive me, Major Goodfellow. Forgive me for everything. I fear I have kept you from dancing with our charming hostess." She pulled her shawl tighter around her shoulders. "Lovely party, Melinda," she murmured.

Julia turned away before a hovering tear could roll down her cheek below her mask. She dove into the press of people where she spied her sister conversing with several more admirers.

Sliding her arm around Carolyn's waist, she whispered in her ear. "The cat's out of the bag. Melinda knows we are here. We have got to go now before she takes it into her flighty head to make a scene."

Carolyn squeaked a little "oh!", then smiled at her

companions. "Oh, dear, gentlemen, I fear I have over-stayed my time, and my mama would skin me alive if she knew. We have to leave your fine company, but with much regret."

"Miss Carolyn," protested one of the men.

Julia stepped into the breach. "I am so sorry, sirs, but I fear my sister speaks the truth. It has been a very great pleasure to have met you all. Come on, Carolyn."

Before the officers could say anything else, Julia pulled her sister out to the front hall. Once in the cloakroom, Julia sent word for Perkins to meet them outside the front door. The maid in attendance couldn't understand their haste in departing when some of the guests were only just arriving after late supper parties.

"My sister is feverish," Julia quickly confided to the servant, "and we don't want to infect anyone, do we?"

The young woman backed away. "No, miss, we surely don't."

Once they donned their cloaks, they swept past the door-man and down the steps to the windswept street. Perkins awaited them on the curb with his lantern held high. He looked both surprised at their early departure and greatly relieved.

"Now, this is the first bit of good sense that you two have shown all day. Let's be off before the provost's patrol comes round. We don't have passes to be out this late." He started briskly down the sidewalk. Julia and Carolyn hurried after him.

Though Julia was a Confederate, Rob discovered that he could not be angry with her, despite his deep aversion to the Rebels. She had not deliberately deceived him, but had merely sidestepped his questions with quotations from

A Midsummer Night's Dream. He regarded Melinda, who returned him a smile of pure triumph.

"They're playing a waltz, Major," she hinted. She tried to take his useless arm again.

Rob stepped back, leaving a small but definite space between them. "I do not dance, Miss Winstead. In fact, I find that the pleasure of the evening has somewhat palled. Since I will no doubt be sullen company for you, I beg you to excuse me."

Melinda gasped. Rob roamed throughout the rooms, looking for Julia and her sister, but both the Chandlers had vanished. Questioning the doorman, he learned that the two young ladies had left only a few moments ago. Rob stepped out onto the front landing and surveyed the street, but the sidewalks on both sides were bare save for a mangy cat that slunk down the far wall in search of a garbage rat.

The cold air sharpened Rob's senses. Melinda's spiteful words to Julia had angered him. Even though the lovely Miss Chandler was a Confederate, she was also the most intelligent company he had enjoyed in quite some time. China doll-like Lucy Van Tassel paled in comparison to Julia's accomplishments. Lucy never opened a book, much less quoted Shakespeare. Nor had she ever displayed any particular talent other than gossiping and changing her clothes five times a day. For the first time since her abrupt termination of their engagement, Rob realized how lucky he had been to escape a lifetime with Lucy.

Not that he was interested in Julia, he told himself. She was a Southern sympathizer, and therefore, beyond further consideration from him. She had been merely a charming diversion on an otherwise deadly evening. Yet, she had looked so wounded by Melinda's words. He, like a tongue-tied dolt, had said nothing to champion her honor, especially since he was so acutely aware of her innocent virtue.

Julia must think that he concurred with Melinda's sentiments against her. In fact, he abjured them. But he had not
been quick enough to tell Julia that, nor to bid her a proper
good-night. He should have done that much, at least.

Rob stared down the street again. The skulking cat had
disappeared. The only signs of life were the music and
laughter inside the Winsteads' house behind him. Rob
opened his timepiece and read its dial by the flicker of the
gas lantern over the front door. Nearly midnight. He
snapped shut the watch with a snort. Three hours at the
ball were up; his time was now his own.

He would make amends to Julia right now, before any
more time passed. The Chandler sisters had only left a few
minutes ago. If they lived nearby, he might be able to catch
up with them in time to give the lovely lady a proper
apology. But which way did they go? He turned back inside to get his greatcoat.

"The Chandler house?" the doorman repeated Rob's
question. "They's Seesech, Major, sir. Those kind of folks
stay to themselves, they do. You don't want any part of
that family."

Rob swallowed his impatience. "Miss Julia dropped her
fan this evening. I wish to return it," he fabricated, itching
to be off now that he had made up his mind for action.

The doorman gave him a fishy look. "The Chandlers
were not invited to this here party. That's a fact."

Rob controlled himself. He had never before spoken directly to an African servant, and he was afraid to press the
man lest he lose his temper. Instead, he lowered his voice
as if to impart a great secret. "Miss Julia and her sister,
Carolyn, came in disguise. They haven't been to a party
in years. No harm done—except, of course, Miss Julia losing her fan." He hoped the man wouldn't ask to see the
nonexistent item.

The doorman considered Rob's explanation for a moment, then nodded. "That's what old Perkins said down in the hall. Said old Mrs. Chandler would have had a fit if she knew what her girls were up to, but I didn't think he meant this party. Miss Julia, as I recollect, was a nice enough child, very polite to everyone. If she lost her fan here, I expect she'll feel mighty low about it."

When the man paused for breath, Rob added fuel to his plea. "I hope for Miss Julia's sake that the fan does not belong to old Mrs. Chandler."

The doorman shook his head. "Lordy, that child will be in a world of trouble if that be the case. You go along now, Major, sir, and see that Miss Julia gets it back right quick."

Elation made his blood flow faster. "Which way do I go?"

The doorman pointed to the right. "Down to the corner, turn left. That's Prince Street. Go on two blocks. The house is in the middle on the left side. Red brick with black shutters. Got a double door in front."

"And the number on the house?" Rob prodded.

"Now how am I expected to know that, Major, sir? I'm not allowed to read, you know." The doorman's face turned as blank as an ebony mask.

Rob considered bribing the servant with a twenty-five-cent piece, but thought better of the idea. He might be insulted or he might be telling the truth, which would be a waste of Rob's time and money. Thanking the fellow, Rob got his greatcoat from the antechamber, then departed the Winsteads without a formal goodbye to the host, or telling his cousin Ben where he was going. Since the way sounded short, Rob chose not to retrieve his horse from the warm stable just yet. No point in allowing Buster to catch a chill while Rob made his apologies to the lovely Miss Julia.

He didn't stop to think that for the first time in many months, he was running *to* something, rather than away from something.

Chapter Six

Sitting cross-legged in the middle of the double bed she shared with her sister, Carolyn brushed out her hair. "What a divine time! I don't believe I have ever had a finer night in all my born days. And I didn't step on too many toes, either."

Julia sat at their vanity table, also brushing her hair, though her strokes were not as vigorous as Carolyn's. Her head throbbed with a dull ache—the champagne's after-effects. When she stared into the looking glass, it was not her face that she saw, but that of the handsome Major Robin Goodfellow, or whomever he was. She wished she knew his real name. She chewed her lower lip. No, it was better that she didn't, since she had made such an idiot of herself. At least, she would never see him again.

As if reading her thoughts, Carolyn asked, "Who was that Yankee you spent the whole evening with?"

Julia shrugged and massaged her neck. "I have no idea. We traded names from Shakespeare, not our own. I thought it was safer that way."

Carolyn shook her head. "Julia, you are a caution! Even at a party, you can't forget all that heavy reading. You think too much to enjoy yourself."

Julia smiled ruefully at her reflection. What she was thinking would shock Carolyn to fits, and it had nothing to do with English literature. Her cheeks grew warm. *He said he would kiss me many times and in many places.*

Carolyn persisted. "It is a good thing that Mother didn't see you. She would have locked you in here for a month of Sundays for being so free and easy with that man."

Julia turned around and stared at her sister. "Me? And who was dancing and flirting—and drinking champagne— with flocks of the enemy?"

Carolyn stuck out her tongue at Julia. "Pooh! I had to let those poor boys see what they are missing by living up North. I hear that Yankee girls are sour in looks and disposition. They wouldn't know how to have a good time even if it came knocking on their front door."

Julia only half-listened to Carolyn's explanation. She preferred to muse over the devastating smile of her mystery man. And his lips! The ones that refused to ruin her. She tingled with a delicious thrill at the idea of his mouth pressed against hers. But it would never happen, she reminded herself. No proper girl should be kissed like that until she's engaged, and Julia would never consider engaging herself to a Yankee.

Carolyn tossed her brush on the daybed, then slipped under the satin eiderdown quilt. "Well, I am going to sleep. All those Yankee boys wore me to a frazzle. Ooh, my toes will ache so in the morning!" She giggled as she snuggled deeper into the covers.

"Good night, sleep tight, don't let the bedbugs bite," Julia intoned absentmindedly, reciting the little rhyme that had been their bedtime ritual since both girls were small children.

"'Night," Carolyn murmured from under the quilt.

Julia returned to the mirror. Once again, Rob's face rose

in her mind. Again, she recalled his firm, sensual lips. She ran her finger over her own, then sighed. She wished there had been more time at the ball. He might have tried to kiss her if he had drunk some of that eggnog. She shivered, not with the night's cold, but with the speculation of forbidden delights. She sighed again. *I should have thrown myself at him....*

Rob studied the front of the Chandler house. The dark windows facing the street indicated that the family had all retired. Much to his surprise, he felt a sharp stab of disappointment, though he had no firm idea what he would have done had the lights still been on. A gentleman didn't make social calls at midnight.

A large cat, silver-gold in the street's gaslight, brushed against his boots, then ambled down the narrow cobbled alleyway that ran between the Chandlers and their next-door neighbors. Rob watched the animal disappear around the corner of the house, drawing his attention to a faint glow in the rear garden. His heartbeat accelerated. Without considering the consequences, he followed the cat's path down the alley. In a brick archway of the rear garden wall, a narrow wrought iron gate opened to a brick path that led up to the Chandlers' back door. Sitting on the kitchen steps, the cat licked its paws with an air of ownership.

Rob traced the glow to one of the second-floor windows; its light fell gently on the garden. His sense of adventure stirred. He pressed down the latch and swung open the gate. The cat looked up, but did not hiss or give any other sign of alarm. Drawn by the light, Rob stole into the garden, and closed the gate behind him. He slid along the high brick wall and stopped when he came to the privy house in the furthermost corner. From this darkened vantage point, he could just make out the indistinct shape of a woman sitting before a mirror with her back to the window. An oil lamp flickered beside her; the looking glass caught the light and reflected it out—to him.

Rob gave a slight start. The woman looked like Julia. Her hair color was unmistakable. Yet there could be other members of her family who bore her resemblance. "Turn around," he whispered in the darkness. "Come to the window." What would he do if she did look out?

The chill of the ground seeped through the soles of his boots. Rob gave himself a shake. What a damn fool he was to loiter in a girl's garden like a lovesick swain!

As he turned to leave, his sudden movement startled the cat. With a low yowl, it hopped from the stoop to the side lattice that supported a dry, brown vine. Displaying swift agility, the cat climbed up the lattice like a ladder to the windowsill above—the same window where the oil lamp still burned. Once perched on his place of safety, the cat scratched at the glass pane like a dog. Holding his breath without realizing it, Rob waited to see what would happen.

Julia cocked her head; again she heard the sound that had disturbed her musings. She smiled to her reflection. The scratching at the window signaled Tybalt's impatience. Outside on the ledge, the orange striped cat stared in at her with wide amber eyes. He lifted his paw and scratched the glass again. Julia unhooked the latch then lifted the sash. A wedge of cold air blew in through the opening.

"Hello, Tybalt," she greeted him in a low voice. "Too chilly for you tonight?"

Mewing an answer, the cat slipped inside and landed softly on the floor. Julia started to lower the window, then stopped when she saw something flash in the darkness below. The hairs on the back of her neck prickled. Warning spasms of alarm erupted in the pit of her stomach. She had the instinctive feeling that someone was down there, though she could see no discernible shape in the garden's shadows. Her first impulse was to wake Perkins. The bounty of the holiday season was enough to tempt many a burglar, especially now that Alexandria was full of louts from the North.

Something flashed again. A man stepped out from the overhang of the large magnolia tree, took off his hat and bowed to her. Covering her mouth, Julia swallowed her scream. Replacing his hat, he stepped closer.

Julia gripped the window frame. "Who…who's there?" she whispered through the opening.

"What light from yonder window breaks?" the man asked in a low, but distinct voice. "It is the east and fair Julia is the sun," he continued, improvising the opening lines from the balcony scene in *Romeo and Juliet.*

Julia released her breath. Though the speaker's face was in deep shadow, she instantly recognized his Northern accent. Her heart leaped to her throat and blood pounded against her temples. Casting a quick glance at the sleeping Carolyn, she knelt on the floor by the narrow open window.

"You have changed your identity, Major Robin Goodfellow. Are you now Romeo?" she responded, praying that her sister would not wake up.

He chuckled. "My name, dear saint, is hateful to myself, because it is an enemy to thee." As if to accentuate his point, the brass buttons of his uniform greatcoat caught the light of the moonshine and flashed in return.

Julia hugged herself. This unsuspecting Yankee was certainly taking his life in his hands to come into their garden, especially in the dead of night. Though Jonah Chandler was a mild-mannered man, he would not hesitate to use the shotgun hanging in the back hall to protect his family.

"You had best go quickly before you waken my father. He has a gun," she warned.

The major chuckled again. "There is more peril in thine eye, than in twenty of his swords," he continued, using Romeo's words.

Julia wanted to scream at him, this time in frustration. Didn't this Yankee have any sense at all? Perhaps midnight visits were a common practice in New York, but such outlandish behavior just wasn't done in Virginia. The man was apt to get his handsome head blown off.

"You are too rash, sir," she told him. "So then, good night," though she hated to close the window and turn away from him. This would never happen to her again, especially if she married boorish Payton and had to live in the midst of his tobacco fields.

The major stepped more into the moonlight, then went down on one knee. "Wilt thou leave me so unsatisfied?"

A new, unexpected warmth surged through her, not only by the seductive suggestion in his voice, but also by his sheer boldness. Had he come to ruin her now? A dizzy current of heat raced through her blood. Her body tingled. This Yankee was a romantic lunatic—and perhaps, so was she.

Raising the window a little higher, Julia leaned out. "You are the most thick-headed person that I ever met," she whispered louder. "Don't you know that you could be killed for a prowler if anyone hears you?" She refused to wonder why she wanted to save this Yankee's life. Men like this one had killed sweet Frank. Yet Julia knew that she would feel very guilty if the major were shot in her garden because of her.

Rob tilted up his face, the white of his teeth gleaming

as he grinned at her. "I have night's cloak to hide me," he said, not seeming the least bit worried.

Carolyn murmured in her dreams. Julia shot another swift glance at her. Even though her sister was a heavy sleeper, this insane conversation would certainly waken her if it continued. Julia knew that she should shut the window and be done with the man, but she couldn't do it. He enticed her; his boldness tempted her to do something equally rash in return. Should she ask him now to have his wicked way with her?

He stepped closer to the foot of the back steps. "Wouldst thou withdraw?" he called softly, almost tenderly.

This night would never happen to her again. There was a war between them. Tossing aside her common sense, Julia acted upon the most daring idea she had ever had in her sheltered life. She leaned out the window again. "Stay under the tree in the shadows. I'll be down in a minute."

Julia didn't look at him as she shut the window, but she had the distinct impression that he grinned before he retreated under the magnolia, thick with its evergreen, glossy leaves. She didn't consider what she was about to do. Instead, she imagined his lips upon hers. Hastily, she twirled her hair up in a knot, then tossed a dressing gown over her nightdress. She swept up a knitted afghan from the foot of the daybed and threw it around her shoulders.

As she slipped her bare feet into her fur-lined slippers, Carolyn stirred from the depths of the four-poster bed.

"Where are you going?" she asked in a sleep-thickened voice.

"To get the cat," Julia replied, lighting a candle. "Go back to sleep."

Yawning, Carolyn snuggled down again. As Julia left

their room, she hoped that her sister wouldn't notice that Tybalt was curled in a furry ball next to her pillow.

A few moments later, Julia stepped onto the back stoop. She lifted her candlestick higher, allowing the light to spill deeper into the silent garden. Its flame flickered in the light breeze. Then she saw him move under the tree. Gathering her courage, she descended the steps carefully in case they were icy. She halted just inside the magnolia's screening boughs. After all, she didn't want to get too close to the man, in case his manner turned threatening. He had been a perfect gentleman up until now—but he *was* a Yankee. Nor did she want to give him the idea that she was a loose woman. Now that she faced him, she was suddenly unsure what to do next.

The major stepped just inside her candle's glow. "I am glad that you removed your mask, Miss Julia. Beauty should never remain hidden."

His deep voice caressed her, and a spiral of nervous excitement corkscrewed down her spine. She fumbled for a suitable reply. Given the late hour and her shameful state of undress, there was nothing she could think to say. Instead, she fell back on Shakespeare's words.

"The mask of night is on my face, else would a maiden blush paint my cheeks." In fact, her cheeks were on fire.

"Thank you for coming down," he said, though he did not attempt to move closer to her. "I was running out of quotations."

Julia wiggled her toes inside her slippers. "I must admit, I have never heard so much Shakespeare spoken in one night."

He cocked his head. "Haven't you attended any of his plays? Surely Ford's Theater or the National must produce a few of his works in between their comedies." He stepped closer to her light.

Julia sucked in her breath. Without his mask, the man was even more handsome than she had imagined. The classical lines of his face were softened by the hint of humor that shone in his dark eyes and lingered at the corners of his mouth. He looked taller in the darkness and even more broad-shouldered than she remembered from the ball.

At his question, she shook her head, and turned away. Suddenly, she was too shy to look at him. The courage provided by the champagne had disappeared. She moistened her lips. "Before the war, my parents often attended the theater in Washington, but since then, none of us has ventured into…" She caught herself before saying "that Yankee city." Instead, she finished lamely with "there."

He nodded as if he understood. "I see. Someday, there will be peace again, Miss Julia. Then I do hope that you will have the opportunity to see Shakespeare enacted on the boards."

Julia closed her eyes to block out the sight of his blue uniform. She pulled her afghan closer to her body. "I, too, long for that day."

A silence fell between them. Julia tried to think of a lighter topic of conversation, but the cold of the night crept into her consciousness. She clamped her jaws together to keep her teeth from chattering.

He cleared his throat. "I came to apologize for my behavior at the Winsteads."

His words caught Julia off guard. "What do you have to regret, Major? You were every inch a gentleman. I am the one who acted in such a scandalous way."

He grinned, then replied, "When Miss Winstead spoke in such a vile manner to you, I did not come to your defense. I was remiss and I am most sorry for it."

Julia lifted her chin and met his gaze with a steady eye.

"Why should you be? Melinda's accusations were correct, Major. I am a Confederate."

He studied her for a long silent moment. Julia forgot the chill of the air. Anxiety tore at her insides. Would this admission of hers be the undoing of the careful shield that her parents had maintained for the past two years while living in Union-occupied Alexandria?

Taking a step backward, she confessed, "I was warned never to trust the Yankees. They say that you are a wicked people. It appears now that I was well advised. Do you intend to clap me in manacles, sir? Am I to be arrested for my loyalty to my birthright?" She stretched out her hands to him and bared her wrists. The candle shook in her grip; its flame danced erratically.

He stepped closer to her. Only then did she notice that his right sleeve hung empty. She recalled that he had kept that same hand in his pocket during the whole time at the ball. Was he injured?

Without saying a word, he took her free hand in his left one. Instead of a rough grip, as she had expected after her taunting, his touch was gentle. His lips curled up in a smile.

"I see no treason here," he murmured, turning her hand over. His thumb massaged her open palm.

Her throat closed up, and her knees weakened under her nightdress. Her nerves felt as if they were being pulled taut to the breaking point. At the same time, she found his simple caress to be the most intimate thing that she had ever experienced. She wondered if he was going to kiss her now—hard, brutally—just as he had described.

Just then, something small and white fluttered on her nose—a snowflake. A second and a third followed in quick succession. Both Julia and the major looked up to the sky.

"Why, the moon has disappeared," she observed with surprise.

More snow fell, dotting them with gentle white flakes like confetti.

"And you are chilled to the bone," he remarked. His eyes were dark and full of power, yet tiny laugh lines crinkled at their corners. He continued to stroke her palm. "I may be a wicked Yankee, Miss Julia, but I am not a murderer. I have no wish for you to freeze to death on my account."

Julia gulped. "Then I am free to go, sir?"

The glow of his smile warmed her, despite her anxiety and the freezing temperature. "Only if you promise to meet with me again tomorrow at a more suitable time and place."

His suggestion was a bold challenge, one that Julia found hard to resist. "I might. Where and at what time?" Hearing her own voice, she could hardly believe she had just uttered such reckless words.

"Market Square on the corner of King and Washington Streets at three o'clock? And I promise that I will behave like a gentleman, and not like one of those Yankees whom you fear."

"I'm not afraid," she corrected.

He chuckled. "Methinks the lady doth protest too much," he murmured, staring at her hand as if he had never seen anything quite so wonderful before.

"I do not think that quotation comes from *Romeo and—* oh!" she gasped as he brushed his lips across the bare skin of her palm. Her breath caught in her throat. The shock of his kiss ran through her whole body. Blood drummed in her ears; a wave of giddiness broke over her. She would surely expire.

He looked up at her through his long dark lashes. "Will you dare to meet me in broad daylight, Miss Julia?"

She balled her hand into a fist to keep it from shaking. Then she lifted her chin a notch. "Of course I will, Major, if only to prove that you do not frighten me."

He slowly released her. "Good, I am glad to hear that." He touched the brim of his hat with his fingers. "Until tomorrow at three. And may I suggest that next time you wear gloves? Your hand is very cold."

With that observation, he turned toward the back gate. Julia clutched her candle tighter. "Major!" she called after him.

Pausing, he looked back to her. "Miss Julia?" he asked with a quizzical lift of his dark brow.

Julia cleared her throat. "I fear you have the advantage as I don't know your real name. I highly doubt that you answer to Major Romeo."

He laughed but with a bitter note. "You are correct, Miss Julia. My cousin would attest to that fact. I am Robert Montgomery of Rhinebeck, New York, and I bid you a good night." He cocked his head, then spoke again, this time in Shakespeare's sweet words. "Sleep dwell upon thine eyes, peace on thy breast."

"And to you, Major Robert Montgomery," she whispered.

He touched the brim of his hat again, then let himself out of the gate. It closed with a small click behind him as he disappeared amid the swirling snow. All the warmth of the night went with him. Just then, all the church bells in the city tolled the hour of midnight. Christ Church began its complicated peal to ring in the New Year—1864. Roused by the bells and the cold, Julia hurried through the back door and up the stairs to the safety of her room.

She was well and truly out of her mind. Mother would surely die if she knew she planned to meet a Yankee in public tomorrow. But she would—and not just to get rid of Payton!

Chapter Seven

"Oh, my heart!" Clara Chandler dropped her coffee cup. Missing the breakfast table and the corner of the Oriental carpet beneath it, the delicate English bone china smashed against the bare floor. Hot coffee pooled around the broken bits of the rose-pattern design.

Jonah set down his fork on his plate before giving his complete attention to his wife.

Clara stared at the scathing letter she held in one hand while she clutched her bosom with the other. This time there was no need for subterfuge. The loathsome words written by Melinda Winstead were vile enough to bring on a true seizure. "I shall die," Clara moaned, dropping the blue notepaper.

Jonah caught it in time before it landed in the puddle of coffee. "Hettie," he called over his shoulder. "Please fetch my medical bag and some smelling salts, as well."

The housekeeper needed no further explanation. She dashed out of the breakfast room before the doctor had finished speaking.

Closing her eyes, Clara slumped in her chair. "We are undone, Jonah," she moaned as he unfastened her dress and loosened her stays. "We will never be able to venture outside our doors again. How could she have done this to us?'' Clara would have wept, but she had no spare breath for it.

Jonah cut through the knot in her corset lacing with his pocketknife. ''What has Carolyn done now, my dear?''

Clara shook her head. ''Not Carolyn,'' she gulped. ''Julia!''

Her husband pulled apart the whalebone corset. Then he helped his wife from her chair to the low burgundy cut-velvet sofa nearby, where he laid her down, resting her head on the padded arm. Hettie returned with the doctor's satchel and the vial of spirits of ammonia. Jonah took the latter, uncorked the bottle and waved it gently under Clara's nose. She reacted to the mind-clearing fumes with a start.

''You want to get Miss Clara up to bed, sir?'' Hettie whispered.

''In good time, Hettie,'' Jonah replied. ''She needs to rest some before she climbs the stairs.'' He looked at the servant. ''Please tell Julia that I require her presence at once.''

Clara groaned at the sound of her eldest child's name. ''How can I possibly look at her?'' she cried. Her body shook with her emotion. ''She has all but killed me.''

Jonah lifted her wrist and took her pulse. ''I will speak to Julia. You have no need to involve yourself. Just rest easy, my dear.''

Clara did not bother to stifle the sobs that she knew always unmanned her husband, but allowed her tears to flow freely. ''She has betrayed us. Our family will be talked about in every decent parlor by this afternoon. We will never be received by our friends again, I just know it. We might have to move away.''

Her eyes filled, even though the idea of leaving Alexandria did have some positive merit. She had longed to go ever since the war began.

Jonah patted her hand. "No, we won't. I am sure that this tempest, too, shall pass."

Clara glared at her husband. "It will not, sir," she corrected him in a more hardy voice. Her anger at Julia gave her the strength to pull herself upright. "This atrocity will follow us like a tail follows the dog."

Just then their erring daughter appeared at the door, her face ashen. "Mother?" She rushed to Clara's side and reached to take her hand.

Clara curled her fingers into a ball and tucked her hand under a fold in her skirts. "Do not touch me, you...you Jezebel!"

At these words, Julia looked even more stricken. "What is the matter? Papa?"

Jonah held out the crumpled letter. "I have no idea. Read this, since I do not have my spectacles about me. Then, perhaps, you will be good enough to explain it."

Clara covered her ears with her hands. "Oh! I cannot bear to hear it!" she whimpered, but for once, no one, not even Hettie, gave her any attention. The loathsome contents of the letter were far too intriguing.

Julia scanned the note quickly. "Oh!" she murmured.

Clara narrowed her eyes, then looked away as Julia read:

"'Dear Mrs. Chandler, it pains me to be the bearer of bad news—' Ha!" Julia added. "Melinda Winstead revels in disasters, as long as they are not directed at her."

"Go on," ordered her father.

Out of the corner of her eye, Clara caught sight of Carolyn peeking round the door. She was too angry at Julia to bother to reprimand her younger child over the bad manners of eavesdropping.

Julia cleared her throat. "'—but I feel it is my Christian

duty to inform you of the most shocking behavior of your daughter, Julia.'" She paused a second time, much to the annoyance of her mother. "Papa, if Melinda is a Christian, then I am a Punjabi."

Jonah blew through his clipped, steel-gray mustache. "Please, Julia, no more remarks. Finish Miss Winstead's letter."

Julia cast a glance at Clara, but her mother refused to acknowledge her. Clara's pride had been rubbed raw, and she was in no mood to heal the injury so soon.

"'Last evening, your daughter had the unmitigated boldness to attend the ball given by my parents—a ball to which your family was specifically not invited. While there, Julia imbibed too many glasses of champagne. So affected by this unaccustomed amount of libations, she then made free of her person with a number of our male guests, who naturally took such behavior at face value, and treated her as nothing more than a common woman of the town.'" Julia gasped with horror.

Clara shuddered. She took the smelling salts from her husband's slack hand and waved it again under her nose. Neither Jonah nor Hettie noticed Clara's distress. They were transfixed by the letter. Clara commenced to fan herself, but no one looked her way.

"Is there more?" Jonah asked in a strangled tone.

"More slander, you mean, Papa?" Julia retorted.

"I will be the judge of that," he replied. "Continue the letter."

Julia rattled the paper as if she could shake away its filth. "'I am sorry to report that we were forced to evict your daughter from the premises. All our guests were much amazed by her most scandalous behavior, since it is well known that she comes from a good family, despite our present breach. Forgive me for the pain that this letter will cause you, but I felt compelled to inform you at once of what transpired last evening, since I am sure Julia will say nothing. I trust that you will attend to this heinous matter forthwith. Melinda Winstead.' What a piece of trash!'' Julia sank to the floor amidst her billowing skirts.

''Ooh!'' wailed Clara, this time in earnest.

Jonah signaled Hettie. ''I do believe that Mrs. Chandler will feel much better if she were taken up to her room. Go on, Clara, my dear. I will deal with this.''

Clara was tempted to resist because she was anxious to hear what Julia had to say for herself. On the other hand, she really did feel quite faint. If Julia even admitted to half of Melinda's accusations, Clara knew that she would be sick to her stomach.

Hettie slipped her arm around her shoulders. ''Come along now, Miss Clara,'' she crooned, practically pulling her off the sofa. ''You know what the old folks say,'' she continued, helping her cross the room. ''A mole don't see what his neighbor might be doing,'' she intoned, loud enough for every listening ear to hear. ''And I do believe we have a passel of moles in this story.''

Julia's shoulders sagged under the weight of Melinda's venomous lies. She slowly reread each word. The ink on the paper practically dripped with poison. She barely noticed her mother's departure, nor her father's ominous silence. Her vision blurred with tears that she refused to shed. How could Melinda be so cruel, so hateful? True, Julia had drunk too much champagne and had offered herself to Major Montgomery, but he had recognized her virtue and saved her from embarrassment—and worse. Neither Julia nor Carolyn had done anything to spoil the party, much less the scandalous behavior that Melinda accused her of. Then she realized that Carolyn's name did not appear in the letter, even though her sister had been much more prominent on the dance floor.

What had she done to deserve such particular spite from Melinda?

Dr. Chandler cleared his throat, breaking into Julia's thoughts. Looking up at her father, she was stunned to see the anger in his usually gentle eyes.

"Well?" he asked in a very quiet tone. Ice practically fell from the single word.

Julia shook her head slowly. "Lies, Papa," she whispered, barely able to keep her anger at Melinda in check. "Hateful, horrible lies."

Her father tugged on his mustache. "Did you attend the Winsteads' ball last night?"

She bit her lower lip before replying, "Yes." She made the quick decision to leave Carolyn out of the situation, if possible, and she prayed that Perkins would say nothing. Carolyn got into enough trouble as it was.

Dr. Chandler's white eyebrows rose with his surprise. "Alone?"

Julia swallowed. "Perkins escorted me there and back. I only stayed for an hour or two."

Her father sat down hard on the sofa in front of her, as if the shock of her admission had sapped his strength. "How could you have done such a thing, Julia? It's not like you at all. How could you have made such a display of yourself?"

Julia held out the letter to him. "I only drank a little champagne, Papa, and I did not make a spectacle of myself, I swear it to you."

"Do not mince matters with me, young lady. You went to the Winsteads' without an invitation."

Julia took a deep breath. "I did have an invitation, Papa," she replied in a low voice. "I will not reveal who gave it to me for that will only cause further distress to another party, but I *did* have an invitation."

Her father narrowed his eyes. Julia couldn't remember the last time she had seen him so angry. She trembled.

"You did not have our permission to go," he enunciated.

She gave him a level look. "And would you have granted me permission, if I had asked you?"

"Of course not. The Winsteads have not spoken to us since Sumter—not until now." He eyed the letter as if it were a clod of horse dung in the middle of his Oriental carpet.

Julia nodded with grim satisfaction. "Exactly why I didn't ask you."

Her father stared over her head for a moment before he said. "You have practically killed your mother. She truly does have a weak heart, you know. I am appalled by your shocking behavior."

"Papa, I did nothing to disgrace our family. I was not drunk, nor did I make a fool of myself, nor did I act like...like a hussy, as Melinda claims." Julia's ears turned red. Did Major Montgomery consider her a hussy, especially after his midnight visit?

Her father waved away her protests. "That is not the point, Julia. You went to a party to which you were not invited, and without our permission. You were out on the streets after dark without a pass from the provost marshal. What if you had been stopped by one of the guards? Or worse? You know our city is not safe for respectable folk. You attended without a chaperone, among people who have known our family since before you were born. People will gossip. How could you do this to your mother? She will not be able to go out in public for fear of the scandal you have caused."

Julia was tempted to tell her father that most of the people at the ball were not the ones who kept company with her mother, but she decided that nothing she could say would make any difference. "I'm sorry for the distress I have caused, Papa. Truly I am."

With her apology, the doctor softened a fraction, though he continued to pull at his mustache. Julia glanced at the door to see if Carolyn still lurked behind it but, for once, her sister had the good sense to silently disappear. Julia would deal with Carolyn later. In the meantime, she wondered what she could possibly do to amend the situation.

Dr. Chandler cleared his throat again, a sign that he was about to say something important. Straightening her shoulders, Julia watched him with an unwavering eye.

"It pains me to the quick, child, but you must be punished for such an infraction of manners. No, I do not believe that you acted with a loud or lewd behavior at the Winsteads'. It appears to me that Melinda is in a boiling fury because you invaded her home, and she is striking back in the only way that she knows how. I cannot say that I blame her anger, I only hope that her stories have not circulated any further than this house."

Julia sighed with relief, thankful that her father had faith in her.

"But," he continued in a harsher tone, "the fact of the matter is still your blatant disobedience to your parents' wishes and your serious lack of good manners. How can we possibly convince Payton to marry you if he thinks you are reckless, disobedient and wanton?"

Julia's heart leaped with joy. In her anger at Melinda's lies, she had forgotten her real reason for attending the party. The Yankee major had been too kind to smear her reputation, but this former friend had no such reservations.

Melinda's letter and the gossip it would generate had ruined Julia most admirably.

She hoped Payton thought she was all those things and worse. Julia said nothing aloud. There was no point in angering her father any further by reiterating her refusal to marry her cousin.

"Since it is clear that we cannot trust you, I fear we must keep you under lock and key, for your own good, and for our peace of mind."

Julia stared at him, her mouth open in horror.

"If we were Catholics, I would send you to a convent without delay, in the hope that the nuns could discipline you," he continued without a sign of emotion. "Since we are not, the best I can do is to send you to your room where you will stay until…" He wavered for only a moment. "Until I say otherwise."

"Papa, please—"

He shook his head at her interruption. "You may come downstairs for meals and for exercise in the garden, but the rest of the day, you will stay in your room. There you may contemplate the injury that you have done to your mother's health, to your future and to our family's good name."

Julia gasped at his harshness. "Papa, you have always been a fair man, ready to listen to both sides of the story whenever Carolyn was in trouble. Is this fair—to treat me in this way without any mitigating points in my favor?"

He passed his hand over his eyes as if the sight of her was too painful for him. "What else can I do, Julia? Your impetuous action has left me with very little choice. Your mother is right. You should have been married a year ago. The duties of a wife and mother curb wild impulses."

Julia rose to her feet. "Papa, all I did was attend a party for a few hours. I wore a mask and behaved myself. Is that such a crime? I did not steal their silverware, nor did I cause a ruckus. I did not slander the Winsteads, though Melinda has no qualms about slandering me. I was not disrespectful to a single soul.

"Papa, I am loyal to the Confederacy. I long for Virginia to be free from the grip of the Yankees, but more than anything else I long for peace. I am sick of being walled up inside this house, when I know that others my age are going to balls and picnics and teas and to…to the theater! Papa, do you realize that I have never seen a play? How long will it be before I can live a normal life again? Will I never have the same pleasures that Mother had when she was young? I think not. I will be too old by the time this war ends."

Dr. Chandler's anger left his eyes, though not from the set of his shoulders. "War asks us all to make sacrifices, Julia. For the loss of your youthful times, I am sorry. For the death of your young beau, I grieve. But no matter how weary we become of the privations that we must bear, we must continue to endure for the love of Virginia and those principles of independence that we hold so dear. For me, it has meant the decline of my medical practice, as well as the loss of many good friends. Your mother has lost the social life that she dotes on, and her health has suffered for it. The sons of many of our friends have already given their life's blood for the sake of the Confederacy. Frank died in the first flush of his manhood. Is it too much to ask you to give up dancing and the theater?"

His words hurt Julia far more than a shout. The reminder of Frank especially wounded her. She clutched the silver locket. How easily she had forgotten the boy who had told her that he loved her. More hot tears welled up in her eyes, and she allowed them to fall freely. "I am so sorry, Papa," she whispered.

He nodded. "I know you are, my dear, but the fact of your disobedience remains. You must be punished, not only for your own sake, but also as an example to Carolyn, lest she take it in her head to run wild in the streets."

A small flame of resentment flared up in Julia's breast. Why should she alone suffer the blame when it was Carolyn's idea to go in the first place? Because if she hadn't gone, Carolyn would have perhaps gotten herself into worse difficulties. Julia remained silent.

With a sigh, her father touched her elbow. "Come, this unpleasantness will pass. Once you are married to Payton and safe at Belmont, this episode will be nothing but a shadow."

She would never marry Payton.

Only after she returned to her room did Julia remember her promise to meet Major Montgomery at three o'clock that afternoon. Somehow, she had to send him a message with her regrets, so that he would not think her fickle. Julia did not pause to consider why the Yankee's good opinion meant so much to her.

Chapter Eight

A merry tune, expertly whistled, wafted through Colonel Lawrence's half-open office door. Surprised by the levity and the early hour on New Year's morning, he rose from his desk and cast an inquisitive glance into his outer room where his officers toiled to decipher the latest Confederate code and relay the gathered information to the proper Federal command. The colonel lifted his bushy brows with surprise when he saw that the music came from his usually dour major. What was even more surprising was the unaccustomed smile on Montgomery's face.

Lawrence strode out to the antechamber on the pretext of searching for an agent's field report. He paused by the major's desk. ''I presume that you enjoyed yourself last night, Montgomery,'' he muttered, as he flipped through some unimportant documents that lay near at hand.

The major cocked his head. ''Tolerable, sir, most tolerable.'' He did not bother to stifle his smile.

Lawrence shot him a sidelong glance. ''So I see. What a change! To what do we poor mortals owe the pleasure of your good humor?''

''A woman, sir,'' sniggered Lieutenant Johnson before

his cousin could reply. Montgomery frowned at his high-spirited relative.

"Cherchez la femme." The colonel nodded with a grin of remembrance of his own past times in petticoat company.

"A lady, sir," Montgomery corrected the lieutenant.

"And a very pretty one, as I recollect," Johnson added, ignoring Montgomery's scowl.

Better and better, thought Lawrence. It was high time that the major pulled himself out of the doldrums and started living again. "Indeed?" Lawrence prompted.

Montgomery glanced around the office. Every junior officer, and most of the civilian clerks, had stopped their work to listen. He flushed under his tight collar. "It was nothing, I assure the colonel. While I do admit that Miss Julia Chandler possesses a pleasing countenance, my interest in her company was purely—" He cleared his throat. "Purely official business," he muttered. "In short, I was feasting with the enemy."

Lawrence suppressed a grin. "Indeed?" he echoed. "I did not think that a dance or two would be of interest to the War Department, nor that a pretty girl could be considered an enemy. Please explain yourself, Major."

The colonel enjoyed Montgomery's sudden discomfiture. It proved that the boy was a human being, instead of a well-educated waxwork.

Montgomery swallowed before replying. "Miss Chandler is a Southern sympathizer. I considered it my duty to…um…keep an eye on her in case she…that is…" He coughed to cover his obvious embarrassment. "Our meeting was a chance encounter," he concluded in a rush. "Nothing more."

"Chandler," Lawrence repeated the name to himself, while several of the clerks chuckled aloud. The colonel had heard that name before, but he couldn't remember where. He turned back to his office. "Very well, Major. I apologize for my interruption of your work. Proceed." He shut the door behind him.

Lawrence lowered himself onto his cracked black leather chair. Chandler, Chandler, where had he heard that name? He would have to look it up. The colonel wrinkled his nose as if he had just smelled a foul gutter stench. Spying was a nasty business. Yet the first two years of warfare had demonstrated the necessity for this deplorable form of combat. It was an ironic twist of fate that Lawrence, who hated all forms of lying and cheating, found himself assigned to the War Department's new secret service, Office of Military Intelligence—the brainchild of the Honorable Edwin Stanton, the Secretary of War.

His mind roved over the past few months, plucking out the few instances when the subject of feminine spying had arisen. Major Montgomery's new alliance with Julia Chandler could be beneficial. The colonel took out a sheet of his official stationery from his letter holder. He dipped his pen into the ink bottle, then composed a brief note to Pinkerton. Lawrence needed a lot more information about the Chandlers of Alexandria before taking any action.

Pulling his woolen muffler tighter around his neck, Rob berated himself for his poor choice of a meeting place. Alexandria's Market Square was an ideal spot for an assignation with a gently-bred lady, but not in the depths of winter. The snow flurry of the previous evening had dusted the gabled rooftops like confectioner's sugar, but the cobbled thoroughfares looked more like dirty molasses. The thermometer had plunged since yesterday. Stamping his feet to keep warm, he scanned the crowds of citizens and soldiers who strolled along King Street. Inside his greatcoat pocket, he carried a small box of sweets from one of the Federal City's finest bonbon shops.

"Excuse me, sir," said a voice directly behind him.

Rob whirled around and stared into the ebony face of a dignified-looking matron, clothed in a gray woolen dress with double skirts, a thick knitted shawl of a vivid orange hue and a white kerchief tied around her head. She carried a willow-work shopping basket that held several small parcels.

He touched the brim of his hat to her with his good hand. "May I be of assistance?" he asked.

The woman gave him an appraising look before she replied, "That depends on whether you are Major Montgomery or not."

Surprised that this stranger knew his name, Rob nodded. "I am, and you are?"

She pursed her lips. "I've come from Miss Julia Chandler, though why I let her talk me into this fool trip, I don't know." She shook her head.

Rob swallowed down his growing misgiving. "Is she ill?" he asked. Perhaps she had taken a chill after spending such a long time with him in the wintry garden.

"Oh, she's in fine fettle—too fine, if you ask me. She's managed to displease *both* her parents."

Rob knotted his brows. Had their meeting last night been discovered? "I trust that she has not suffered for it."

The woman raised one eyebrow. "That she has, sir. Her father has confined her to the house, and says he won't let her out until she is good and married."

Anger rose in Rob's breast. Though he barely knew the lady, in his estimation, Julia was a sweet, gentle girl. "What was her crime?"

The woman cocked her head. "Oh, I expect that you know all about that, Major Montgomery, since I think you were at that Winstead party last night. Miss Julia had no business going to that ball, but I am not surprised that poor child did. Like my mama always said, the best watermelons holler at you from over the neighbor's fence.'' She gave him a meaningful look.

Rob tried to sort out exactly what the servant meant. Had their tryst in the garden been discovered? Or was it only Julia's attendance at the ball that had caused her incarceration? ''And her sister?'' he asked. ''Is she locked in, too?''

The woman's face took on a shrewd expression. ''Miss Carolyn? Now what do you know about that child?''

Rob realized that he had just stumbled into a patch of quicksand. He chose his answer with care. ''I know that Miss Julia has a sister named Carolyn. I only wondered if she, too, shared the same fate.''

A hint of a smile touched the woman's lips. ''I can see that you have the gift of a silver tongue, Major, but it won't do you a speck of good now. Miss Carolyn is like a cat. She has nine lives and always lands on her feet. On the other hand, Miss Julia is shut up tighter than a drum, and she'll stay that way until Mr. Payton comes to get her.''

Rob narrowed his eyes. ''And who is this Payton fellow?'' He had a sinking feeling that he already knew.

The maidservant didn't seem surprised by his question. In fact, she looked as if she had expected it. ''Why, he's her cousin from down Richmond way. He's the one her family is fixing to marry Miss Julia.''

Rob suppressed an oath. Payton must be the toad.

''I had no idea that Julia was engaged to be married. She neglected to mention that fact to me—at the ball,'' he probed.

''That's because she doesn't know that her mama wrote to Mr. Payton this morning and told him to come get her. He's a bad mixture—been that way since he was in short pants. Miss Julia would rather hug a skunk than hug him. All my young lady wanted to do was to kick up her heels a bit before she's too old.''

"Why doesn't she just say no, if she doesn't like the man?" he asked, remembering the sudden swiftness of his own broken betrothal to the feckless Lucy.

The woman snorted. "I don't know what folks do up north, Mr. Major, but down here in Virginia, proper young ladies marry the men their fathers pick out for them. But not Miss Julia, she did the picking first time round. But Mr. Franklin Shaffer got himself shot dead. All the good boys have become mighty scarce these days ever since you Yankees started killing them. Mr. Payton may be the scraping at the bottom of the barrel, but at least he's still breathing.''

"I see." No wonder Julia had seemed so desperate last night!

"In any case, Miss Julia asked me to give you her regrets that she couldn't meet with you this afternoon—though she should be ashamed of herself to go off after a man—especially a Yankee soldier!—without her parents' knowledge. That's what trashy girls do, and my Miss Julia is not one of those, you understand what I'm saying?''

Rob nodded. "Rest assured that I never considered her anything but a fine, respectable young lady.''

He started to give the woman a verbal message in return, but thought better of it. Julia was in enough trouble as it was. For all he knew, this servant might go straight to Julia's father with her tale. Rob delved into his inner breast pocket and pulled out his small memorandum book and pencil. He rarely used it, since writing with his left hand was a chore, especially in public, but he felt compelled to send Julia a safe message in return. He prayed that the servant couldn't read. Under her interested gaze, he extracted the silver lead pencil from the book's side pocket with his teeth. Flicking his wrist, he opened to a blank page. Ignoring the woman's stare, he placed one foot on a carriage block, balanced the little book on his knee and printed out his short message.

"Does her room overlook the street?" he asked as casually as he could manage. He wanted to be absolutely sure where she was located before he visited the garden again.

She chuckled. "Like my mama always said, a wise fox knows where the yard dog sleeps. The girls' room is in the back of the house."

"I'll come again by moonlight tonight. Ten o'clock. You know the place," he wrote. He hoped that Julia could decipher his scrawl. He tore the page from the book, folded it between his fingers, then handed it to the woman.

"Please give this to Miss Julia for me." He returned the booklet to his pocket. Then he took out his little box of candy. "And give her these from me as well, if you would be so kind."

She took the box, sniffed the lid and then shot Rob another one of her shrewd looks. "You sure know how to win a woman's heart, Major Montgomery. Judging by the look of you, I expect you've had a lot of practice. Now, you listen to me real good. If you double deal with Miss Julia's heart, you will have to answer to me, Hettie Perkins, you hear?"

She reminded Rob of a ruffled mother hen. He gave her a winning smile. "My ears are good, Hettie Perkins. I will keep your words in mind."

"See that you do."

He fished in his trouser pocket and felt a quarter. "Take

this for your pains, ma'am. And commend me to Miss Julia.''

Hettie eyed the silver coin. ''You expect to buy my approval of these shenanigans, Mr. Major?''

He admired both her loyalty to her mistress as well as her sagacity. ''No, I expect you to buy some gewgaw here at the market that might attract your eye. The day is cold, and I appreciate your time.''

Hettie plucked the quarter from his fingers. ''I expect I can find something of interest.'' She dropped the coin in the pocket of her apron. ''See that you remember what I told you.'' With that final warning, Hettie shifted her shopping basket to her other arm, then turned into the square.

Rob watched as she disappeared among the vendors' ramshackle stalls. Only then did he consider what he had just done. Julia was not only a Confederate, but also an engaged woman, though not of her own free will. By all rights, Rob should have nothing more to do with her. The box of caramels made a fitting thank-you gift for a pleasant evening. But Rob didn't want it to end there. He had to see Julia again, even under the difficult circumstances engendered by her parents. She made his heart sing. He not only looked forward to spending another freezing night in the Chandlers' garden; he relished the challenge.

Not even rereading the sadly beautiful lines from Shakespeare's *Romeo and Juliet* could keep Julia's attention from straying time and again to the small mantel clock that ticked away the afternoon hours. Bless Hettie for agreeing to meet with Major Montgomery even though he was a Yankee. Now Julia waited with nervous dread for her return. Hettie had promised to be back by 3:30 p.m. It was nearly four o'clock now.

Maybe the major had not kept his appointment; perhaps

he had only toyed with Julia's emotions last night. Maybe he had been unavoidably detained, and Hettie had missed him. Maybe Hettie had not recognized him, despite the detailed description Julia had given her, even mentioning the major's disinclination to use his right hand. Perhaps Hettie had not gone to the market; maybe her kitchen duties had prevented her from leaving the house.

The more Julia stewed over these possibilities, and a dozen others like them, the less interested she was in Shakespeare's star-crossed lovers.

She was acting like a ninny. She shouldn't care a fig for the man. He was a Yankee—and she despised Yankees.

Julia let her book slide to the floor when Hettie opened the bedroom door. She balanced a silver tray that held a pot of tea together with a tea cup and saucer.

Relief flooded Julia. It wasn't because she was dying for a cup of tea. "Did you see Major Montgomery?" she asked in a breathless undertone.

Hettie drew in a deep sigh, as she set down the tray on a small round table before the fire. "Like my mama always said, good looks don't split rails. Lordy, child, you have no earthly idea how to pick a man. First Frank and now this one."

Used to Hettie's maxims, Julia clapped her hands with joy. "So you did see him! Did you give him my message? What did he say? Was he angry that I wasn't there? Did you think him handsome? Well, what did he say, Hettie? Please, I am all in a tizzy for your news."

The housekeeper sat down on a rocker and stretched her feet toward the blaze in the hearth. "Have mercy, Miss Julia! Your questions take my breath away. It was cold out there in the marketplace."

Kneeling by the rocker, Julia took the woman's hands

in hers. The teapot had warmed them. "Don't tease me, Hettie. What did he say?"

"I thought you asked me if I thought him a handsome man? How can I answer two questions at once?" Smiling, she patted Julia's shoulder. "Rest easy, child. Of course I found him. A man that tall, wearing a Yankee uniform with one hand stuck in his pocket all the time is hard to miss. As to his looks, you are a better judge of that than me. All I can say is that I found him to be a man of character." She chuckled. "Oh, yes, indeedy, quite a character!"

Julia frowned. "Did he say something cheeky to you?"

Hettie only chuckled again. "Not at all, though I expect that he could be very naughty, if he wanted. Yes, indeed! He's got that devilish look about him! Like my mama said, a hungry rooster don't cackle when he finds the worm."

Julia bit back her impatience. "Please tell me, what did he say?"

Hettie shrugged. "Oh, he's a man of few words. Didn't say much at all, except to ask after you, and—" Pausing, she fumbled in her apron pocket. "He gave me this note. I expect he thought I couldn't read—which I can't, of course," she added with a sly grin. Julia knew that Hettie was as well-schooled as herself.

She eagerly unfolded the scrap of paper and pored over the words. Though he had printed, his letters were difficult to decipher.

"I expect that he's not used to writing with his other hand," Hettie observed, as she poured the hot brew into Julia's cup. "His scribble is enough to make your eyes water."

Julia's heart skipped faster as she reread his brief message. He really did want to see her! She shivered with anticipation.

Hettie added two spoonfuls of sugar. "I suppose you are going to be fool enough to keep that appointment?" she asked in an offhand manner.

Julia glanced up at her beloved confidante. "Now how do you know I am going to meet anyone?"

Hettie stirred the cup. "I expect a little bird told me so." She lifted a white damask napkin from the tray, revealing a small blue velvet box with gold letters stamped on the cover. "And that same lowdown, no-account Yankee brought this for you, though why, I don't know."

With a cry of glee, Julia pounced on the box. She had never before received sweets from a gentleman. "Velati's Bonbons! Oh, Hettie, this is the finest confectioner in Washington." She lifted the lid and nearly swooned at the sight of the contents. "Caramels! Mmm! Good enough to make the angels weep!"

Hettie rocked in the chair. "You'd be wise to hide that pretty box or your mama will make you weep for sure if she sees it. In the meantime, drink up your tea and think of what you're going to say when you see this major of yours."

"I'll thank him for the caramels, of course." Julia gave a sugary grin.

"I expect so," said Hettie, closing her eyes. "Just don't take too long expressing your gratitude."

Chapter Nine

The church bells of Alexandria struck ten as Rob let himself through the Chandlers' back gate. For safety's sake, he had left his horse at the public stables just off Washington Street, so that no inquisitive neighbor would spy it hitched outside Julia's house and wonder about the Chandlers' late evening guest. Throughout his evening meal at Lyle's Tavern, Rob pondered why he felt compelled to see Julia again. At the very least, he risked the taint of scandal should his visit be discovered. At the worst, Dr. Chandler could fill his body with buckshot and finish the job another Confederate had begun seven months ago at Gettysburg. Yet a sense of urgency drove him to keep this reckless tryst. Just this last time, he promised himself.

Rob crept along the wall to the cover of the friendly magnolia tree. With a small sigh of relief, he ducked under its boughs. Then he scanned the second-floor windows for a light.

"Good evening, Major," said Julia in the shadows.

Rob froze; his mind sharpened. Narrowing his eyes, he peered through the gloom in the direction of her voice. "Miss Julia?"

Her laugh answered his question. "I could be, if you so desire."

Rob stepped closer to the shrouded form next to the tree trunk. "I do indeed crave the company of Miss Julia Chandler," he replied, in a voice grown husky. He tried to spy her face in the depths of the large hood that covered her glorious hair.

"Then I will answer for her, and you may take my words as hers." So saying, she opened the shutter of her dark lantern. The candle within shed a little of its feeble light between them. She pulled back her hood, then allowed it to drop to her shoulders.

Her warm smile would have melted a heart of stone. Rob's human one thumped against his chest. Though scudding clouds covered the moon, light from a distant street lamp made Julia look even more beautiful than he had remembered. Her extraordinary green eyes glowed with a fire that made him forget the bitter coldness of the night. Her lush lips curved upward at their corners, tempting him to forgo his good intentions and taste their nectar. His gaze fell to the creamy line of her neck and lingered there. He longed to plant a row of kisses along the sweet route to her hidden breasts.

Rob gave himself a mental shake. He had been out of women's company for too long. His lustful thoughts did not honor the lady standing before him. He cleared his throat. "You surprised me. I had expected to see you at your window as a forlorn captive. Instead, you are down here like Queen Titania in her bower."

An unexpected emotion flared within Julia. At the sound of his voice, a warm flush washed her cheeks. It was so strange that this man—a Yankee—could affect her so much, when other men's voices did nothing to shake her accustomed calm. Even Frank's cheerful voice had sunk to a whisper with the passage of time. When Rob lifted his dark eyes to meet hers, Julia experienced a buoyancy to the depths of her soul. Last night, she had thought that she was ill, but now she realized that her flushed face and rapid pulse were symptoms of a sickness in her heart. Some of her novels likened love to a disease, but she had always presumed that the authors used their poetic license. Now, with her cheeks fevered, her blood pounding against her temples and her breath coming in short gasps, she believed that every word she had read on the subject didn't half do justice to the real thing.

How could she be falling in love with this man? She barely knew him. She had to remember he was a Yankee.

Yet, she found that she could not flee from him any more than she could stop her blood from flowing. This near-stranger exuded a sexual magnetism that she had never before experienced—not even with Frank. She felt giddy as if she had taken a glass of champagne. Julia wet her dry lips. She must pull herself together before she lost complete control of her wits. Thank heavens Rob's reference to Shakespeare's fairy queen had given her the conversational opening that she desperately needed.

"I pray thee, gentle mortal, speak again," she replied, quoting from *A Midsummer Night's Dream*. "My ear is much enamored by thy note."

He chuckled. "Methinks I should have brushed up on the Bard, instead of reading dull reports this morning. But, since this is not a midsummer's eve but the coldest night in January, I will come to the point—when we last met, I noticed that your hands were cold."

Before she could frame a reply, he took her hand in his. She inhaled sharply at the touch of his warm skin, but did not pull out of his grasp.

"Ah," he murmured, as he caressed the back of her hand. "I see that they are still cold. I will remedy this situation."

He gently released her, then reached inside his coat and withdrew a small package. "Please oblige me by accepting this small token of my…my concern for your health and well-being."

Julia looked from his face to the gift in his hand. His unexpected gesture flattered her, though she knew that she should not accept anything more from him. After all, they had never been properly introduced, nor did he pay his call in her family's parlor under the stern gaze of her parents. She bit her lower lip.

"You are most kind, and far too generous, Major Montgomery. You have already sent me the most wonderful caramels that I could ever eat. But I must—"

A sudden fear flashed in his eyes. "Please don't reject my poor offering, Miss Julia. Upon my word, I mean no offense."

Julia's curiosity, as well as her desire to please him, rose at his imploring words. She accepted the tissue-wrapped package, allowing her trembling fingers to brush over his. Once again, excitement rippled through her veins at their touch. She quickly untied the ribbon and pulled away the paper.

"Gloves!" she exclaimed, fondling the thick fleece-lined suede.

He nodded. "A perfectly respectable gift to give to a lady, especially one with cold hands," he added.

"But these are quite expensive," she whispered before she remembered that one never spoke of the cost of things, especially a gift. "It would be wicked of me to accept them."

"It would be very wicked of you to reject them," he whispered.

His seductive voice sent a delicious chill down her spine. In that instant, she realized that her feelings for him had nothing to do with reason. For the moment, she would hang up her common sense. Besides, his gift was greatly appreciated—and so was the giver.

"True, Major," she replied, pulling on the gloves with satisfaction. "I do try to avoid wickedness whenever possible."

When she looked at him again, she was startled to see that he had drawn closer to her so that their shoulders almost touched. The faint whiff of his bay rum cologne disturbed her—in the most pleasurable way. For a brief instant, she fantasized being held close in his embrace. His eyes gleamed at her. In her confusion, she glanced down and saw that his right hand was still deeply embedded in his coat pocket. Here was a subject that not only intrigued her, but would also distract them both from tripping further into the dangerous sensual quagmire that dawned before them.

"I sincerely hope that your hands are not too cold." She sounded stiff and unnatural.

"I was injured," he said with a steely edge in his voice. Instantly, Julia regretted her words. His pain was not only in his hand, but in his soul.

"It tears my heart to think of it," she whispered, not knowing what else to say. "I am so sorry."

"So am I," he snapped, then coughed. "Forgive me, Miss Julia, I didn't mean to be so sharp with you. My hand was shot up at Gettysburg, and I am not yet comfortable with the fact that I can never use it again."

Gettysburg! The name of the dreadful battle screamed in her memory. The South had lost so many of her sons during those three days of carnage. She studied the Yankee beside her in a new light. Naturally the major would have been on the other side—shooting at her friends. She gave him another sidelong glance. She sensed that he was not proud of the part he had played in that bloodbath. Her heart softened.

"Is your wound so truly bad?"

He looked away. "You may take my word for it. My hand isn't fit to be seen by a lady." The drooping line of his shoulders bespoke his shame.

She touched his sleeve. "You have forgotten. I'm not a lady. I go where I am not invited," she whispered, then added. "Misery weighs less when it is shared."

He said nothing but pulled his hand out of his pocket. Then he removed his glove. "It will disgust you." Bitterness dripped with his warning. Pain carved merciless lines in his face.

Steeling herself for a fearful sight, Julia stepped closer and took his hand in hers. The warmth of his skin surprised her. She had expected his hand to be like a dead, cold fish. She held her lantern closer.

"Oh!" her breath caught in her throat at the sight.

"I did warn you," he said, almost angrily.

His little finger was missing from the top of the first knuckle, and his ring finger lacked its tip. The hand itself had lost its proper shape, as if a gigantic hammer had flattened it. The skin on his palm had knitted badly, causing his fingers to curl inward a little. His wrist bore a huge white scar where a bullet had smashed through it. Yet she could feel solid bone under her fingers instead of fragments.

Julia was tempted to kiss the scar as if that simple act could smooth away his festering hurt, but she decided against her impulse. The major might misconstrue her sympathy, and take more liberties with her than she was willing to give him—at least for now.

Instead, she covered his hand with hers. "It is not as bad as you think, Major Montgomery. Perhaps time will surprise you."

"I doubt it," he replied, but he did not snatch his hand away as Julia had expected. In a gentler tone, he continued. "At least, you did not shriek at the sight. For that, I thank you."

By the thickness of his voice, Julia suspected that other people in his life had done exactly that when they were confronted with his injury. How cruel of them!

Removing his hand, Rob quickly shoved it back in his pocket.

"I wish that this horrible war was over." Julia sighed. "Before anyone else gets hurt."

"Amen to that prayer."

She pursed her lips. "Do not misconstrue my sentiments, Major," she said, hoping that she wouldn't offend him. "I am a Confederate down to my bones. I can't help feeling the way I do."

"Which is?" he asked, in a cold, exact manner. He withdrew his good hand and shoved it back in his glove.

She looked across the dark garden. "The Confederacy has no wish to conquer the North. Whatever would we do with you people?" Turning toward him, she boldly looked into his eyes. "We only want to separate from the United States, to be free to pursue our own destiny. Why do you want to trample the South underfoot? Does your government love us Southerners so much that it is willing to send so many young men to die in order to keep us under their thumbs?"

He stiffened as though she had struck him. "I fight to

preserve this nation in its entirety, North and South. And to free the slaves, of course.''

Julia bowed her head with resignation. There was no way she could explain to this man from New York the long, complex social history that bound the black and white Southerners to each other. He would never understand. In truth, Julia barely understood it herself. When her father had given Perkins and Hettie their freedom papers last January, her mother had predicted a slew of dreadful repercussions. To date, nothing had happened. Hettie and her husband continued to serve the Chandler family just as they had done before. Only now, Papa paid the Perkinses for their work.

''I wish it were in my power to end this madness tomorrow,'' she told him in honesty.

''On that point, we both agree, Miss Julia,'' he replied with quiet emphasis.

''Then let us speak of other things, Major,'' she said more brightly. Better to leave the war's ugly reality outside her snow-frosted garden.

His expression softened and a smile found its way to the corners of his mouth. ''Very well, Miss Julia. To begin again, please call me Rob, not Major Montgomery. Let's leave the army outside your gate.''

Julia relaxed, cheered by his willingness to put aside their political differences and agree to disagree. It seemed a very intimate thing to call him by his Christian name. She was honored by his trust.

Time and the sub-freezing temperature surrounded them unnoticed. For the next hour, Julia and Rob huddled on a garden bench under the magnolia and conversed on ordinary subjects: of childhoods filled with pranks and schoolwork, of the common foibles of maiden aunts, of favored pets, unruly siblings and of holiday merriment. At length, a stiff wind off the Potomac River blew through Alexandria's streets and over the Chandlers' back wall. Julia shivered in its icy breath. Putting his arm around her, Rob drew her close against his warm body. Julia shivered again when she felt the hard muscles of his chest, even under several layers of heavy wool. His thigh brushed against hers. She inhaled sharply at the contact, then coughed to cover her confusion.

"You will catch your death of cold and it will be all my fault," he murmured; his warm breath fanned her cheek.

Julia's heart raced like a bolting horse. She shivered all the more, though it had nothing to do with the biting wind. Laying her head against the cold buttons of his greatcoat, she thought she could detect the faint beat of his heart, and it thrilled her. *What am I doing?* In that moment, she knew that her hatred for all Yankees had shattered like broken glass.

"You should go inside," he murmured in an odd, husky voice.

"You are right—I should," she concurred, though she did not move. She was in paradise, albeit a cold one.

"May I see you again tomorrow?" he asked, pressing his cheek against the top of her head.

How comforting that felt! And how very right, as if she had been created for exactly this man. "I fear that I will still be housebound," she replied.

He chuckled. "As you are now?"

She smiled into the folds of his greatcoat's shoulder cape. "Exactly."

"Then may I come again to your garden, just as I did tonight?"

She sighed with contentment. "Our garden attracts all sorts of birds, even blue ones."

He grinned. "I do not have a singing voice, but I will endeavor to keep you amused."

Julia quivered at the word *amused*. The way he said it made the promised entertainment sound very seductive. Her common sense suddenly reared its head. What was the matter with her? Resting shamelessly in the arms of a man, who was her enemy?

Julia lifted her head to say good-night, and found, to her shock, that his lips hovered very near hers. His tongue flicked out between his teeth, then retreated. He tensed under his coat.

Heavens above! He was going to kiss her!

Her throat tightened. "This…this is too rash," she stammered. "Much too sudden."

Raising his head, he released a long, slow breath. "Forgive me. I nearly forgot myself." He stood up, taking his warmth from her.

Julia experienced an odd twinge of disappointment. Rising from the bench, she attempted to ease the ticklish situation. "The hour has grown very late. I share a bed with Carolyn and I am afraid that she might notice my absence. I would not, for the world, wish any more harm fall on you from a Confederate gun. My father used to be an excellent shot."

He gave her a wry smile. "I appreciate your concern, Miss Julia. But tomorrow night? May I come again at ten?"

Julia was afraid to voice her consent. Instead, she merely nodded.

He touched the brim of his hat. "Then, a thousand times good night until tomorrow's night comes again."

Before she could whisper, "Good night, Rob," he strode out of the garden, just as if she had sent him on his way with a flea in his ear. He did not look back when he lifted the gate latch, nor did he wave from the alleyway. In less than two minutes, he was gone from sight. Julia touched her bare lips that had no sweet kiss lingering on them.

Chapter Ten

All the way back to his rooms at Ebbitt's Hotel, and throughout the rest of that dark night, Rob could not get Julia Chandler out of his head. The analytical part of his brain told him that she was of no interest to him. Julia was a Southerner—a breed apart, as his mother would have said. Rob had been raised to believe that all Southerners were a lazy, shiftless people, who now fought to keep their slaves to do their work and wait upon them. Yet, Rob had difficulty fitting Julia into that description. He found her to be a highly intelligent woman, though extremely sheltered. Considering her desire to teach school, she did not strike him as shiftless. Then again, he had only met her three times, and always under unusual circumstances, to put it mildly. His mother and assorted aunts would have been scandalized if they knew he was wooing a Confederate lady.

Rob bolted upright in his narrow bed. Was he really wooing Miss Julia? Beads of sweat broke out on his forehead, despite the fact that his bedroom was chilly. Mr. William Ebbitt practiced the utmost thrift when it came to heating his establishment at night. Rob returned his head to his pillow and pulled the thick woolen blanket high under his chin.

Of course he wasn't wooing Julia, or any other woman. After his nasty experience with Lucy Van Tassel, he had sworn off matrimony for good. Lucy's emphatic rejection forced Rob to realize that he would remain a bachelor all his life. His nephews and nieces would have to fulfill his desire for children.

So, his nagging conscience asked, if he wasn't wooing Julia in her father's garden, what was he doing there? Making small talk while they froze to death? Thanking Julia for the pleasant time he had enjoyed at the Winsteads' ball—three times over? What about the caramels? A mere courtesy gift. And the gloves? Her hands were cold. And the promise to return tomorrow night?

Rob had no answer to that question—at least none that he cared to examine closely. Squeezing his eyes shut, he willed his mind to think of something relaxing like drifting clouds and fields of waving grain. The last thing he remembered before sleep finally claimed him was the way Julia had looked at him when he had shown her his hand. A gentle kindness had shone in her face. Warm gratitude filled his heart.

In the cold light of dawn, his memories of the Chandlers' garden refused to go away. While buttoning his shirt with his left hand, he paused to study his right. In the dark last night, Julia could not have fully seen the damage that one of her countrymen had done to him. Perhaps she did not comprehend the extent of the scarring, nor realize that some of his fingers were virtually frozen into their half-curled position. It had ceased to look like a hand to Rob. In his own mind, he called it a claw.

Julia was only being kind. Her gentle heart didn't allow her to see him as he really was. She pitied him, that was all. With that distasteful thought, he struggled into his uniform frock coat. In the mirror, a grim-faced major of the United States Army looked back at him.

That was who he was—her enemy. He had no business pursuing this…relationship with such a gentle lady. They were too divided by their backgrounds and beliefs. This friendship could only lead to tears or trouble. Best to end it now and save both of them from grief. He would not accept pity, even if it was wrapped in kindness.

Rob clamped his jaws together so tightly that a small nerve in his cheek throbbed. He had made his apologies to Julia for his lack of courtesy at the ball. He had sweetened his shortcomings with caramels. He had, for a brief moment in time, allowed himself to live again as the man he had once been, before that blistering day at Gettysburg changed him forever. As it was, he had pushed his advantage almost too far with that innocent lady. His gift of the gloves was enough—in fact, they had been far too much for propriety, but that was now over.

His mirrored image squared his shoulders. Oak leaves embroidered in gold bullion on his shoulder boards flashed in the pale light of the winter's morning sun. His military rank reminded him of his job in the secret service. Consorting with the enemy, even one as sweet as Julia, was against the rules of war. He knew the next action he must take, and it wrung his heart, for he realized how hurt Julia would be when he did not keep his appointment that evening.

"It is the best thing that I can do for her—for both of us," he said aloud to the man in the looking glass. "And I am a vile cad for it."

Briefly, he considered writing her a short note to explain his reasons for ending their friendship, but he had no way to send it to her without risking interception by her parents.

Of course, there was the maidservant, if he could find her again. No, the break must be complete and final—like a battlefield amputation. He glowered at his right hand. Maybe he should have let the doctor saw it off instead of stupidly hoping that one day it would be whole.

He would never allow himself to be that foolish again.

In the dark night, the chimes in the tower of Christ Church tolled half-past ten. Julia burrowed her chilled face into the fur collar of her cloak. What had delayed Rob? He had promised to be here by now. Perhaps the freezing weather had made the roads between Alexandria and Washington difficult to traverse at night—especially when so many of the water-filled ruts had frozen over. His horse must take its time to pick its way around them lest it break an ankle in the dark.

She shivered. At least her fingers were warm. She smiled at the fleece-lined gloves that protected her hands from the bitter wind, so much better than her muff. How very thoughtful Rob was! Especially for a Yankee!

Julia shook her head. She couldn't think of Rob as a Northerner. In the dim light of the garden, his coat lost its blue color. It could have been black—or even dark Confederate gray. How wonderful it would have been had Rob been born on this side of Mr. Mason and Mr. Dixon's survey line! If he had been a Southerner, Julia knew she would have married him in a heartbeat. Poor Frank, for all his charm, did not hold a candle to Rob.

Julia pulled her cloak tighter around her. Rob couldn't possibly marry her. Not only was he a Yankee, but he had never even hinted at his feelings for her. Perhaps she had been just a bit of fun to him. Julia bit her lower lip. Here she was—a silly, moon-crazed girl standing in a frigid garden waiting for some will-o'-the-wisp to come by and dally with her once again for his own amusement.

Her cheeks burned. How could she have been so stupid? She had been so anxious to find someone nice to ruin her that she had not used the eyes that the good Lord had given her. She should have seen straight through that handsome smile of his and all those honey words immediately. Was her heart to be bought by a box of sweets and a pair of gloves? She had been out of civilized society for too long, and had forgotten how to spy a snake in the grass.

Of course, Major Montgomery wasn't coming tonight! He never intended to return. Julia should be thankful that the man possessed enough decency not to pursue his obvious advantage over her.

What a foolish ninny I have been! Picking up the hem of her skirts she dashed to the back steps. The frosted autumn leaves crackled underfoot. She would count this experience as a very good lesson learned. Major Montgomery was nothing more than a rascal and a Yankee!

The next morning, a soft tap on the bedroom door pulled Julia out of her self-pity. The cold sunlight illuminated the pages of her book, but her eyes did not see the words for the sheen of tears in them.

She cleared her throat. "Who is it?"

"Carolyn," her sister replied. "May I come in, Julia?"

Julia closed her book. "I have a headache, Carolyn. I'm afraid I am poor company this morning."

Carolyn retorted with a rude word that she must have picked out of a gutter. "I know you're crying and I highly doubt that it is over a headache." She jiggled the door-knob. "Please, Julia, let me in. Mother has launched into another one of her tantrums, and I need to hide until she takes a nap."

Sighing, Julia pulled the key out of her pocket. "Just a minute," she called as she pinched some color into her cheeks. Then she opened the door.

"Your eyes are red," Carolyn remarked, sitting down on the bed. "Don't bother to cry over Payton. He's not worth it."

Julia lifted her chin. "I am not crying over that stupid boy. In fact, I've barely given him a second thought."

Carolyn settled herself among the bolster pillows. "Well, it's plain as milk that you're not crying over this phantom headache."

Julia snorted. The transparency of her feelings annoyed her. "Who says that I have been crying over anything at all? I may be coming down with a cold. I do declare, Carolyn Anne, your imagination has run away with you again." She lay down on the counterpane next to her sister.

Unfortunately, her sister was too intelligent to believe her. "Oh, frivle-fravle! You haven't cried like that in a year of Sundays. Not since the time you learned that Frank had been killed. You have a broken heart, sure as you're born. I can hear it flapping inside you. Tell me all, Julia. You know you'll feel better if you do." She lowered her voice to a conspiratorial whisper. "I am *very* good at keeping secrets."

Julia sighed. It would be a relief to unburden her soul, to have a really good cry with Carolyn and then put the whole horrid episode behind her. She rolled on her side to face her sister.

"You're right, Carolyn. I am pining, though I don't think that I am filled with utter despondency. At least, I certainly hope not," she added.

Carolyn's blue eyes grew wider. "Someone at the ball?"

A lump rose unbidden in Julia's throat. She nodded while she tried to swallow it down.

Carolyn knitted her brows. "But who? There were no decent boys there, only a roomful of crowing Yankees. What a mass of finery and vulgarity they were! Though I have to admit that some of them could dance well enough. My stars, Julia! Did you ever hear such accents come out of anyone's mouth like those Northern boys spoke? They set my teeth on edge. I told my dance partners, 'Don't say a word, honey, just smile.'"

Julia nodded. The lump in her throat grew larger. Her chest felt as if a wide belt had been pulled tight around it. She bit her lower lip.

Carolyn studied her sister's face. "Hellfire, Julia! Is that what you're crying over? Some *Yankee* boy?"

"He's not exactly a boy," Julia croaked. She blew her nose and scolded herself for her weakness. "He's twenty-seven."

Her sister's eyes narrowed. "But he's a Yankee just the same, even if he was fifty and had pots of gold under each arm. You can't trust them a lick. They are all polecats, every last one of them. What's come over you?"

Julia sniffed into her hankie. A fresh set of tears filled her eyes. "I told you that I wasn't feeling well."

Carolyn snorted. "You're as healthy as a horse. Don't you start having the vapors like Mother. It's too tiresome. You get hold of yourself and you'll be fine soon. Why, I bet that Yankee is nothing more than a whiskey-drinking, tobacco-chewing varmint."

Julia balled her wet handkerchief in her fist. "He may be a lot of things, Carolyn, but I don't think he drinks whiskey, nor chews tobacco—at least not in the presence of a lady. He did have a certain amount of good manners."

Carolyn tossed her blond curls. "Ha! I daresay he drinks

whiskey all the time—and not in a julep, either.'' She wrinkled her nose. ''Be that as it may, the New Year's Ball is over and done now. Your good-mannered Yankee is back in Washington, probably laughing up his sleeve at you while he tells tall tales to all his friends.''

Julia's temper flared, blotting out her tears. ''Rob isn't that sort at all. No matter what he may think of me, I doubt he would be so cruel as to banter my name around some oyster bar.''

Carolyn lifted one brow. ''Oh, it's *Rob* now, is it? Let me tell you about this Yankee Rob. He has *robbed* you of your good sense, that's what! And cruel? I've heard such stories of cruelty that those people have done to our poor Virginia that it would make your hair stand on its ends.''

Julia's cheeks grew very warm. ''You don't know the first thing about him, Carolyn. This man is kind and he, too, has been hurt.''

''Fiddlesticks!'' Carolyn mimicked. ''I don't care a fig for his little ole feelings. Look what he's done to you! That weasel has made you lose your wits and cry your eyes out for the likes of him—all in one night.''

''He's not a weasel!'' Julia snapped. ''And it wasn't just in one night. Oh!'' She stopped herself, but Carolyn pounced on her slip of the tongue.

''What have you gone and done, Julia?'' she gasped.

Julia knotted her handkerchief between her fingers. ''I've seen him several times since then,'' she replied softly. ''In our garden.''

''Over Papa's dead body!'' Carolyn gasped. ''He'd just up and die if he knew that a Yankee had stepped foot inside our home—even in the garden.'' She put her hand to her mouth. ''I can't believe how you've changed. You have never done anything so outrageous in your entire life.'' Her voice sank to a whisper, ''What did you do in the garden?''

Julia's ears burned. ''Nothing! We sat under the tree and talked. He is very witty and charming. He can even quote Shakespeare very well.''

Carolyn shook her head. ''I highly doubt that an introduction, even from Mr. William Shakespeare, would cut the mustard with Papa. You have lost your mind entirely!''

Colonel Lawrence furrowed his brow as he reread the memorandum from Secretary of War Stanton. Ever since the inconclusive battle at Antietam, President Lincoln had grown increasingly concerned over the lack of good military leadership. The appalling losses at Gettysburg and the new policy that prohibited the exchange of prisoners had exacerbated the problem. The President wanted to redress this situation before the Spring campaign heated up. Forced into action by executive pressure, Stanton and his civilian advisor, Allen Pinkerton, had come up with a dangerous solution.

Lawrence pulled off his glasses and rubbed his eyes. He firmly believed that civilians should stay out of military affairs. This rash scheme was going to cost him a good man, not to mention the number of other lives at stake.

He stared out his window at the gray morning. A few hardy pigeons winged their way toward Lafayette Park in search of food for the day. Washington, with its soot-stained gray buildings, its muddy streets and an overflowing population, looked particularly grim this morning. The usual optimism of the New Year was muted by the discouraging news that, a week ago, Richmond celebrated the triumphant return of that wily Confederate general, John Hunt Morgan, who had successfully tunneled out of the Federal prison in Columbus, Ohio. Lawrence pulled out his wrinkled handkerchief from his hip pocket and blew his wet nose. The Federal City was not only the center of government, but also a cesspool of dangerous vapors and noxious air. Whatever had possessed America's founding fathers to erect their capital city in the middle of a pest-infested swamp?

"Lieutenant Johnson!" he barked to his aide whose desk was just outside his half-open door.

Within a minute, the perpetually cheerful young man appeared before the colonel. After wiping his fledgling mustache clean of coffee, he snapped a salute worthy of West Point's parade ground. "Sir!" he chirped.

In the face of such youth and high spirits, Lawrence suddenly felt very old, although he was only in his early forties. The years of warfare had already tinged his dark hair with streaks of steel gray. He sighed.

"Lieutenant, I believe that you were at the Winsteads' ball on New Year's Eve?"

Johnson grinned. "A most enjoyable affair, sir."

"By any chance, did you engage the Chandler girl in conversation?"

Johnson's grin broadened. "I spoke with a number of charming young ladies, sir. I regret that I also imbibed liberally of our host's well-medicated eggnog. As a result, I am afraid that I lost track of names."

The colonel sighed. Why was he sent so many green young officers who had no notion how and when to gather useful information?

"Lieutenant, may I remind you that even when you are off duty and enjoying a social hour, you should always remember where you work and why we are here? It is at balls and receptions, in saloons and restaurants, even in the depths of the lowest brothel in Swampoodle where we learn the most useful information that our generals need to engage in this infernal war. It is a proven fact that some of the Confederacy's most effective spies are women, very comely young ones. No matter how much you enjoy yourself, remember that you, Lieutenant Johnson, are the eyes and ears of the United States. Do I make myself clear?''

Johnson gulped under his tight collar. His grin disappeared. ''Yes, sir. You might ask Major Claypole, sir. He was there and, as I recollect, he spent most of the evening hugging the wall. I do not believe that he knows how to dance, sir,'' he added with a snicker.

Lawrence rumbled in the back of his throat. ''Send him in, Johnson. You are dismissed.''

The colonel sighed while Johnson disappeared to fetch the major. Lawrence had wanted to avoid including the man in this delicate matter, even indirectly. Scott Claypole may have been born to a middling farm family in Ohio, but, unfortunately for Lawrence, he was also the beloved nephew of Edwin Stanton, Secretary of War. Claypole proved to be uncommonly intelligent and ambitious for one of his social class. Since joining the army as a second lieutenant, he had worked his way into his present rank with surprising speed. Claypole always seemed to be in the right place at the right time. His name had often appeared in dispatches, usually accompanied with high recommendations for advancement. At Antietam, a year ago September, an unlucky but opportune bullet had killed Claypole's immediate superior, allowing the young man to take command of his unit under fire. His field promotion to captain quickly followed. Since the battle of Fredericksburg, he was a major, even though he had been stationed in Washington at the time. Lawrence narrowed his eyes. The colonel had the uncomfortable feeling that he needed to watch his back when this man was around.

No doubt Claypole wanted to be a general before the war ended.

"Sir, you wished to see me?" Claypole asked.

The colonel fiddled with a pencil. "You attended the Winstead ball?"

Claypole smiled. "Indeed, sir. It was a very jolly evening."

"Mmm," Lawrence rumbled. "As did Johnson and Montgomery?"

The smile never left the major's face. "On your orders, sir."

The colonel nodded. "On the day following, you mentioned something about Johnson, or was it Montgomery? I cannot now recall what it was you said."

If anything, the smile on Claypole's face broadened. "I merely remarked that Major Montgomery quite surprised me, sir. After protesting to all of us that he did not care for the company of ladies, he spent the entire evening speaking with a very pretty specimen. A Miss Julia Chandler, as I was told." He paused.

The colonel shifted in his seat. The little brick city of Alexandria shielded many Secessionist vipers behind its veneer of gentility. Though Confederate sympathies ran underground there, the feelings were strong and not easily squashed, despite the daily presence of the Federal army and an active provost marshal. In Lawrence's opinion, the whole town should have been cleaned out of Southerners two years ago. It wasn't safe to have such a tinderbox of rebellion sitting so close to Washington.

According to the Pinkerton detective, one of the known Southern sympathizers in Alexandria was the Chandler family, a name that cropped up occasionally in his reports. Nothing specific, merely whisperings of their allegiance to the Confederate cause. Most of the time, his agents wrote of Mrs. Jonah Chandler, who had the nasty habit of berating any poor Union soldier she met on the streets. Apparently the woman wielded an acid tongue.

Then there was something about one of the daughters—a young minx barely out of pinafores who played pranks on the local provost guards. Harmless tricks, to be sure, but nevertheless they showed a certain lack of respect for the very people who were there to protect the good citizens of Alexandria. Could this Julia Chandler be the same prankster?

Lawrence cleared his throat. "Was there something more about the major and this Miss Chandler?"

Claypole's smile segued into a slow smirk. "Indeed, sir, though as a gentleman, I hesitate to elaborate on the private behavior of a fellow officer."

Claypole was as much a gentleman as a pig in a mud wallow, the colonel thought. His family relationship had gone to his head. He folded his hands on his desk and leaned forward. "You have my permission to elaborate, Major. Indeed, it is my order."

The man licked his lips as if he were about to indulge in a savory feast. "The long and the short of it is that they were quite thick with each other all evening. Heads close together, whispering…things, if you catch my meaning, sir."

He was either insinuating that Montgomery was seducing the woman or that they were exchanging information. Both options made the gorge rise in Lawrence's throat, especially since Montgomery's military record was exemplary.

He glowered under his brows at Claypole. "But you have no clear idea what they were…um…discussing?"

Claypole's eyes grew wide with assumed surprise. "Colonel, sir, I would never *dream* of eavesdropping upon a private conversation. I was merely surprised by Major Montgomery's...warmth toward the young lady.'' His eyes glittered as he leaned closer to Lawrence. ''I found the major's behavior even more surprising when he left the party almost immediately after the departure of Miss Chandler and her sister.''

Lawrence felt as if a rock had hit him hard against his chest. Of course, young bucks will dally when and where they can, especially during wartime. Years ago, the colonel had enjoyed one or two dalliances himself when he was fighting the Indians in the west. But his marriage to his beloved wife had put an end to all such immoral pastimes.

Unlike Claypole, Montgomery came from an old Knickerbocker family. Lawrence could not conceive of him indulging in despicable vices. He struck the colonel as a cut above the rest, most especially Claypole. That virtue was precisely why the colonel now wanted Montgomery for Stanton's mission.

Lawrence narrowed his eyes at the young man on the other side of his desk. ''So you are accusing Major Montgomery of licentious behavior with a young woman?''

Again, the major expressed a wide-eyed look of astonishment. ''Not at all, sir. I know nothing of any behavior of that sort on the major's part. On the other hand—'' He glanced over his shoulder at the half-opened door, then lowered his voice to just above a whisper.

''There *is* the possibility that the major may have fallen into the tender snares of the delightful Miss Chandler. She is a Southerner. A pretty face, fluttering lashes and a cooing voice asking him what he does in this office all the livelong day. A slip of the tongue, and Miss Chandler stores this tidbit in her memory until she can relate it to Confederate ears. I understand this sort of thing happens with depressing regularity here in Washington. I know for a fact that Major Montgomery did not return to Ebbitt's Hotel until the small hours of the following morning. We have rooms on the same floor,'' he added, by way of explanation.

As much as he disliked the fact that Claypole would even suggest such a disturbing scenario, Lawrence was forced to admit that the possibility existed. In any event, the colonel's question had been answered. Montgomery had struck up a friendship with one of the Chandlers. "Tell Major Montgomery I wish to speak with him,'' he snapped at Claypole. "You are dismissed, Major.''

Claypole straightened up, saluted his superior, then left the office with almost a jaunty step. Lawrence had the overwhelming urge to wash his hands and perfume the air behind him. He studied Stanton's letter once more and wondered what Montgomery's answer would be to the horrific proposal it contained.

Chapter Eleven

More than a week had passed since Rob made his resolution not to see Julia again. Yet he could not forget her. Her face haunted his dreams; temptation plagued his days. Why couldn't he forget her as easily as he had done with the numerous girls of his youth? Julia had only been an evening's diversion. But her spirit refused to leave him in peace. Shifting in his hard chair, Rob tried to focus on the latest Pinkerton report.

"The colonel requires your presence, Major." Claypole leaned over Rob's shoulder, breaking into his reverie.

Rob bit back his annoyance, not at the colonel's request, but at Claypole's behavior. He covered his papers with a file folder, then stood so abruptly that he forced the man to stumble backward. "Thank you, Major," he replied in a crisp voice. Claypole grated on Rob's nerves; so smug, so sure of himself because he was Stanton's kin.

Without giving Claypole another glance, he strode to Lawrence's office. Only after he had saluted the colonel did he wonder what matter could be so urgent on the colonel's mind.

Lawrence looked weary, as if he hadn't enjoyed a good night's sleep, though that was the usual expression with most of the senior officers in the Federal army—at least the ones who were out in the field in the thick of the war. "Sir?" Rob prompted him.

The colonel stared at him for a long moment, then said, "Close the door, Major. What I have to say is somewhat…delicate."

Rob steeled himself for news that his mother had died. Her health had always been a cause of concern for the family. Her lungs had never been strong and the cold winds blowing off the Hudson River made her condition much worse. Yet, being a proud descendant of hearty Dutch settlers, she had steadfastly refused to leave New York for warmer, more healthful climes.

Rob squared his shoulders, and lifted his chin. "Sir?" he asked again as Lawrence continued to stare at him. "Is it about my family?"

The colonel pursed his lips. "No, Major. To the best of my knowledge, they all enjoy good health."

A wave of relief swept over him; he barely heard the colonel's next sentence.

"It is your friendship with Miss Chandler that I want to discuss with you."

Rob raised his brow "Miss Chandler? Is *she* ill?" How did the colonel know of Julia?

Lawrence looked up to the pressed tin ceiling then back to Rob. "Major, I have it on good authority that you have struck up a friendship with Miss Julia Chandler of Alexandria. Is this true?"

Heat rose up Rob's neck and enveloped his ears. He hadn't felt this uncomfortable since he was nine years old and had been caught helping himself to a full glass of brandy from his father's decanter. He cleared his throat. "Miss Chandler is a very fine young lady, sir. Well brought up and from a good family."

The colonel nodded as if he already knew quite a bit about her. Rob hoped he wouldn't inform her parents about their rendezvous.

"I can assure the colonel that nothing improper has passed between us," Rob continued in a rush. Julia did not deserve to be further punished for his rashness. "We have met only—" he hesitated for a fraction of a moment "—once. At the New Year's Ball given by Mr. George Winstead. The same ball that you ordered me to attend, sir."

Lawrence nodded again. "So I was informed. And at this party, you and Miss Chandler spent a good deal of time together?"

A tight knot formed between Rob's shoulders. Did the Colonel know about those dangerous moments he had experienced in the supper room alcove? "We did. Miss Chandler is an exceedingly bright person and has read a great many of the same books as I." His mouth twitched at the memory. "I don't believe that I have quoted so much Shakespeare since my school days."

Lawrence's penetrating stare turned to one of astonishment. "You were whispering Shakespeare into that woman's ear all night?"

"Some of it was."

"And the rest of it, Major?" Lawrence lifted one of his brows. "Understand me, I am not in the habit of prying into the affairs of my officers, unless there is a compelling reason to do so. I do have a compelling reason. What *else* did you and Miss Chandler discuss?"

"We spoke of the other guests, and the weather, of course." Also, Miss Chandler had begged him to seduce her.

Lawrence cocked his head like a terrier on a scent. "Nothing else?"

"Nothing more that I can recall, sir." Rob swallowed the lie. "May I ask the colonel what is his reason for his interest in my social life?"

"Mmm," rumbled the colonel. He pointed to the straight-back armchair opposite him. "Sit down, Major. I have a proposal I want to discuss with you."

Wary of the colonel's sudden shift in the conversation, as well as his offer of the chair, Rob perched himself on the end of the seat. "Sir?"

Lawrence untied a bundle of documents that lay in front of him. He scanned the topmost paper. "You are a man of action," the colonel began. "First and Second Manassas, Antietam, Fredericksburg, Gettysburg. You have been cited in dispatches for bravery in the field on several occasions."

Rob's ears burned at the recitation of his past accomplishments. "That was a long time ago, sir." Inside his coat pocket, his useless hand ached as if the Rebel's minié ball had just ripped it apart again. "Ghost pain," the surgeons called it. Rob massaged his forearm. "My days in the field are over."

The colonel regarded him in silence for a few moments. Rob shifted his weight on the wooden seat. The room felt stuffy.

"Do you enjoy working behind a desk, Major?"

Rob snorted. "It's tolerable, sir."

"But not to your liking?"

Rob cleared his throat, more worried about the reason behind the colonel's interest than the question itself. Were they going to send him home on permanent medical disability? "I am pleased to serve the United States in any capacity that I am able."

Lawrence raised both his eyebrows. "Is that a fact?" He leaned forward, his brown eyes hooded like those of a hawk inspecting its prey. "Would you be ready to leap into the jaws of hell for your country?"

Fireworks of excitement swirled inside Rob's chest; his heart thumped like a racehorse at the starting post. He had not experienced this rush of anticipation since the second morning at Gettysburg, when he took command of the Rhinebeck Legion on a rocky hill called Little Roundtop.

"I would, sir, if a one-handed man is needed."

The colonel flashed him an odd smile. "As long as your mind is fully operational, it does not matter how many hands you possess."

Rob tensed his shoulders. His breathing grew more rapid. He did not dare to hope that the colonel was going to send him back into the action. "There is nothing wrong with my mind."

"Good." Lawrence held up a sheet of paper. Rob saw the words: "Edwin M. Stanton, Secretary of War" on the letterhead. "I have just received orders that are effective immediately. You will presently understand why time is of the essence, but first I must caution you that anything I tell you from now on must be kept in the strictest confidence. Not even your cousin is to know what is said here."

Rob gripped the arm of his chair with his good hand. "You have my word, sir."

"Even if you decline to accept the task?"

The taste of adventure filled Rob's mouth, intoxicating him. "Yes, sir, though I am most anxious to be of any service."

"The task is dangerous. You could lose your life."

Rob disregarded the Colonel's warning. He had been in a number of life-threatening situations in the past three years, but nothing had killed his spirit so much as the six months he had spent in an office. The suggestion of danger only whetted his interest.

"What does the Secretary have in mind?"

Lawrence nodded, as if he approved. "President Lincoln has become increasingly concerned over the high casualty rate our army has sustained during the past year. Most particularly, he is worried about the growing scarcity of junior field officers—men who thrust themselves into the forefront of the battle to give encouragement to their troops. Men like yourself, Major."

Rob silently acknowledged the compliment.

"The cadets at West Point are eager young pups, full of idealism, but they lack sufficient seasoning," the colonel continued. "The current crop of second lieutenants are too wet behind the ears to be of much use."

Lawrence's voice dropped into a conspiratorial tone. "Rumor has it that General Grant will be put in charge of the army in the not-too-distant future. He's a fighter like a bull terrier. He will need a lot of qualified field officers when he takes command for the springtime campaign. The question is, where do we find these men before the roads dry out and the war heats up again?"

Rob presumed that the Secretary of War didn't mean to empty all the hospitals of wounded officers. "From abroad?" he ventured, though he couldn't imagine his own boys being willing to take orders from someone with a foreign accent. They would want a good man from New York to lead them.

"A thought," the colonel agreed, "but not practical given the lack of time. Pinkerton has come up with a viable solution, though as I warned you, it is a highly dangerous one for all concerned."

Rob curled his lip. "What does a civilian detective know about training army officers?"

Lawrence barked a laugh. "My thought exactly. No, Pinkerton, with the Secretary's blessing, has suggested that since the Confederates are unwilling to give us back our officers whom they have captured, we will go down to Richmond and get them ourselves.''

Understanding flooded Rob. ''The prisoners of war?''

Lawrence nodded again. ''In Libby Prison, right in the heart of the Confederate capital.''

Rob's imagination raced with the possibility. It could work, if planned well. ''How?''

''We understand, through a trusted informer, that a major prison breakout is already in the works. Who is planning the escape and when are unknown, as yet, but the goal is to free as many men as possible. Mr. Pinkerton suggested that we arrange for an officer—one battle-hardened and briefed in escape tactics—to be placed inside Libby. There, he will help the organizers. He will have memorized the fastest routes out of Richmond and will know where caches of clothing and provisions are hidden along the way.

''We need someone who has a quick mind, who is able to improvise and who will remain cool under pressure. We need a man who will willingly go into the hellhole of Libby for as long as it takes. Also, he must be someone who will not break under torture, if it comes to that. Are you interested in volunteering, Major?''

Rob could barely contain himself. It was salvation for a dying soul. ''I am your man,'' he replied, his voice quivering with pent-up excitement.

The colonel relaxed against the back of his chair. ''I had hoped you would say that, Montgomery. I will be honest when I tell you that I do not relish sending anyone into the Confederate prison system.''

''When do I leave?''

''As soon as you have memorized the maps that Pinkerton has prepared. The United States is most fortunate to have loyal citizens in Richmond—one in particular. It is she who has provided most of the necessary information. She will be your contact as she visits the prison under the guise of charitable works. Her name is Elizabeth Van Lew, known as Miss Lizzie. She is an elderly spinster—''

Picturing his mother trying to organize anything more complex than a picnic, Rob groaned.

Lawrence cocked his head. ''Do not be so quick to judge this woman's abilities. I have read reports of what she has already accomplished and she sounds quite capable of anything, including murder. She affects the guise of an eccentric old biddy, but make no mistake, Miss Lizzie is a good deal more intelligent than many men I know. Most importantly, you can trust her.''

Rob mulled over the various aspects of Stanton's plan. ''Very well. I'm a fast study. If I have the maps and other information this afternoon, I can be ready to go in a day or two. How will I be sent to Richmond, sir?''

The colonel's mouth hardened into a thin-lipped smile. ''The most obvious way, Major. You will be captured. Our agent in Fairfax City has the ear of Mosby's Rangers. He will let it be known that an important member of General Grant's staff—one who is privy to the plans for the spring advance on Richmond—will be in a certain place at a certain time. The Confederates will be eager to have the information they think you know.''

Rob felt as if a hand had closed itself around his throat. ''I see what you mean by the possibility of torture, sir.'' He attempted to sound lighthearted. ''They will not be amused when they discover that they have made a mistake.'' He knew that Mosby occasionally hanged his prisoners.

Lawrence tried to look cheerful. ''By that time, you will be in Richmond. Once they discover that you are no use to them, they will toss you into Libby. It's the only prison there strictly for officers. As to torture, let us hope that the Confederate officers will live up to their reputation of being honorable gentlemen. Are you still interested?''

Thinking of his life during the recent bleak months, Rob nodded. ''Have you chosen the place of my capture? Surely you do not expect Mosby to come riding up Pennsylvania Avenue for me.''

Lawrence sighed. ''Hardly. This is where your Miss Chandler enters into the picture.''

Chapter Twelve

A sickening lump formed itself in the pit of Rob's stomach. While he had no fear of personal danger, Julia's safety loomed as a paramount importance to him, despite his vow to forget her.

"What about Miss Chandler, sir? I fail to see what help she can give. As a matter of fact, I have not pursued our acquaintance. The young lady and I were too much—" He groped for the right word. "Our politics are at opposite poles. I realized that a continued friendship would lead to grief."

Lawrence sat back in his chair. "Ordinarily, I would never presume to dictate the social affairs of my men, Major Montgomery, but we are not living in civilized times. I am asking you to resume your friendship with Miss Chandler, and entertain her with all the formidable powers of that charm of yours."

Rob opened his mouth to protest, but the colonel held up his hand.

"Hear me out, Major. My reason is far from frivolous. We must place you in a position to be captured by Colonel Mosby. You will be apprehended while at the home of a known Southern loyalist. I am quite certain that Mosby's men will have no trouble locating the address. They probably know it already."

White anger overcame Rob, and he leaped to his feet. "Julia Chandler is an innocent young woman, sir! To use her trust for such a nefarious purpose is a callous act."

Lawrence folded his hands together as if in an attitude of prayer. "Indeed, Major. War is also a callous act, and it turns us into beings that we are not by nature. Families tear each other apart like hunting dogs over a fox. Brothers kill brothers in the name of patriotism, and friends betray each other with a smile—and a kiss."

Rob gritted his teeth. "It sickens me to use a sweet young woman for such a devilish purpose. Isn't there some other way?"

Lawrence shook his head; he would not meet Rob's eyes. "None that we can use so quickly, and time is of the essence. Your countrymen languish in hell, Major Montgomery. They pray daily for release," the colonel whispered. "Your President wants them out, and General Grant needs them desperately."

Closing his eyes, Rob wished that he were back home in Rhinebeck. The Hudson would be frozen hard by now and he could skate up its winding course halfway to Montreal, leaving the war with its bloody maw and gut wrenching decisions far behind him. The air was crisp and clean in the wilderness of the North Country.

"Major?" Lawrence's voice shattered his daydream. "Will you do it?"

Rob swallowed down the bile in his throat. "Yes, sir," he replied in a hollow tone. His conscience screamed reproach. "While I loathe the idea of Miss Chandler's involvement, I understand the reason for it. I pray that she too, will understand it eventually. May God forgive me for such a breach of trust."

Rob lowered his eyes to hide the deep regret he felt grip his heart. "When do you want me to see her?"

Claypole watched as Montgomery returned to his desk. The man looked as if he had been whipped, taken down a peg or two. Scott chuckled to himself. Then he shunted aside his personal feelings and chewed over the possible reasons for Montgomery's hangdog look. There had been no raised voices behind the colonel's door, so Claypole presumed that the New Yorker had not been reprimanded for some military misbehavior.

There was something in the wind, he knew it. Perhaps it could be used to his benefit.

He stretched in his chair, then got up and sauntered around the maze of desks and filing cabinets until he reached Montgomery's area. He noted that both the major's hands, the good one and the bad, were hidden under the desk. Montgomery stared at his inkwell with a grim look that would make a weak man shiver. Claypole had no qualms about disturbing the major's dark musings. In fact, he relished the idea of irritating this pompous son of old New York.

"Seems like the world landed hard on your shoulders, Rob," he said in a companionable voice. "You look like a man who might be in need of a drink."

A muscle jumped along the major's jawline. He didn't give him the common courtesy of looking at him. "It's only past eleven, Claypole," he rumbled. "Too early in the day."

Claypole forced himself to laugh in a pleasant manner. "Never too early for a medicinal tot."

Montgomery closed his eyes. "Go away, Claypole."

Though the major was often morose, he was never this touchy. His behavior confirmed Claypole's suspicions;

something big was in the wind. He refused to give up in spite of Montgomery's rebuffs. If he could only lure him to a saloon. A few shots of whiskey might loosen the major's tongue.

He leaned over Montgomery so that his voice wouldn't carry. "If you are in need of a sympathetic ear, I have two for you. Misery is—"

The major's glare froze the rest of Claypole's offer on his lips. "Leave me alone! I am already bound for hell without your help."

With a stiff smile pasted on his face, Claypole backed away. He held up his hands, palms out. "No harm intended," he lied. Then he returned to his own cubbyhole where he watched Montgomery.

A few minutes later, he saw the major take out some of his personal note paper from a side drawer. He dipped his pen into the ink bottle, then began to write furiously across the page. Claypole nodded to himself. Writing to home again. From the look of things, Claypole guessed that Montgomery had received new orders that were not to his liking.

The rattling of her bedroom doorknob in the middle of the morning caught Julia unawares. Hettie had already cleaned the room and taken away the nighttime slops. Carolyn was at her French and drawing lessons with Madame DuSault on Wolfe Street. Julia rose when her parents swept into the room. By the set look on her mother's face and her father's downcast eyes, Julia instinctively knew that this unexpected visit did not bode well for her. Perhaps they planned to exile her to Strasburg in the Shenandoah Valley to live with Mother's elderly Aunt Charlotte.

Julia forced her lips to part in a smile. "Good morning, Mother. Good morning, Papa. This is a surprise," she added truthfully. Behind her mother's back, Papa returned a wan smile.

Mother seated herself on Julia's chair before she gave her daughter the full brunt of her attention. "I do hope that this past week's solitude has been instructive, and that you have now learned the virtue of obedience," she began in a haughty tone.

Julia refrained from the temptation to point out that she had always been the obedient daughter, and that it was Carolyn who needed discipline. Why stir up another storm? From the expression on her mother's face, Julia knew that anything she said would be interpreted as disrespectful. She pressed her lips together.

Mrs. Chandler smoothed out her gray watered-silk skirts, then continued, "I have just received the most delightful letter from your cousin Payton. Despite your skylarking and unbridled behavior, he has graciously agreed to make you his bride—immediately."

With a gasp, Julia stumbled backward against the bedpost. She gripped it lest she collapse under the weight of this dire announcement. She glanced at her father, but he would not meet her eyes. Julia masked her inner turmoil with a deceptive calmness.

"This is hasty news, Mother."

Mrs. Chandler gave her daughter a slow, feral smile. "So it is, and not a moment too soon. Marriage will do you a world of good. It will give you the discipline and maturity you so obviously lack. There'll be no more gadding about town and dragging our family's name in the dust behind you."

Mother, with her love of drama, had blown the episode of the ball all out of proportion. But the situation could have been a lot worse, if Major Montgomery had not been a gentleman.

"Payton says that he will obtain a pass from the provost marshal in Richmond, so that he may come through the lines to get you. He expects to arrive in Alexandria in a few days. I have already contacted the sexton at St. Paul's. You and Payton will be married there two weeks from Saturday." Opening her fan, her mother waved it back and forth as she elaborated her plans.

"Since it is wartime, as well as the bald fact of your infamous conduct, the service will be small. Family only. Carolyn will stand up for you and I am sure that Payton will produce another witness, if necessary. Afterward, a small wedding breakfast here. We do not have the wherewithal of the Winsteads. Then you and Payton will return to Richmond on the afternoon train." She frowned to herself. "Of course, you will have to make several station changes. I hear that some of the rail lines are torn up. You may have to spend your wedding night in Fredericksburg."

Julia gulped for air. The whirlwind of Clara's plans made her head spin. "Mother, you have given me no time. How can I possibly marry a man that I have not seen in years? What if I dislike him? We will need some time to get to know one another again."

Mrs. Chandler continued to fan herself as if she had not heard a word. "You can wear your blue taffeta morning dress. It suits your coloring quite nicely. And I suppose you will have to wear Grandmother Lightfoot's pearls. Family tradition and all that, but I want them back before you leave this house. No sense in losing them on the train, is there?"

Julia swallowed down the scream that hovered in her throat. Her cherished vision of teaching classrooms full of eager children dissolved. "Papa?" she implored her father.

He gave her a sweet, sad look before he shook his head.

"Your mother is right, my child. In these unsettled times, we are fortunate to find you a proper husband—a man who is willing to overlook your lapse in behavior."

Julia's distress veered sharply to anger. "Of course Payton is willing to overlook anything that I might have done, since he knows that I will be inheriting my legacy soon. It's my money he's after, not me. He was always greedy when he was a boy. Once I caught him searching through Carolyn's little purse for spare change."

"Hold your tongue, Julia!" Two bright red spots appeared in Mrs. Chandler's cheeks. "How dare you utter such filth! My aunt would turn in her very grave if she heard you accuse her grandson of thievery. Payton is a fine gentleman, well set up with a large plantation, livestock, servants and fine furnishings. He has no need for any more money, though of course, we are giving him something to take you, now that you have soiled your reputation—and ours!"

She shook out her handkerchief and began to wail loudly into it, though Julia suspected that her mother's eyes were bone-dry.

Leaning her head against the cool wood of the bedpost, she felt exactly like a rabbit caught in a narrowing mesh trap. "I had no idea you hated me so much, Mother," she murmured under her breath.

"Hate you!" her mother caterwauled. "When all I have ever done is work hard for your benefit? Good schooling, pretty clothes, music lessons! Oh, Jonah," she beseeched her husband. "What a serpent we have nurtured in our bosoms! Such ingratitude! I am awash with sorrow. Oh, dear! Oh, my heart!" Gripping her chest, she held out her hand to her husband. "I do fear that I am having palpitations. Take me to my bed."

Julia's father helped his wife to her feet, muttering his

usual soothing nonsense. Hettie, who had been listening in
the hall, took Mrs. Chandler's arm. Feeling strangely un-
moved, Julia watched in silence as Hettie helped her
mother down the hall. Then she said, "Papa, I am truly
sorry, but I cannot marry Payton Norwood. I want to teach
in a school."

Her father didn't look surprised by this admission,
merely sad. "I don't know what to say to you, Julia. Your
mother is set on this match. For the sake of her health, I
cannot overrule her. Perhaps your reluctance is unfounded.
Payton may have grown up into a good man. Do not judge
him until you have seen him again. As for teaching school,
I am afraid that is impossible. You were reared for the life
of a plantation mistress. You must forget that idea, Julia.
It will only make you unhappy."

Then he left, without allowing her one more word of
protest.

In the waning light of a January afternoon, Rob loitered
on the corner of King and North Royal Streets near Alexandria's Market Square. He pulled his woolen scarf
tighter around his neck while he scanned the crowd of late
shoppers, hoping that the Chandlers' maidservant was
among them. His perfidious note to Julia burned inside the
pocket of his greatcoat.

Before leaving Washington at midday, Rob had visited
Mr. Chandlee's card and stationery shop inside the elegant
Willard Hotel with the idea of buying a peace offering for
Julia. He had chosen a gilt-edged book of Shakespeare's
sonnets for her when his conscience reprimanded him.
How could he betray her trust again with a pretty present,
while he used her friendship for a coldhearted purpose? At
their meeting in her garden, he should keep himself as
aloof as possible, and pray that Mosby's men captured him

quickly. The less time he spent in Julia's seductive company, the better it would be for both of them.

Rob stamped his feet to encourage his sluggish blood to warm his near-frozen toes. Yesterday's *Washington Evening Star* reported that this winter was an unusually cold one. And he intended to spend most of it inside the dank walls of Libby Prison! He must truly be fortune's fool.

"My, my, my," squealed a high-pitched feminine voice behind him. "Look, Mama! I do believe that we have stumbled upon the handsomest officer in the entire Federal Army. Good afternoon, Major Montgomery."

Puzzled, Rob turned to confront two well-dressed ladies swathed in colorful velvet cloaks, fur hats and muffs. It took him a few moments before he recognized the hostess of the New Year's Ball and her daughter. Then he touched the brim of his hat with his good hand.

"Good afternoon, Mrs. Winstead, Miss Winstead. It's a bitter day to be out and about," he remarked, casting a furtive glance over their shoulders in search of Hettie Perkins.

Mrs. Winstead tittered. "So it is, Major, but we had a few errands to run."

Giving Rob an especially warm smile, Melinda moved close to him. "What Mama means is that we have been so cooped up in the house ever since the party, we simply had to get outside and breathe. I just couldn't stand those old walls a minute longer, no matter how cold the weather is. Alexandria is so boring in the wintertime—unless there are some *interesting* people who come to call—like yourself."

Before he could react, she looped her arm through his good one and snuggled closer against him. Rob masked his impatience. "No doubt many of your friends are also equally bored with the cold and the snow. I am sure that they hope that you and your mother will pay them a call.''

Mrs. Winstead tittered again, though she looked a little colder than before. Melinda tightened her hold on Rob. ''The very thing!'' she cooed. ''Why don't you accompany us home, Major Montgomery, and we shall enjoy a dish of tea and sweet cakes while we laugh at Old Man Winter?''

Rob experienced a sharp sinking feeling. He had no desire to postpone his distasteful mission any longer than necessary. With a quick twist, he freed his arm from Melinda's grasp.

''Thank you for your kind invitation, Miss Winstead, but I fear I am in Alexandria on official business. I was looking for the Chandler family cook, a Miss Hettie Perkins?''

''Dear me,'' said Mrs. Winstead, huddling deeper into her cloak. ''I expect she would be home by now. Just as we should be home by now,'' she added, giving her daughter a meaningful lift of her brow.

''Yes, Mama,'' Melinda replied, though she made no move to depart. ''We'll leave in two shakes of a lamb's tail. But first, we must convince this gentleman that he would feel much better to stretch out his feet in front of our fire. No point standing out in the middle of a public thoroughfare looking for a nobody, Major. You'll catch your death of cold before you see her,'' Melinda added. ''Besides, meeting Hettie won't do you a parcel of good whatsoever. If it's Julia Chandler you want, you're too late.'' Her charm descended into gleeful spite.

A stab of fear twisted in Rob's gut. ''I beg your pardon, Miss Winstead? Has Miss Julia left town?''

Melinda laughed without warmth. ''Not yet. But just

this morning, a little bird told us that Julia is to be married very soon. Fancy that!''

Behind his back, Rob clenched his good hand into a hard fist. So Julia's cousin, the toad, was hopping up to Alexandria to claim his princess. This unpleasant turn of events had happened faster than Rob had expected. "She is engaged?''

Melinda gave him a smug look. "I highly doubt that she knew it herself—until very recently. Obviously her family was quite mortified by her brazen appearance at my party. Such a blot on their good name! Why, everyone in Alexandria was talking about Julia's shameful conduct. The only man that would have her after that trick appears to be her second cousin. I expect the Chandlers will pay that poor boy a pretty penny to take her off their hands.''

Listening to Melinda's gloating voice, Rob's anger grew into a scalding fury. "Exactly *what* do you mean by that? I found Miss Chandler to be a most refined young lady, unlike many others I have recently met.''

His thinly-veiled insult rolled off Melinda like water from a duck's back. "Rubbish!'' she purred. "Julia Chandler was never a prize catch, even before the war started. She's always spent more time with her nose stuck in a book than attending to important things, like learning good manners. At every party we attended, she couldn't wait to show off her book-learning, so that no one else could get a word in edgewise. With her hair pulled back and those spectacles on her nose, it's no wonder that all the boys didn't pay her any mind, except poor Frank Shaffer. I have no idea what he saw in her, but it doesn't matter now. Frank died before he could propose. Since her reputation is in shreds, Julia is very fortunate to get an offer—even if it is her cousin.''

Rob glared at Melinda and her cold-faced mother. "Any

man who marries Miss Julia Chandler would find himself most fortunate.''

Melinda curled her lip, but before she could make a retort, her mother tugged her sleeve. "The wind is picking up, my dear. I do declare that my feet have turned into ice. We must be going now, Major Montgomery. *So* nice to have seen you again. *Do* come calling on us when you are not on official business."

Melinda looked mad enough to spit nails. She managed to throw Rob a final barb before her mother dragged her up King Street. "Forget Julia Chandler, Major. I am sure she has forgotten all about you, especially now that she is practically a married woman. Heaven help her poor cousin!"

As his anger simmered down to a dull ache in his heart, Rob felt a chill more numbing than the wind blowing off the river. He knew that Julia would be unhappy in a forced marriage with a cousin merely to save her family's face. It was criminal to toss away such a fine woman as Julia for some misguided notion of honor—the same sort of fanatical notion that had pushed this blood-soaked war into its fourth senseless year. Southerners were all crazy, he concluded.

The pale sun sank down to the lavender horizon. One by one, the vendors in Market Square closed up their shops and trundled away their carts. The pedestrians thinned as people hurried home to their warm hearths and hot suppers. The street lamplighter began his rounds of the city. Rob found himself alone with his thoughts. A soldier wearing the armband of the provost marshal stopped and saluted him.

"Evening, Major," he drawled in a Midwestern accent that bespoke of flatlands filled with cornstalks. "Are you lost, sir?"

Rob returned his salute. "Now that you ask, I believe that I am," he replied with a grim note in his voice. "Can you direct me to the nearest place where a man might get a drink and something to eat?"

Grinning, the guard pointed behind Rob to a red-brick building across North Royal Street. "There's the City Hotel, sir. I reckon you'll find what you want there." He stepped closer and lowered his voice. "Unless you are in the mind for a bit of fun with your meal? Mrs. Shaw's Firehouse is down near the wharves on Quay Street."

Rob shook his head. "I've had my fill of feckless women for the day, Corporal. Good night." He stepped off the curbstone before the beardless youth could suggest another one of Alexandria's bawdy houses.

The City Hotel offered Rob the hospitality he sought—companionable noise, air heady with cigar smoke, a drop of good whiskey at a larcenous price and a surprisingly good oyster stew for a fair price. He ate his meal in silence, oblivious to the hubbub common to a saloon in a soldier-filled town on a cold winter's night. Only Melinda's words, "Julia will be married," repeated themselves over and over in his fevered brain. Nursing his second tot of whiskey, he stared into the red-orange flames in the huge fireplace. The din around him receded as the voices inside his head grew louder.

Why should Julia's impending nuptials trouble him? He certainly had no intention of marrying her, nor anyone else for that matter. He never planned to see her again until his duty demanded it. Despite her delightful conversation and great beauty, Julia was a Confederate at heart, he reminded himself.

Julia…married. To the toad.

Sipping his hot whiskey, he allowed the sharp liquid to trickle down his raw throat. Julia shouldn't have to get married if she didn't want to, he reasoned. She was a woman who knew her own mind much better than her parents did. With her brains and cheerful personality, she would be an excellent teacher for children. Rob grimaced as he thought of the elder Chandlers, whom he had never met. How could they be so cruel as to force their daughter into a union with a cousin merely for propriety's sake? Didn't they care about her happiness? He gripped the small glass in his good hand. *He* cared—a lot.

Patting his pocket, where his letter to Julia lay, he reminded himself of his assignment. He must meet with her tomorrow night so the Rebels could apprehend him. This morning, Colonel Lawrence's double agent in Fairfax City had alerted Mosby's Rangers of their opportunity to capture an "important officer on General Grant's staff." Rob snorted. He had never met the famous general in person, and he prayed that none of his captors-to-be had either. His flimsy cover story had to stick, at least until he reached Richmond—and Libby Prison.

Excitement brewed in Rob's gut when he thought of the dangerous time ahead of him. Then Julia's beautiful face rose again in his imagination. He'd certainly never see her again after tomorrow night. He wished that they had met under different circumstances, with no war to divide them, no webs of intrigue to entangle them. There might have been some future for him then. He closed his eyes for a brief moment. Best not to dwell on the might-have-beens. There was no room in his life now for a romance, even if there was a woman who was willing. Rob had always been a realist, accepting his fate in all its grim truth. The day after tomorrow, Julia would be just a pleasant memory to cheer him in his prison cell. By this time next week, she would be married.

Unbidden, a new thought flashed through his mind, startling him from his stupor of self-pity. Nothing was scheduled to happen tonight! No plots, no weddings—only long empty hours until daybreak. He could go to the Chandler garden tonight; if nothing else, he would linger in the shelter of the magnolia. Perhaps, if the angels were kind, he would see her through a window. Maybe she would be wearing a sheer nightgown.

Rob felt a hot stirring below his belt. No! Julia was not a woman for sporting, but for gentle loving. Not that he loved her, he reminded himself. But he *did* like, admire and respect her. In all honesty, he liked her a lot.

Tomorrow night, he knew she would be frightened by the appearance of Mosby's men, even though she was a loyal Confederate. He would not be able to soothe her fears then. Worse, because his capture would take place in the Chandlers' garden, Julia's strict, unforgiving parents would learn of her secret meetings with him—a Yankee. Rob ground his teeth together. Because of him, and the needs of the United States Army, Julia's precious reputation would indeed be lost forever. And he wouldn't be able to apologize—not tomorrow night, not ever.

But tonight, if he were very lucky, he could tell her that he loved her. No, no! That he *liked* her. Love was not an option for him. Lucy Van Tassel had taken care of that.

Rob drained his whiskey, then paid his bill and left the cheerful hotel saloon. The air outside had grown even more bitter in the past few hours. Wrapping his scarf around his neck, he tucked its ends deep inside the collar of his greatcoat. He drew on his leather glove with his teeth, then turned up Cameron Street in the direction of the Chandler home.

For the better part of the next hour, he stood under the magnolia tree, listening to the quarter chimes of the town's church bells marking the passage of the night. In frigid silence, he kept a fruitless watch on the back of the house. Through the dimly-lit windows, he saw Carolyn in her room, and her parents in theirs, but Julia wasn't visible. She must be in a room on the front side, he decided, as one by one the lamps dimmed inside the house.

Just when he was about to give up hope, the back door opened, and Hettie picked her way down the icy steps. She carried a pan of kitchen scraps and a large wooden spoon. Humming under her breath, she walked down to the compost heap at the bottom corner of the garden, scraped the leavings onto the refuse pile, then turned back toward the house. As she passed by his hiding place, Rob called softly to her.

The woman froze on the spot but did not cry out. Instead, she formed the fingers of her left hand into a sign against evil spirits. "Who's there?" she asked in a whisper. "Who comes calling me in the middle of the night? I'm not ready yet, oh Lord, not by a country mile."

Rob stepped out to the path in front of her. "Good evening, Mrs. Perkins," he said calmly, though his heartbeat increased. "I, too, am not yet ready to meet my Maker, but I am very glad to see you."

Recovered from her fright, Hettie drew herself up and narrowed her eyes. "Mighty late to be out, Major. Mighty cold to be taking a turn in someone else's garden, too."

Rob drew closer to her so that their voices would not carry. "You are correct on both counts, ma'am, but I understand that you Southerners don't give us Yankees too much credit for intelligence."

Though her facial features were indiscernible in the dark of the night, Rob saw the flash of her teeth when she smiled. "I never said anything like that, Major, leastwise, not to my recollection. If you're here for Miss Julia, she went to bed early."

"You have read my mind. Do you think that she might possibly be induced to get out of bed and come down here for a visit?"

"And where were you two weeks ago when the poor lamb stood out here all alone like some statue in a park? You broke her heart."

Rob's conscience burned him. "I am most sorry for that lapse, ma'am. I was…that is, I thought it was best to end our friendship. I do hope that Miss Julia did not take ill."

Hettie snorted. "Oh, she's sick, all right. But in her heart—not her body. They're going to force her to marry that no-account cousin, and there's nothing she can do about it. Think you can fix that kettle of fish, Major?"

Rob clenched his jaw, then replied, "I'd like to see her, just once more, Hettie. I know I can't marry her, but perhaps I can give her some courage to go on, to keep her dreams alive."

Hettie scrutinized him with a long, appraising look. "Miss Julia has about run out of tears by now, so I don't think seeing you again will make a particle of difference." Her voice softened. "And if you can put some hope back in her heart and joy in her soul, that wouldn't be a bad thing, either. Like my mama always told me, pigs don't know what a pen is for. I expect that goes the same for folks too young to know what's sensible. You step back into that shadow of yours, Major, and I'll go see if Miss Julia is half as crazy as you are."

Rob touched the brim of his hat to her. "You are an angel."

She gave him an odd look. "Angels are white, or so I've been told."

He called softly after her, "I believe the good Lord likes variety."

Saying nothing in reply, Hettie disappeared through the back door.

Only then did Rob wonder what excuse for this rendezvous could he give to Julia when she came—if she came.

Chapter Thirteen

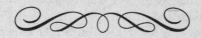

Lying next to her sleeping sister, Julia wondered if this would be her last night as a true spinster. Payton could be here by suppertime tomorrow. They would be declared an engaged couple soon thereafter. And she would have to kiss him to seal the match. She wiped the back of her hand across her lips. Then she heard the door slowly open. Fearful that her mother had truly been taken ill in the middle of the night, Julia sat up and groped for her dressing gown that lay nearby. Hettie entered holding a small candle.

"Is someone sick?" Julia asked. She flung back the bedcovers and searched for her slippers with her toes.

Pointing to Carolyn and putting her finger to her lips, Hettie closed the door behind her. "The only sick person I know of is hiding out in the garden," she whispered. "That man will catch a chill before morning, sure as you're born. He says he wants to see you."

Hettie didn't need to identify "that man." At the thought of Rob, a shiver of delicious expectation rippled through Julia. Part of her reveled in his return, while the other half bristled at the literally cold way he had left her that last time. She should tell Hettie to send him on his way. But she found that she could not say the words. To-

morrow night, she would be engaged. There would be no
more exciting meetings by moonlight for her, only years
of boredom in a loveless marriage.

"Is it very cold out there?" Julia asked, buttoning up
her quilted bedrobe. She opened the cedar chest and pulled
out a spare woolen blanket.

"As cold as sin and then some, " Hettie replied. "I
thought you had sworn off that Yankee after him leaving
you alone like that."

Julia giggled as she pulled on a pair of woolen stockings. "I thought so, too."

Hettie watched her tie the blanket around her shoulders.
"You put me in mind of a beggar woman at the back
door."

Julia brushed the nighttime tangles out of her hair.
"Thank you kindly for the compliment, Hettie, but I am
not planning to seduce him with my beauty. We are merely
friends." She wondered if she ought to pin up her hair but
decided it would take too much time. "How long has the
major been out there?" she asked, examining her face in
the hand mirror.

"By the look of his blue lips, I would say over an hour.
He *did* appear mighty pleased to see me with the supper
scraps." Hettie chuckled.

Julia gave herself one last appraisal in the mirror. Not
her best by any means but what did that matter? She
planned to stay only for a few minutes in the garden. Just
long enough to tell Rob about her engagement and to say
a final goodbye. She turned to Hettie.

"How do I look?"

"Hmm," her confidante replied. "You sure seem to me
like a girl in the clutches of love."

Julia frowned. She wasn't in love with any man. "How
you do run on. After all, Major Montgomery is a Yankee,

and he has never once indicated that he's in love with me. Quite the contrary.''

Muttering ''mmm-hmm'' in response, Hettie led her down the back stairs. At the kitchen door, she looked Julia straight in the eye. ''You can hide a fire, lambkin, but what are you going to do with the smoke?''

Without allowing Julia time to think of a suitable rejoinder, Hettie opened the door and gave her a little push outside. A gust of wind caused the candle to flicker inside the lantern. The frigid air knifed through Julia's few layers of clothing. She gathered the blanket closer around her and hurried down the flagstone pathway toward the huge tree.

Julia didn't see Rob until he stepped out of the shadows right in front of her. Light from the distant streetlamp outlined his tall figure and broad shoulders. Caught by surprise at his sudden appearance, she literally plowed straight into him. ''Oh!''

''Good evening, Miss Julia,'' he said with a smile in his voice. Steadying her on her feet, his hand lingered on her shoulder for a moment longer than necessary. ''Fancy meeting you on such a pleasant stroll. Do you always bowl over your admirers that way?''

Julia inhaled sharply at the contact. Cold, hot, flushed and flustered all at the same time, she found herself extremely conscious of his virile presence. Her heart pounded in erratic rhythms. She cleared her throat, pretending to herself that she was not affected by his proximity. ''I only came out for a minute. I'm getting married in a week,'' she blurted out. ''So this is…I mean, it's…''

A hot ache rose in her throat. Her vision clouded. She gulped hard, trying to control herself. Her heart, acting on its own accord, pulled her toward him, instead of away, as she had intended. Looking up into his handsome, smiling face, something snapped deep inside her. Great sobs racked her body. Scalding tears rolled down her cold cheeks.

Rob said nothing, nor did he look startled by her unexpected outburst. Instead, he opened his greatcoat, and with his good arm, he gathered her snugly against him. In blessed silence, he gently rocked her back and forth while she laid her head against his chest and wept as if her heart had split in half. She drank in the solace of his protection as if she were dying of thirst. He smelled faintly of cigar smoke, whiskey and bay rum cologne that hinted at sultry, exotic climes. She clung to the thick wool fabric of his uniform, her cheek pressed against his rounded brass buttons. He held her a little tighter until her sobs subsided. The warmth of his body heated her in an entirely different way. She inhaled deeply several times to subdue the hammering of her heart.

When Julia felt more in control of her emotions, she trusted herself to look up at his face. "I apologize for making a fool of myself."

His smile echoed in his voice. "I see no fool here, Julia. Only you."

His low tone soothed her. "I am engaged," she began again. "That is, I will be by this time tomorrow night. My cousin Payton is due to arrive in the afternoon. My parents insist that we be…be wed immediately."

She bit her lips to control her self-pity. "I was wrong to have encouraged our…our…friendship." She looked down at her fingers that still clutched the folds of his coat. Under the fabric, she felt his heartbeat. The pit of her stomach churned. "You should not have come back. You must realize that. I can never see you again," she whispered.

Without saying a word, Rob brushed back her windblown hair. Then his fingers trailed down her temple and across her wet cheek with a feather-light touch. His hand

PLAY Lucky 7 and get 2 FREE BOOKS and a FREE GIFT

Scratch off the gold area with a coin. Then check below to see the gifts you get!

NO COST! NO OBLIGATION TO BUY! NO PURCHASE NECESSARY!

The Harlequin Reader Service® — Here's how it works:

Accepting your 2 free books and gift places you under no obligation to buy anything. You may keep the books and gift and return the shipping statement marked "cancel." If you do not cancel, about a month later we'll send you 6 additional books and bill you just $4.47 each in the U.S., or $4.99 each in Canada, plus 25¢ shipping & handling per book and applicable taxes if any.* That's the complete price and — compared to cover prices of $5.25 each in the U.S. and $6.25 each in Canada — it's quite a bargain! You may cancel at any time, but if you choose to continue, every month we'll send you 6 more books, which you may either purchase at the discount price or return to us and cancel your subscription.

*Terms and prices subject to change without notice. Sales tax applicable in N.Y. Canadian residents will be charged applicable provincial taxes and GST.

If offer card is missing write to: The Harlequin Reader Service, 3010 Walden Ave., P.O. Box 1867, Buffalo, NY 14240-1867

BUSINESS REPLY MAIL
FIRST-CLASS MAIL   PERMIT NO. 717-003   BUFFALO, NY

POSTAGE WILL BE PAID BY ADDRESSEE

HARLEQUIN READER SERVICE
3010 WALDEN AVE
PO BOX 1867
BUFFALO NY 14240-9952

NO POSTAGE
NECESSARY
IF MAILED
IN THE
UNITED STATES

was almost unbearable in its tenderness. No one had ever caressed Julia in such a loving way. The delicate thread of renewed trust formed between them in the silence. Julia lifted up her face to him. He traced his fingers across her forehead as if soothing away a headache. Her knees weakened.

"Fair saint, if I profane with my unworthy hand, this holy shrine, the gentle sin is this," he whispered, his breath hot against her cheek. "My two lips, blushing pilgrims, stand ready to smooth my rough touch with a gentle kiss."

The music of Shakespeare's words entranced her, and a delicious glow encompassed her. Rob had quoted from *Romeo and Juliet,* when the star-crossed lovers meet for the first time at a party. She looked up at his face. The smoldering flame in his dark eyes startled her with its intensity. People said that a person's eyes were the windows of their souls. Could it be that Shakespeare's poetry mirrored his inner feelings?

She moistened her lips, then replied with Juliet's words, making them her own. "Good pilgrim, you do wrong your hands too much, for saints have hands that pilgrims' hands do touch." The frosty air around them seemed charged with energy.

Rob pressed a kiss in the palm of her bare hand. The impact of his gentleness shocked Julia. Her pulse skittered like a cat sliding down a tin washboard.

"Have not saints lips?" he asked, his voice husky.

Their intimacy acted like Mother's drops of opium, lulling Julia into a state of blissful euphoria. Her common sense spun out of her head, but she didn't care. It was sweet madness.

"Aye, pilgrim," she responded. Rising on tiptoe, she touched his cheeks, his skin cold beneath her fingertips.

Rob outlined her quivering mouth with a fingertip. "Then, sweet saint, let my lips do what my hand does."

With exquisite slowness, he lowered his mouth to meet hers. His last word was smothered as his lips touched hers like a whispered prayer. Her skin burned at the contact. He gently covered her mouth with his.

Julia's instinctive response shocked her. It was as if Rob had sundered a rusted padlock within her. Her knees suddenly gave way. With trembling arms, she clung to him. She ached for more—something she could not name but knew that she desired above all else. He supported her with his good arm. His uneven breath warmed her cheek as he drew her closer. With her blood singing through her veins, she welcomed his second kiss.

Rob lifted his head. "Thus my sin is purged from my lips by thine." His voice simmered with barely-controlled passion.

She licked her love-swollen mouth with the tip of her tongue, as if tasting a new flavor of ice cream. "Then, do my lips now have your sin they took?" she murmured. She experienced a heady sensation, as if she had twirled round and round on a swing. It grew more difficult to remember Juliet's lines.

Rob chuckled low in the back of his throat. "Sin from my lips? Oh, never, sweet saint! Give me my sin again!"

His grip on her tightened as his attitude became more serious. This time he demanded more. The sheer hunger of his desire took away Julia's breath. She returned his kiss with wanton abandon. His tongue traced along the line of her mouth, then parted her lips with a tender entreaty. Rumbling in the back of his throat, he drank deeply from her.

Hot flames rose up within Julia's breast. Her nipples tingled, then hardened. She melted into his embrace and surrendered to the sweet ravishment of his lips. Emotions she had never suspected she possessed surged through her. A passion, hitherto unknown, radiated from the deepest core of her body. Tremors heated her thighs and the secret place between them. She suckled the sweetness of his tongue like candied ginger, and yearned for more. His was the kiss that her wounded soul had long sought. His were the lips she had dreamt of in years of cold nights.

Julia moaned. Rob withdrew, leaving her with a flurry of soft kisses like snowflakes on her lips, her cheeks, her eyes. He ended with a gentle kiss brushed across her forehead. They stepped apart. Julia placed her hand over her heart as if to keep it from flying out of her rib cage. Her breathing slowed, though her skin sizzled where he had touched her.

"I am truly ruined now," she murmured, drunk with pleasure.

Rob coughed, inhaled deeply then laughed. "I am afraid that I have completely used up my Shakespeare—at least for tonight." He cupped her quivering chin in his hand. "Forgive me for that. I plead temporary madness."

Irked by his apology, Julia turned away from him and tossed her hair. "You are *sorry* for kissing me? Was I that bad? I admit that I have had no previous experience, but still, I thought I was rather good."

He gaped at her, then burst into loud laughter.

Julia sent a quick glance at the darkened window of her parents' bedroom. "Quiet! Do you want to be blasted into kingdom come tonight?"

Covering his mouth, Rob shook his head. "No, Miss Julia, I am not ready for the next world. I did not laugh at your kiss," he explained, drawing her back into the circle of his arm. "On the contrary, your kisses would have sent Shakespeare into rapturous sonnets, if he had been fortunate enough to have met you before I did. No, sweet saint, I was apologizing for my coarse behavior. You should be treated like a lady, not like…um…'' He coughed.

Julia couldn't help but smile. She knew exactly what he meant. "Like a soiled dove?"

"Something like that. Please forgive me."

Exulting in her newly discovered power, Julia cocked her head. "No, Major Montgomery, I will never forgive you for your kiss—your many kisses."

He looked stricken. "Miss Julia, truly I meant no disrespect but…"

She hid her smile. "But you were seized with Shakespeare at the time and lost your wits?"

He cleared his throat. "This is no laughing matter. I meant you no harm. In fact, I find you most…um…"

Julia took a certain satisfaction with his discomfiture. After all, hadn't he left once before with no explanation, and wasn't he truly her enemy? "Cat got your tongue, Rob?"

He snorted. "No, I believe that you had it last."

"Oh," Julia gasped. Her cheeks flushed.

Rob stroked her forehead. "In all seriousness, Julia. I found you most sweet to kiss." He frowned. "Your husband-to-be should count himself very fortunate. I envy the man," he muttered under his breath.

Julia shuddered as if she had been doused with a pail of water. She became aware of the biting cold in the garden. She pulled her blanket closer around her body. "Please don't spoil these last few moments we have together, Rob," she whispered. "I don't want to marry Payton Norwood. But there is not a thing I can do about it."

A cloud of contempt settled on his features. "You

should not be forced into this match, if you don't want him."

Julia sighed. Being a Northerner, how could Rob possibly understand her obligations of duty and honor to her family? "I cannot disobey my parents. My mother suffers from a nervous condition. It could kill her if I defied her wishes."

Even as she spoke these words, Julia wondered whether they were really true. Just how sick was her mother? For years the family and servants had whirled around Mrs. Chandler's whims and commands for fear of "setting her off," as Hettie said. Not once, in Julia's memory, had anyone really stood up to Mother's hysterics and vapors. Carolyn's escapades and her own spurt of independence counted for nothing in the long run. Mother always won in the end. Julia sighed. Tomorrow would be no exception.

"Payton is Mother's great-nephew and my second cousin. She thinks the world of him and his family. Mother is mad about pedigree. Since he's already a relative, I am doubly bound to honor this match." She shrugged. "Who knows? Payton might have turned into a human being since we last met. In any event, I must make the best of it."

Rob grimaced. "You could run away. Come to Washington and I will find you a respectable place to stay—"

"I can't." Julia cut him off before his tempting suggestion took root in her. "I cannot betray my family, and I will not betray Virginia." Her shoulders slumped. "But I do appreciate your concern, Rob." She turned away from him. "Thank you for this most enjoyable evening. I shall cherish it in my heart forever. If only the war had not happened! If only the Northerners had allowed us to go our own way, you and I might have had a different ending to this friendship."

"Julia, I—"

She shook her head. She wanted to finish what she had to tell him before her emotions overwhelmed her. "I must go now before I am missed. Hettie is waiting for me in the pantry."

He turned her face toward him. "Then before you leave, please give me your promise. Please meet me here tomorrow night, at ten o'clock? I want to give you one last gift— a wedding present to remember me by. Will you?"

He sounded very desperate. Julia hung her head as if she carried a huge load on her shoulders. "I will be formally pledged to Payton by then," she whispered.

He stroked her cheek, his touch caressing and very tempting. She lowered her lids.

"But not yet married," he murmured. "It is no crime to say one last goodbye to a gentleman before you make your nuptial vows. Please, this is *very* important to me. Promise me that you will."

"I will try." Opening her eyes, she stepped back from him. "I will try," she repeated. She had to get away from him before her tears overtook her. "Good night, good night," she said, backing away with each word. "Parting is such sweet sorrow."

"That I could say good night till it be morrow," Rob finished Shakespeare's line for her in a hollow voice.

Julia spun away and ran to the steps. She disappeared inside the house without a backward glance. Once in her bed, she vented her sorrow deep into her pillow.

She would never forget this night. It was a comfort to know that there was one man who loved her, even if he was a Yankee. She drifted into a troubled sleep.

Chapter Fourteen

When Julia disappeared inside the Chandler house, Rob felt as if a light had been snuffed out in his soul. Closing the garden gate behind him, he shoved his good hand deep into his pocket and headed back to the City Hotel where he had engaged a bed for the night. His boot heels tapped out a mournful staccato on the icy paving stones, "tomorrow, and tomorrow and tomorrow."

Tomorrow, by first light, he would return to Washington and buy that gilt-edged edition of Shakespeare from the hotel's stationers. Tomorrow would be his last day of freedom for a long time to come. Tomorrow he would pay his lodging bill at Ebbitt's and leave his few possessions in the safekeeping of his landlord. Tomorrow, he would give Colonel Lawrence the letters he had written for his parents and Julia, to be posted in case of his death. Tomorrow he would not think of death.

Tomorrow he would throw himself headlong into the most exciting adventure of his life. Tomorrow night, he would see Julia one last time as he betrayed her gentle trust. He would hate himself for doing it. Perhaps, in the years beyond tomorrow night, she would finally understand and forgive him.

In the City Hotel, war's necessity forced him to share his room with several other snoring occupants. Rob tried to settle himself into a state of repose. Tonight would be his last time in a comfortable bed for many months. He knew his body needed rest for tomorrow's events, but sleep eluded him. As the little city's church bells tolled away the early morning hours, Rob stared out the small window while thoughts of his mission unwound like a spool of thread. Every detail that he had memorized over the past two days returned in vivid clarity.

In his mind's eye, he saw the floor plans of Libby Prison that the clever Lizzie Van Lew had pieced together from her many visits to that dreadful place. The map of Richmond's city streets scrolled through his brain. The back roads that paralleled the James River down to Williamsburg and Newport News marched in cadence with his heartbeat. Once Rob got the escapees beyond Williamsburg, they would be safe behind their own lines. Food and medical attention awaited them at City Point.

Once at City Point…Rob must get them there…as many men as possible…safely to City Point.

Julia! Her beautiful face replaced Rob's nightmares of Confederate gunfire, rats crawling over him in a prison cell, thin gruel to eat instead of the creamy oyster stew that he had enjoyed earlier that evening. Julia's sad eyes reproached him in silence. He didn't want to hear her musical voice ask him why he had betrayed her trust for her enemy's benefit. He expected that his conscience would ask him that question a million times over during his incarceration in Libby.

After the war—it was bound to end soon—Rob promised himself to seek her out. By then she would be Mrs. Payton Norwood. He would knock at the Chandler front door like a proper caller instead of a thief in the night and ask for her address. He would make his apologies to her parents for the havoc that his capture in their garden had brought upon the family. He would make amends as best he could—after the war.

Sometime after the four-o'clock bells struck, he drifted into oblivion.

As expected, Payton Norwood arrived late in the afternoon, and was greeted by his great aunt with cries of joy. Clara ordered Julia to dress in her prettiest gown and to look cheerful.

"Poor you," commiserated Carolyn as she watched Julia unwind a corkscrew curl from the heated tongs. "I peeked over the balustrade when he came in. He still laughs like a mule."

Julia made a face in the mirror. "Could you see what he looked like?"

Carolyn shook her head. "His back was to me and I didn't want Mother to catch me spying. He's taller, but I suppose that is only natural. Papa didn't appear too pleased to see him."

Julia felt a small twinge of hope. Perhaps her father could convince Mother to change her mind and send Payton back to his plantation without her. Julia stood up and shook out her silken skirts and petticoats. The only thing that was going to keep her sane through the next few hours was the knowledge that she would see Rob one more time. She glanced at the little brass-and-marble clock on their mantelpiece. Six hours until ten o'clock.

"Shall we go down and meet my future?" she asked Carolyn with a false brightness.

Her sister gave her another pitying look. "Poor you," she repeated. "At least, Hettie has fixed up a nice platter of roast beef for supper."

The past four years had done nothing to improve Payton except to fatten his body and enlarge his faults. Though his face might have been called fair, it bore an inherent softness that his little, well-groomed mustache could not conceal. The set of his bare chin suggested a stubborn streak. His thick lips curled up at one corner, as if he were always on the verge of a sneer.

When he bowed over Julia's hand in greeting, his fleshy expression melted into a slimy smile. "You make the room feel delicious," he oozed. She resisted the urge to wipe her hand on the back of her skirt.

Clara Chandler spent the next horrible hour oohing and aahing over every little remark that Payton made—and he made a great many remarks, chiefly about himself. As he spoke, he held his head high with the arrogant pride of a man who thinks he knows how worthy he is of other people's envy. He had the annoying habit of drumming his fingers on the arm of the chair if the conversation happened to stray away from the topic of himself. His glances at Julia were positively condescending, as if he expected her to be adoringly grateful for receiving his hand in matrimony. Her skin crawled.

How could she possibly let him touch her? Kiss her? Rob's sweet kisses still lingered on her lips. Oh heaven, deliver her from this pompous fool!

Like his ego, Payton's vanity proved to be monumental. His dark, curly hair had been overly tamed with pomade. Julia noticed that he could not pass a looking glass without pausing a moment to admire his reflection. Upon her arrival in the parlor, he had presented Julia with a box of crystallized fruit, most of which he proceeded to eat himself over the course of the next two hours. Julia wondered if he would have any appetite left for supper, but all of Payton's appetites seemed to be bottomless.

He talked nonstop before, during and after that endless meal. Worse, he did not bother to close his mouth when he chewed his food. Julia barely touched her supper and, by the time the family had repaired to the parlor for coffee, she could not remember what she had eaten. Payton's high-pitched voice droned on and on into the evening. Julia itched to cover her ears and scream.

As the hours wore on, Payton's attention toward her turned from lovesick to lustful. And his bullying behavior that Julia recalled from their childhood had not disappeared. When he "assisted" her to the piano to play after-dinner music, his fingers bit deep into her elbow to assert his mastery. While he turned the pages of her music, he put his heavy hand on her shoulder with an air of possession. His mere touch left Julia feeling violated, ravished, soiled. Pleading a headache, she fled upstairs by nine. Carolyn followed after her.

"I loathe him," Julia cried in a choked voice as soon as Carolyn shut the door of their room. "I'd sooner marry a rattlesnake!" She threw herself across the bed.

Carolyn sat down beside her. "Payton is a wretched piece of work," she agreed in a gentle voice, "but I don't see how you can escape this marriage. Mother will not listen to a contrary word about him. She has set her mind on it, and you know nothing will change her once she gets an idea stuck in her head—not even Papa."

Closing her eyes, Julia wished she could shut Payton out of her life just as effectively. At least, she still had tonight. She recalled the pleasure of Rob's arm around her waist and his warm kisses on her lips. Julia sat up slowly as a plan began to form in her head. She glanced up at the little timepiece on the mantel. Ten past nine.

Julia watched as her sister undressed for bed. Could she count on Carolyn in her most desperate hour of need?

Carolyn pulled the rose-colored ribbon out of her hair. She stared back at her sister's reflection in the looking glass. "My, my, my," she mused. "You are all pink in the face. Now why is that?"

Julia took the brush from Carolyn's hand and began to pull its bristles through her sister's blond locks. "Payton's company has chased all such pleasure from my soul."

Carolyn's blue eyes took on a knowing glint. "Is that why you are blushing? Come on, Julia, tell all. I know there is something. What is it?" Her voice dropped lower. "Are you planning to run away?"

Julia paused, midstroke. "Not exactly." Did she dare to take this course?

Carolyn turned to face her. "What is it?"

Julia stared out the window at the garden below. "We live in a world of reality—not fairy tales. Carolyn, I need your help tonight. Please say you will."

As she spoke, she saw the bushes shake in the far corner of the garden. It looked as if her Prince Charming had arrived a little early.

Lieutenant Jamie Adamson of the Confederate States Army positioned his rangers around the perimeter of the Chandlers' garden enclosure. He took a moment to scan the height of the brick wall that encompassed the three open sides. Seven feet and a bit, he judged. Too high for a man to jump over, but fear of capture sometimes gave one surprising strength. He motioned two of his troopers to station themselves in the rear alleyway in case this Yankee managed to elude his snare. Adamson's commander, Colonel Mosby, would not be pleased if such a prize captive slipped through their clutches.

Hunkering down in the mud behind a particularly thorny rosebush, the young lieutenant felt like a fool. It went against the grain to spy on another man's private business with a young lady, but the war had turned all civilized behavior topsy-turvy. He fervently hoped that the information Mosby had received yesterday evening about this staff member of Grant's was correct.

Adamson also prayed that the Chandlers did not own a zealous watchdog with sharp teeth. While keeping an eye on the wrought-iron gate for the predicted arrival of Major Robert Montgomery, he spent this tense time composing what he was going to say to the Yankee, to the young lady, and most particularly to her family, since Adamson had the unhappy feeling that the good doctor and his wife were in for a very unpleasant surprise when they learned of their daughter's nighttime visitor. He much preferred to fight Yankees in the daylight, far away from the presence of hysterical women.

Just then, the bells of Christ Church struck ten o'clock.

Chapter Fifteen

"Eight...nine...ten!" After counting the final stroke of the grandfather clock in the hall, Julia wrapped her cloak around her shoulders. "I'm going, Carolyn. Remember your promise."

Her sister glared at her. "But he's a Yankee," she whispered with fierce opposition. "How can you even think of lowering yourself? Your reputation will be completely ruined."

Julia gave her sister a sympathetic look. "I know. That is the whole point. If Payton sees me in Rob's arms, he'll have to break our engagement. Family honor will demand it."

"You'll be sent away forever," Carolyn muttered from the depths of their four-poster bed.

"I expect so, but it would be a better fate than marriage to Payton." Julia pulled up the collar of her cloak. "Please don't fail me, Carolyn. As soon as you see us kissing, wake the household, especially Payton."

"Humph," Carolyn snorted. "I don't see how you can bring yourself to kiss that boy."

"Believe me, I would rather kiss Rob for a month of Sundays than kiss Payton once." Julia smiled to herself.

"And Rob's not a boy, Carolyn. He's a man." She picked up the lantern. "One last thing, please don't let Papa shoot him."

Carolyn snorted in reply.

Julia held the lantern close to her as she tiptoed down the dark hall. As she passed the guest room, she saw a dim glow under the door. Payton was still up. Good! Carolyn wouldn't have to wake him. Julia prayed that her skirts would not rustle, and that she would not step on one of the old squeaky floorboards. She didn't want to meet Payton now—not before she kept her assignation with Rob. Afterward, he would not want to see her. She smiled to herself.

Julia swept through the silent pantry and past the larder. Spying her father's squirrel gun on the rack by the back door, she took a few extra minutes to unload it. The round lead bullet dropped to the floor with a loud clatter and rolled away into a dark corner. Julia froze, and cocked her ear toward the floor above her. No sound. With a sigh of relief, she replaced the gun in its rack, then went outside.

The blast of cold night air extinguished her light. She picked her way carefully down the frosty steps covered with straw. Standing on the path, she glanced about the garden. It seemed empty, yet she sensed a presence, almost as if the bushes breathed. She scurried along the flagstones toward the magnolia tree.

"Rob?" she whispered as she ducked under its glossy leaves. He wasn't there.

She was sure she saw someone outside an hour ago, and looked about. Only cold starlight winked at her through the branches. Hunching her shoulders against the cold, her unease grew as she strained to hear the indefinable whisperings that seemed to waft in the air around her. The short hairs on the back of her neck prickled. A premonition of fear seized her. What if he didn't come tonight?

Just then, she heard the unmistakable click of the gate's latch. Julia released her pent-up breath. In a few more minutes, she would be free of Payton Norwood forever.

Rob paused before shutting the gate behind him. Lifting his chin, he sniffed the air, hoping to catch a whiff of oiled leather and damp wool that would signal the presence of the Confederates who were there to capture him. He surveyed the dark garden, trying to penetrate the shadowed corners between the privy house and the compost heap. A dozen men could hide there without a trace, he thought. He swallowed to calm his nerves. He was at the point of no return. From the moment he had said farewell to Colonel Lawrence this afternoon, his path had been set in a straight line toward the cells of Libby Prison. He regretted that the secrecy of his mission even forbade him from giving his young cousin a warmer-than-usual goodbye.

A whippoorwill's call pierced the wind. In the dead of a winter's night, that cry could only be a man-made signal. All Rob's senses heightened, and a spasm of pain spread through his useless hand. Someone moved beside the magnolia. Despite the apprehension for his future after tonight, he smiled when Julia materialized from under the tree's branches. Seeing her in the cold light of the moon, Rob appreciated her slender willowy form, despite the cloak that fell from her shoulders. His blood quickened in his veins as he strode across the frozen ground to meet her. In his pocket, the small book of Shakespearean sonnets bumped against his hip.

I must give it to Julia quickly before—

"Rob," she breathed, her smile radiant. "I was afraid that I had missed you."

He opened his good arm and she walked into his half-embrace as if it were the most natural thing in the world. Slipping his hand around her slim waist, he pulled her closer to him—to keep her warm. Though she wore a wool dress with all its attendant corseting and layers of petticoats, he could still feel the flare of her hips. Rob sucked in his breath. How he longed to savor those delights that Julia's graceful body promised! He dipped his head to hers.

"This is an appointment I could not miss, though the devil himsclf barred the way," he replied with ironic truth.

He suspected that his remaining freedom could be counted in mere minutes now. He had so much to tell Julia, and yet all his lips wanted to do was kiss her.

Julia looked up at him. "Payton arrived. We are truly engaged now, though I have a—"

"Do not speak of him. His name insults your tongue." With those words, Rob covered her lips with his. Julia gasped; her sweet breath filled his mouth. A rush of sensual vitality raced through him. His manhood rose with white heat.

Wrapping her arms around his waist, Julia returned his kiss with a reckless abandon that surprised him. She tasted of clover honey and summer wine—sweet and heady. Hers was a kiss to live for—one that he would cherish in the depths of his imprisonment.

Lieutenant Adamson watched the lovers meld together. The girl confirmed the man's identity when she whispered his name. Adamson groaned with envy. He wished his own sweetheart had half that much passion in her voice when she spoke to him. Drawing his revolver from its holster, he truly hated what he had to do. He sheathed his emotions against the painful consequences he knew the next few minutes would bring.

Just then a shrill scream shattered the stillness. Lights flashed on inside the Chandler house. Shouts and another scream.

The couple broke their kiss, though the woman held the Yankee tight.

Adamson swore. This unexpected disturbance jeopardized his plan to capture the major and escape with as little disturbance as possible. He gestured to his nearest man, who nodded in response and passed the signal down the line. Miss Chandler whispered something in the major's ear, drawing his attention to herself. In less than a minute, the rangers surrounded their quarry. The lieutenant hoped he would be able to take Montgomery without commotion.

Putting his hand on the major's shoulder, Adamson felt his muscles under the coat instantly stiffen. He cocked his revolver. "Major Robert Montgomery, a word with you, if you please," he whispered.

Montgomery looked up from Miss Chandler, but did not release her. In fact, he drew her closer to his body. "Do not harm this lady," he growled. "She is innocent of this business."

Spying Adamson's gun, Miss Chandler screamed, then clapped her hand over her mouth and buried her face in the major's chest. Maintaining an icy calm, Montgomery stroked her hair while staring at his captor. Adamson released a long breath. Though he hated upsetting women, he silently thanked Miss Chandler for her presence. For her sake, it appeared that Montgomery was not going to put up a fight. The lieutenant lowered his gun a fraction, though he did not uncock the hammer.

The noise inside the Chandler house increased in volume. More lights appeared in the downstairs windows.

"Colonel Mosby's compliments, sir. He wishes to meet you as soon as possible," Adamson said quickly, hoping to keep down the noise in the garden. Perhaps the Chandlers' domestic quarrel could work to his advantage if no one inside paid any attention to what was happening behind their house.

Then Jamie noticed that the major's right hand remained in his pocket. Did he conceal a small pistol? Not wishing to make himself a prime target, he grabbed hold of Montgomery's right wrist and yanked out his hand. Instead of the stub nose of a derringer pointing at him, there was nothing but a glove. To be safe, Adamson pulled it off. In the moon's light, he saw the terrible damage done by a minié ball.

"Sweet Lord," Adamson muttered. "Where did you get that?"

"Gettysburg," Montgomery snapped, looking at a spot over the lieutenant's left shoulder.

Lifting her face from the man's coat, Miss Chandler stared at the misshapen fingers. "Oh, Rob," she whispered.

The Yankee clenched his jaw. "Seen your fill, Lieutenant? With your permission, may I put my glove back on? Miss Julia is shocked enough."

Adamson tore his gaze away from the man's injury to look into his eyes. A glare of cold steel returned his glance. With a mumbled apology, Adamson handed over the glove and marveled at the dexterity with which Montgomery pulled it on without releasing his hold of Miss Chandler.

The lights bobbed toward the rear door of the house. Adamson swore under his breath. Now he would have to explain himself to the family. He had hoped to vacate the garden without compromising the lady. That chance gone, now he prayed his rangers could escape with the major before some wakeful neighbor called the Federal provost marshal.

Lieutenant Adamson gave Miss Chandler an apologetic look. "Beg your pardon, miss, but it appears that we have landed you in a heap of trouble." As he spoke, the back door banged open. Several men bounded down the steps.

Miss Chandler shook her head. "No need to apologize, Lieutenant. I have made my own misfortune all by myself."

The major looked down at her with a stricken expression. "Julia, please forgive me. I wish I could have spared you from this."

Placing her hand on his chest over his heart, she smiled up at him. Her lips trembled. "No, Rob, I can't forgive you," she replied in a whisper, "because there is nothing to—"

At that instant, Dr. Jonah Chandler yanked his daughter out of the major's embrace. "Unhand Julia or, by God, I'll kill you." He waved a long-barreled rifle.

Julia gasped. "Papa, please!"

The doctor's outburst galvanized Adamson. Fearing for both the safety of his prisoner as well as that of his men, the lieutenant faced down the angry father. "Lieutenant James Adamson at your service, sir," he said, stepping between Chandler's gun and Montgomery. He touched the brim of his gray felt slouch hat to the doctor.

"I regret this uncivilized intrusion upon your family and property, sir," he continued swiftly, "but I was instructed to apprehend Major Montgomery at this place and hour. Your daughter is a brave woman, Dr. Chandler, and was most helpful in the capture of this Yankee. He is a member of General Grant's staff, and no doubt he has a great deal of information that my commander, Colonel Mosby, will be most eager to obtain. With your permission, we will remove ourselves as quickly as possible and allow you and your family to return to your beds.''

The couple looked at one another with equal expressions of perplexity, while Dr. Chandler, somewhat mollified, stepped back. "Julia helped you?" he asked, with astonishment. "Is that what she's doing out here?"

Montgomery stared only at Miss Chandler. "Did you?" he mouthed silently to her.

Her eyes wide like those of a stricken doe, Miss Chandler pushed herself away from her father. She clutched her throat, but no sound emerged. Lieutenant Adamson hoped that she understood that his lie was meant to save her reputation. He cleared his throat. "Indeed, sir, Colonel Mosby is most grateful for Miss Chandler's assistance." He gave her a fleeting smile.

A numbing sensation crept through Rob's brain. He barely felt his arms being tied behind his back. What was it Julia had whispered to him just as he was arrested? The only words he could remember were, "I am desperate." Had he completely misconstrued her enthusiastic responses toward him? Was she really the spy that Lawrence suspected her to be? Had he been betrayed by a woman once again?

"Did you tell them I would be here tonight?" he asked her.

Shaking her head, she staggered backward toward the house. Though her lips moved, she made no sound, except the rasp of her breathing. She stared at him, at the Rebel soldiers, back to him, then at her father, then to a young fop standing behind Dr. Chandler that Rob presumed was Julia's cousin. Smarting under the lieutenant's revelation, Rob didn't know if he should feel sorry for Julia or be glad that she, in turn, would receive her just deserts.

"Julia—" he began again, but one of the Rebs pushed a gag between his teeth.

Their commander lifted his eyebrow. "Your pardon, Major, but I don't need your help to raise a ruckus."

Rob swallowed. The cloth in his mouth tasted of tobacco and onions. He nodded to the lieutenant. Then he glanced at Julia again. Her eyes glazed over; in the moonlight she looked pale as a ghost. Maybe she knew nothing and this Rebel was trying to be a gentleman.

Two of the troopers grabbed him by each shoulder while a third man prodded him toward the gate with his rifle barrel. Mosby's Rangers had not earned their reputation for daring swift raids by loitering too long in one place. The closer Rob got to the gate, the faster the soldiers pushed him. He stretched his neck to look at Julia one last time. He saw her shake off the younger man's arm from her shoulder. Standing alone, she appeared as fragile as a glass figurine.

Outside in the alley, two other rangers held the reins of a number of horses. His three guards roughly pushed Rob up into the saddle of one. The book he had brought for Julia bumped against his leg. Rob bit down on his gag with frustration. There had been no opportunity to give it to her.

He tried to see her through the gate, but his escort allowed him no time. Without waiting for their commanding officer to join them, they took off down the street at a brisk trot away from the river, pulling Rob's horse behind them. When his guard picked up speed on the edge of the city, Rob forced his thoughts away from Julia. Gripping his mount with his knees, he hung on as his escort dashed them through the sleeping farmland. Once incarcerated in Libby Prison, Rob would have ample opportunity to analyze tonight's events. For now, he needed to use every ounce of his strength to stay in the saddle.

A heaviness stole over Julia's senses. She could hear the Confederate officer speaking to her father, but his words sounded muffled, as if he talked though a goose-down pillow. The grim expression on Rob's face froze her voice. He believed she betrayed him, that she had arranged for his capture.

She tried to tell him that he was wrong, but no sound came from her throat. Her fingers lost all feeling. Her feet refused to walk in a steady line. Her vision blurred so that Rob's form melted together with those of his captors—blue and gray together. She wanted to stop them so that she could assure Rob of her innocence, but the shock of his capture had dulled her wits. The sudden appearance of the Confederates was not what she had planned.

Payton hung his arm around her neck. She could smell strong brandy on his vile breath. He growled something in her ear, but his words sounded like gibberish. She struggled to free herself.

She had to go to Rob before they took him away.

But instead of running to the garden gate, her legs gave way on her. For the first time in her twenty years, Julia crumpled into a faint.

Payton caught her before her head hit the flagstones. With a grunt, he scooped her into his arms.

"I'll take her inside, Uncle," he called to her father. "A lady is not used to guns and violence." He directed this remark to the lieutenant who eyed Julia with more than casual interest. Had Julia kissed him, too? As Payton carried her up the back steps, he rued the necessity that compelled him to marry her. Once they were back at Belmont, he would keep her under lock and key. He would be the only man she would ever see again. He would make her pay dearly for this night's embarrassment.

When Payton had first spied Julia and the Yankee with their arms around each other, his anger exploded within his brain. She had not looked at him this evening with one-tenth of the interest she had for that varmint. Payton craved to horsewhip them both, then shoot the man and make her watch him die.

Shifting her weight in his arms as he negotiated his way through the pantry, he glanced down at her. Julia's face looked all the more angelic in repose. His gaze lingered on her lips—lips that had kissed the Yankee, but had not yet kissed him, her own fiancé.

"You will rue this night a hundred times over. *That* is my wedding vow to you," he swore.

He kicked open the door that led from the kitchen into the hall. When he saw his aunt and younger cousin on the staircase, he rearranged his features from hate to concern. This misadventure of Julia's could work in his favor, he realized. Now that she was truly degraded, he could ask his uncle for a much larger sum, as well as Julia's legacy. He needed every penny he could get to pay his creditors, especially since Confederate inflation had sent his debts sky-high. Payton's poor luck in Richmond's gambling dens had already used up his inheritance.

Yes, not only would he make Julia pay for his injured pride, but so would her family. They would settle a fortune on him to get rid of her now.

Payton flashed Clara a wicked smile as he carried Julia up to her bedroom. "No need to worry, Auntie," he said in a soothing voice. "She's only fainted. We stopped that Yankee before he could ravish her."

Clara's high-pitched squeal of alarm acted as a healing balm on Payton's punctured honor.

Chapter Sixteen

"Your parents wish to speak with you in the parlor," Hettie informed Julia the following morning. The housekeeper's face wore a sympathetic expression. "They've been talking about you since dawn."

Julia turned away from her window where she had been gazing down at the garden. How could such a peaceful-looking place have been the scene of such cataclysmic events last night? Yet her own plan—to be caught in kissing a Yankee—had worked beautifully, except that she had not been able to warn Rob in time. Her surprise fainting spell may have saved her temporarily from her parents' wrath, but she had to face them now. The dark wakeful hours between Rob's capture and this morning's summons to the parlor had only stiffened Julia's resolve to lead her own life. Though she would probably never see Rob again, especially since he thought she had betrayed him to Mosby's men, she rejoiced that, at least, she didn't have to marry Payton.

She tried to give Hettie a flutter of a smile, but her stomach churned at the thought of the interview to come. "Is Payton with them?"

Hettie wrinkled her nose as if she smelled something

rotten in the back of the larder. "No, he ate a big breakfast, then said he was going for a walk. When a raccoon drinks water, you know he's fixing for a fight," she added.

"Is that another one of your mother's sayings?"

Hettie nodded solemnly. "And everybody downstairs drank plenty of water this morning at breakfast. Coffee, too."

The mention of food made Julia's stomach rumble, though she had little appetite—at least, not until after she had faced her parents. She patted her hair in place then walked to the door. "Once more, dear friends, into the breach," she muttered the opening line of Henry V's speech before the Battle of Agincourt.

Dr. and Mrs. Chandler greeted their elder daughter with severe expressions. Both Julia's parents wore dark clothing, as if in mourning, and their attitudes matched their somber attire. Of course they were angry, as she had expected. She stiffened her shoulders for the verbal blows to come.

"I hope you are satisfied with yourself," Clara began. Her eyes narrowed into angry slits. "Your behavior last night was unforgivable."

Julia said nothing, but cast a quick look at her father. He refused to return her glance. Julia held her silence until her mother had finished everything she intended to say.

"I cannot imagine what wicked spirit has possessed you this past month, but you will no longer be our concern. Once you are gone from this house, I never want to see nor hear from you again. Your disgrace has pierced me to the heart."

Julia inwardly flinched. Though she had expected her mother to be angry, nevertheless her finality cut to the quick. When the silence lengthened, Julia cleared her throat. "I am sorry to have caused you so much distress,

Mother, Papa.'' She again looked to her father, but he appeared to be made of stone. ''It was not my intention to do so.''

Her mother clenched her hands so hard that she shook. ''Of course not! You did not give us a second thought, when you threw yourself at that...that man. Vile Yankee! You should count your blessings that Payton is a true Christian gentleman, and far too good for you. It surprises me that he did not reject you on the spot. Instead, that sweet boy insists he loves you and will give you a good home. A week from Saturday, you will be married to dear, kind Payton, and he will take you back to Belmont. It's far, far more than you deserve.''

Julia nearly gagged. Payton didn't love her! She had seen his face when he dumped her on her bed last night and it wasn't full of kindness, but a much more base emotion. Lifting her chin, she stared down at her mother. ''I regret to add to your displeasure, but I refuse to marry Payton Norwood.''

A strangled cry rose out of Clara's mouth. For the first time, Julia's father looked at her. His frown deepened.

''Payton is a worthy bridegroom for any girl, Julia,'' the doctor said, in a bruised tone dredged up from the pit of his melancholy.

Clara found her voice. ''Payton is far too good for you! All the girls in Richmond are just dying to marry him. So handsome, so polite, so intelligent!''

Julia steeled herself for the sake of her future. ''Let the Richmond girls keep him, then. But I will never have that false loon for a husband, not on Saturday next, not ever.''

''Ungrateful wretch!'' her mother gasped, pulling out her handkerchief.

Before the crocodile tears could commence, Julia hurried ahead, her words tripping over themselves. ''I loathe

Payton. Being married to him is not going to make this situation any better, except for Payton. You think he is so good and kind to marry me even though my good name is ruined? He doesn't care a fig for me. What he lusts for is Grandmother's ten thousand dollars that will be mine on my birthday next month. That's why he still insists he wants to marry me. But he'll never have that money! I intend to use my inheritance to open a school for girls. Payton may want to marry me, but I refuse *him*. This is *my* life, Mother, and I will choose to live it as I see fit—not as *you* command.''

''You will die in the gutter like one of those…loose women!'' Clara shouted. ''That's where you will end up if Payton doesn't take you. No one will want a brazen hussy to teach their daughters. You will starve, do you hear me? Starve, for we have washed our hands of you. See how you like that!''

Though her mother's vindictiveness inflamed Julia's temper, she fought to remain calm. She had never before seen her so overwrought. ''Believe me, I have done nothing wrong. But it *will* be a crime if I am forced to marry Payton. He will beat me as he does his slaves and dogs. I refuse to be saddled with a husband I despise, and live out my life in sorrow, merely to give you membership into Richmond's social circle. That's really what you want, isn't it, Mother?''

With the scream of a harpy, Clara launched herself out of her chair. She flew at Julia with her fingers curled into claws. Her husband grabbed her around her waist before she had the chance to touch Julia.

Dr. Chandler shook his head as if he bore an unbearable weight. ''Hush, Clara, hush now. You will only do your heart more injury,'' he soothed. ''There, there, be still now, and we will get your laudanum for you. You will sleep. It will be good for you. Hush now.''

His wife's eyes bulged, though she calmed in his arms. All the while, she stared at Julia with a silence that unnerved her daughter. Julia took a horrified step backward. Her mother was truly mad!

Her father stroked Clara as if she were a kitten, while he spoke to his daughter. ''Julia, you do not understand your position. Your rash actions have taken away your choice in this matter. As your parents, we must do what is right to save you from yourself, if that is necessary. Your infatuation for that…man in the garden has led you astray from all that you have been taught.''

The sudden realization stunned her. ''That's true,'' she said aloud. ''You taught me to hate the Yankees. I was told that they were crass bullies who envied us and who wished to crush us. I have discovered, much to my shock, that not all Northerners are evil. In fact, some can be more civil than Southerners on occasion.''

Her mother went white. Bright red blotches appeared on her cheeks. ''Hold your tongue, Julia May!'' she shrieked. ''You have lost your mind. No matter, that will be Payton's problem, not ours, thank heavens.'' She struggled again in the doctor's embrace. ''Mark my words, you *will* be married next week. Between now and then, you will be locked in the second bedroom. You are forbidden to join us for meals, nor may you walk in the garden.'' She shuddered convulsively at the mention of the place. ''You will not speak to any of us again as we have no desire to communicate with you. From this moment on, you are *dead* to the Chandlers. Do you hear what I say? Dead! Dead! You are dead!''

Julia felt as if she had been slapped in the face. Hot tears pricked her eyes, but then she noticed that her mother watched her as closely as a cat at a rathole. A thin smile of triumph flitted across her mother's face.

She was gloating! She thought she'd defeated her, and that Julia would fall on her knees and beg for forgiveness. Astonished by her mother's downward spiral, Julia blinked back her pain. She turned to her father. "Is this your decision as well, Papa?"

Dr. Chandler closed his eyes for a moment before he nodded. "Our hearts are blistered with sorrow by your behavior, Julia. It is beyond comprehension. You were always such a good girl—until now."

Julia shot a quick glance at her mother. She noted that Clara remained dry-eyed and triumphant. It was all a game to her—one that she had to win! The realization was an awakening experience that sent Julia reeling.

"Yes, Papa," Julia replied softly. "I always did everything you asked of me, so that Mother would not have one of her fits." She looked at Clara, as if seeing her for the first time. "I grew up terrified that it might kill you if I did something that upset your nerves. That's the way you wanted it, isn't it, Mother? All these years, you have ruled our family like a tyrant, using your delicate health as a two-edged sword over our heads."

"How dare you speak to me like this!" Clara shook her fists. "Oh, Jonah! I had no idea that we had harbored such a viper in the bosom of our family."

Julia was tempted to point out that her mother was the true viper, but looking at the distress on her father's face, she saw that she had already gone too far.

"I will *not* marry Payton," Julia reiterated in a monotone. Her energy drained away from her, leaving a heavy feeling of lassitude in its wake. Without waiting to be excused, she turned toward the hall door. All Julia wanted now was to lie down and sleep.

Clara tried to lunge after her, but Jonah held her tighter. "Your insolence is intolerable! I do not care a whit what you want. A week from Saturday at ten in the morning, you will be married to poor, dear Payton at Saint Paul's, even if we have to drag you through the streets of Alexandria behind our carriage to get you there."

"Now, dear," her husband soothed in the singsong voice that he used with his cantankerous patients. "She will change her mind once she has had time to consider. You'll see. Let us find your laudanum bottle. Hush, my sweet. Be still as a mouse."

Julia opened the door to the hall. She would never reconsider. But Lord only knew how she would get out of there.

Hettie hovered outside. The servant hugged the girl in a tight embrace. "A one-eyed mule can't be handled on his blind side," she murmured in Julia's ear. "Pay your mother no mind now, child. It's the devil in her mind that's done all her talking. You go to bed, and I'll mull you some cherry bounce that will help you sleep."

Julia wrapped her arms around Hettie's shoulders and rested her head on her ample breast. "Oh, Hettie, what am I going to do?"

Still holding Julia tight against her, Hettie helped her up the stairs. "Bide your time and wait for a better day, Miss Julia, just like I've done all my life. You have yourself a good cry, then sleep some. After that, we'll put our heads together and hatch us a good plan."

Julia didn't have the strength to argue with her. Sleep was what she craved. Once rested, she could turn her brain to the knotty problem before her.

"Come hell or high water," she vowed to the housekeeper under her breath, "I will not marry the loathsome Payton."

Hettie massaged her shoulders. "'Course not, child."

After drinking Hettie's warm, sweetened brandy, Julia slept for nearly twenty-four hours. The weekend dragged by like an overloaded cart on a rutted road. Clara spent much of the time sedated in her room. Payton disappeared among the inhabitants of Alexandria for hours on end. Jonah occupied his days reading his newspapers, both Unionist and Confederate, while smoking on his pipe. Carolyn kept her sister informed of the family's changes of moods, as well as the news of the day beyond the confines of the Chandlers' front door. Though Julia spent her days examining the problem of her future in a logical manner, no reasonable idea came to mind.

On Monday afternoon, while their mother took another laudanum-induced nap, Carolyn paid one of her clandestine visits to her sister, bringing newspapers and caramels. "You could run away," she suggested. "Go to Aunt Charlotte in Strasburg."

Julia shook her head. "I am sure Mother wrote to her the first thing, telling her how wicked I had become. I'd be chased off Aunt Charlotte's front porch with a broomstick just like a pesky raccoon."

Carolyn nodded. Idly, she turned the page of the latest smuggled copy of the *Richmond Enquirer*. With a small cry, she sat upright on the bed, clutching the newspaper.

"What did you say your Yankee's name was? Montgomery?"

Her eyes closed, Julia massaged her temples. It hurt to remember him. "Major Robert Montgomery. He's from someplace in New York."

Carolyn whistled through her teeth, a habit she had picked up on her unchaperoned jaunts around Alexandria. "Could it be Rhinebeck?"

Opening her eyes, Julia stared at her sister. "The very place! How did you guess?"

Carolyn folded back the paper. "No guesswork at all. Look down the last column on the right, near the bottom of the page."

Julia's hand trembled as she took the newspaper. She polished her spectacles on her sleeve before squinting at the tiny, blurred newsprint.

"Among the recent prisoners incarcerated in Libby Prison this week is Major Robert Montgomery of New York's Rhinebeck Legion who was apprehended by Colonel John S. Mosby late on Friday evening. It had been assumed that Montgomery was a highly placed staff officer under the command of Union General Ulysses Grant. Alas, the perfidious Yankee proved to be merely an invalid soldier employed in the Federal Quartermaster Department. He can now spend his new leisure time in contemplation of the tasty victuals that he will no longer enjoy in the Federal City's Willard Hotel."

"Oh!" The paper fell from Julia's hand.

Carolyn gave her sister a pitying look. "I've heard that Libby is the very worst prison in the whole South. Your major is likely to die there." She made a face at the idea, then added in a gentle voice, "I am truly sorry for it, Julia. He may be a Yankee, but at least he made you happy."

Julia hugged herself as if she could squeeze out her misery. "Don't talk like he is already dead, Carolyn."

Carolyn retrieved the newspaper and folded it. "There's nothing we can do for him here. And I highly doubt that Payton will let you go visiting him when you are living at Belmont."

A brilliant idea hit Julia so hard, she nearly slipped off her chair. In the blink of an eyelash, she knew exactly what course of action she would take—and it had nothing whatsoever to do with Payton Norwood.

She forced herself to settle down so that she could think straight. "Run and get Hettie, Carolyn," she asked as excitement ignited her hope.

The girl stared at her sister with anxiety. "Have you taken ill?"

"No, you little goose! I've finally turned the corner of my life. Hurry up and don't ask me questions now. There is very little time left and a world of things I must do. Get Hettie and don't talk to another soul."

Carolyn cast Julia a second worried glance, then raced out the room, banging the door behind her. Julia heard her footsteps thudding down the stairs. New life welled up inside her. She made a list of all her jewelry in her small satin-lined jewel case in her top bureau drawer under the handkerchiefs. She underlined the string of pearls that Papa had given her for her sixteenth birthday. They ought to fetch a good price at a Yankee pawnbroker's.

Chapter Seventeen

Libby Prison, Richmond, Virginia
Late January 1864

"Fresh fish! Fresh fish!" cried a dozen voices at once. Then a hundred more took up the refrain in the rooms overhead.

Two days after his capture in Julia's garden, Rob stood before Major William Long of the Confederate States Army and adjutant of Richmond's infamous prison for Union officers. Rob couldn't recall the last time he had eaten a full meal, nor when he had been allowed to lie down and sleep for more than three hours at a stretch. Despite his fatigue, he straightened his shoulders and gave Long a crisp military salute, albeit with his left hand.

"Major Robert Montgomery, Rhinebeck Legion, New York," he stated, staring straight into the gray eyes of the man on the other side of the desk. "Pardon my salute, Major, but some of your boys took care of my right hand at Gettysburg." He gave the adjutant a cold smile.

More voices overhead shouted "Fresh fish," and banged their tin cups against the floor planking. Rob looked up at the ceiling. "I didn't know you served fish on your menu for supper. What kind?"

Behind him, a young prison guard sniggered. Even Major Long permitted a half smile to flit across his face. "We haven't had fish here since last September, Major Montgomery. It's *you* who is our latest catch."

"Oh," replied Rob crisply, to cover his chagrin. "Then I am honored by the welcome of my brother officers." He wished Lawrence had given him a better briefing on Libby's rituals. From now on, he would hold his tongue until he learned the customs of this cloistered society.

Long scanned the report that had accompanied Rob on his journey from northern Virginia—miles jostling on horseback, followed by more miles lying bound on the floor of a train's unheated cattle car.

"I see that Colonel Mosby was misinformed," Long remarked at last. "It appears that you are not a member of General Grant's staff, as the colonel was led to believe, but merely a flunky in the Quartermaster's Department." He regarded Rob with a penetrating look. "Pray enlighten me. How on earth could Colonel Mosby have been so wrong about you, when he is usually so right?"

Rob decided to play the part of a "bombproof," the derisive name for officers who sought safe desk jobs instead of the hazards of field command—men like Major Scott Claypole. Relaxing his stiff posture a fraction, he assumed Claypole's annoying mannerisms.

"To tell you the truth, Major, I was as surprised as the colonel. More so, in fact, since I was…shall we say, *interrupted* in the midst of a promising tête-à-tête with a most delightful young lady." The young guardsman perked up and drew nearer in hopes of hearing more lurid details.

Ignoring the beardless pup, Rob continued to weave his

cover story. "I have nothing to do with General Grant, and have never even had the pleasure of meeting him. So you see, Major, I am utterly useless to you, and I said as much to Colonel Mosby. I must confess, he did not take too kindly to the mistaken identity. Nor did he offer an apology for my inconvenience."

In fact, Mosby had lost his temper, both at Rob and at Lieutenant Adamson. The Gray Ghost baldly accused Rob of lying and a great many other devious crimes as well. The heated interrogation had lasted until dawn before Mosby grudgingly accepted Rob's identity as a mere supply officer. No breakfast was served the prisoner except a cup of the foulest-tasting excuse for coffee he had ever drunk, followed by the harsh ride across open countryside to Catlett Station.

Major Long lifted a brow. "Inconvenience? Well, I would not count on seeing your young lady again in the near future. You will bide a while with us." To the guard, he ordered, "Take the major upstairs and put him in the central gallery." To Rob, he added, "I do hope that you get along with Pennsylvanians, Major. You'll be sharing quarters with quite a number of them. Reveille is at five, breakfast at six, roll calls are at eight and four in the afternoon, supper at six and tattoo at seven. See that you don't miss anything. My sergeant-at-arms is very touchy about punctuality."

As the guard pushed him toward the far door, Rob asked, "What time did you say was dinner, Major? I'd hate to be late for that."

Long narrowed his eyes. "There is no dinner here, Major. Good day."

The young guard sniggered again as he prodded Rob up a narrow flight of open stairs. "You're in hell now, Yankee."

With bewildering speed, Rob left the last vestiges of normalcy in the adjutant's office, and entered into a nightmare existence at the top of the stairs. The second floor of the former tobacco warehouse and ship chandler was comprised of three long galleries, divided from each other by bare brick walls. Cast-iron stoves inside large fireplaces at each end of the galleries provided a feeble heat. Despite the huge number of men packed into each gallery, the room was chill as stone. Wind from the nearby James River whined through the open-barred windows that lined the outside walls of each gallery.

A lanky lieutenant colonel, wearing a dog-eared uniform, stepped out of the crowd and extended his hand. "Welcome to Hotel de Libby, Major," he said with a grin. "You've arrived just in time. We were about to commence this evening's entertainment, cootie races." The men around him laughed, though there was no mirth in their eyes.

Rob returned the handshake with his left. "Rob Montgomery, sir. I hope you gentlemen will not mind having a New Yorker in your midst."

"So long as you don't snore much," shot back one of the men.

The lieutenant colonel nodded. "Hamilton's my name, Rob. The boys call me A.G., and I'm a Kentuckian by birth and breeding—a *Northern* Kentuckian." He pointed to a spot on the floor along the outside wall. The "bed" was a single rolled blanket without the addition of a cot or straw mattress.

"You can sleep over there since the youngster who was using it last night doesn't need it anymore." A.G. paused for a moment; a tic quivered along his jawline. "The wind will keep you wakeful, I'm afraid, but when we all lie down, it gets nearly tolerable in here. Just holler when you want to turn over.''

The stark conditions of his new surroundings appalled Rob, though he did not betray his shock. Until he could learn who was planning the breakout, he would watch, wait and pray that he could get these lean, hollow-eyed men back home.

That night, in the few hours of sleep that he could manage, Rob dreamt of Julia Chandler.

Two mornings after the painful interview with her parents, Julia quietly dressed in the gloom of pre-dawn. Thanks to help from Hettie and Carolyn, she was ready to make her bid for freedom, though it cut her to the quick to realize that her disappearance would cause her beloved Papa great pain and fill her mother with fury. On the other hand, she didn't care a fig what Payton would think once he realized that his golden goose had fled her coop.

Since her planned escape route compelled her to travel with little baggage, Julia dressed with care, putting on two layers of everything. The double skirts, petticoats and, especially, the tight bodices made her appear considerably heavier than she was. In a small carpetbag, she packed toothbrush and powder, her hairbrush, tortoiseshell comb and a small ivory-backed mirror, a small bottle of lavender water, a clean set of underdrawers and camisole, a spare chemise, a half-dozen handkerchiefs, her spectacles and a pair of wool stockings. She hated to part with her precious books but necessity forced her to be sensible. A woman on the run could not be encumbered with a library.

Carolyn watched her from the warmth of the four-poster bed. ''I'll hide your books,'' she said with sympathetic understanding, ''so Mother won't burn them in a fit of pique. Someday you'll be back..." She trailed off with a sniffle.

Julia paused in her preparations to give her sister a quick hug. "I do hope so, lambkin." With her own eyes welling up, she turned back to her little bag. "I'll take my Bible for comfort, and Mr. Browning's poems for diversion," she continued, stuffing the two small volumes deep inside the bulging satchel.

"You're sure you want to do this?" Carolyn asked her yet again. "Once you leave, you know that Mother will never let—"

Julia interrupted her. "I know I can't stay here and marry Payton. In Richmond, maybe I can find some employment. I understand they need nurses badly in the hospitals."

Carolyn made a face. "I would faint at the sight of blood."

Julia didn't want to think about the grim scenes she knew those houses of suffering held. She would find out soon enough. "Once I have found a place to stay, I will go to the Libby Prison. I am sure I can persuade the guards to let me visit with Rob. I'll bring him some extra food and whatever else he will need. I've got to prove to him that I didn't betray him to those soldiers."

Her sister sighed. "You must truly love that varmint to run off after him like this."

Julia fastened the bag's latch with a snap. "I don't love Rob, Carolyn. You make me sound like one of those sugary heroines in those novels of yours. But I do feel very responsible for his capture. It's only right that I try to make his imprisonment as comfortable as possible."

She paused before the tall dresser where Frank Shaffer's silver locket lay in its velvet box. Julia held up the trinket. The little heart twirled on its black velvet ribbon. For nearly three years, she had worn it faithfully, but that time was now past.

"Rest in peace, sweet Frank," she whispered to the locket. "Thank you for teaching me how to love. I will always remember you." Then she returned it to its box, burying the treasure deep in the top drawer under her handkerchiefs.

Julia pulled on her green velvet cloak. It was a snug fit over all her other clothing. She tied on her hat, then put on the wonderful gloves that Rob had given her. Lastly, she took up her reticule. Inside, the proceeds from her pieces of jewelry and her meager pin money amounted to less than seventy dollars, most of it in small greenback bills and the rest in a mixture of silver and copper coins minted by the Federal government. The pawnbroker assured Hettie that Federal money was worth a lot more than the pink shinplasters that the Confederate Treasury printed.

A soft knock on the door startled both girls, then Hettie peeped in, holding a lantern. "Are you about ready, Miss Julia? Old Sam will be down the street any minute now and you need to be on the corner."

The little clock on the mantel showed 4:25 a.m. by the single candle's light. With one final glance in the mirror, Julia straightened her hat. Then she wrapped the plaid wool shawl around her shoulders and picked up her carpetbag. It weighed more than she had anticipated, but she couldn't stop to repack it now. "Ready," she replied in a shaky voice. She crossed over to the bedside and hugged Carolyn. "Don't cry, honeylamb. You are not supposed to know I've gone."

Carolyn wiped her nose on her nightdress's sleeve. "Don't worry about me, Julia. I'll be fast asleep in my own bed." She got out of the four-poster that she had shared with her sister since she was barely out of infant clothes. She stuffed the bolster pillows under the sheet to approximate the shape of a sleeping body. "That will fool them for a while."

Julia cupped Carolyn's chin in the palm of her hand. "Promise you won't tell them where I've gone? Mother will send Payton after me, if you do."

"Won't breathe a word. Cross my heart and hope to die." Carolyn shrugged. "How could I know anything? I was across the hall asleep in my own bed when you sneaked out of here like a thief in the night," she added, mimicking their mother's voice. She blew out the candle. "I will miss you something fierce."

Julia hugged her again. "And I will think of you every day. Please remember me in your prayers. I love you, Carolyn."

Hettie tapped her foot. "We've got to go, Miss Julia." Just then, a faint call drifted up from the street. "There's Sam now." She pulled Julia out into the hall. "You get back in your own bed, Miss Carolyn, or you will give us all away. Lordy, stop sniffling, both of you," she whispered, shutting the bedroom door with a soft "click."

Suddenly, there was no more time for Julia to think or reconsider the drastic action she was about to take. Once she left her home, she knew she could not return. The shame and scandal of running away would be too painful for even her gentle father to bear. Hettie pushed her past the closed doors of her parents' suite and Payton's room. The two women hurried down the back stairs, through the pantry and out the rear door.

On the back stoop, Hettie hugged Julia, then looped a small basket over her arm. "Some bread and butter, apples, cold chicken, hard-boiled eggs and caramels. You make that last, 'cause I don't expect there will be much between here and Richmond that's fit for a lady to eat."

She kissed her on the forehead. "Now you behave yourself and tell Old Sam that next time he comes by, I'll place a double order for eggs, you hear?"

Julia's heart was too full to voice her gratitude lest she dissolve in tears. She hugged Hettie for a third time, then dashed down the steps. Lifting her multiple skirts to allow her more speed, she raced to the back gate. She could hear the clip-clop of Old Sam's horse as he pulled the heavy egg-and-chicken wagon up Columbia Street. They would pass the corner of Prince at any moment. Hettie had cautioned Julia several times that Sam would not loiter there for her. Even though he was a freeman, the penalty for "kidnapping" a white woman from her home would be very stiff for him, no matter what Julia would say in his defense.

She reached the intersection just as the cart passed by. Old Sam, looking younger than she had expected, pulled the horse to a stop, then jumped off the seat. With a mumbled "morning" to Julia, he snatched her bag out of her hands, and tossed it among the willow-work coops of his feathered wares. The chickens, startled from their sleep, squawked their indignation, breaking the silence of the slumbering neighborhood.

"Hettie said—" Julia began, but Sam gave her no time to talk. Without preamble, he grabbed her around the waist and hoisted her into the back of the cart. The chickens screamed louder. Sam pointed to an old blanket behind the pile of coops. "Get under that and stay there, miss, and you let my hens do all the talking. I'll tell you when you can come out—and not before, you hear?"

Julia nodded, them stumbled her way to the blanket. Sam hopped back in his seat, snapped the reins and the cart jerked forward. Jolted by the sudden movement, Julia sat down hard on the floorboards, just missing a stack of the occupied coops. She pulled the blanket over her head and curled herself into as small a ball as she could, considering the amount of clothing she had on.

Above her hiding place, Sam bellowed, "Chick-ens! Fresh, lively chickens! E-e-e-gs! I got eggs this morning!"

For hours upon hours, Old Sam wended his way around Alexandria hawking his wares. The cobblestones of the city's streets jolted the cart and rattled Julia to the bone. Though the day was as cold as the previous week, she felt hot and stuffy under the foul-smelling blanket. She had never realized until now just how pungent a large number of confined chickens could be.

At first, she feared that the horrid smell would make her gag. Then she worried that the swaying, rocking wagon would upset her already nervous stomach. Eventually, she grew used to the smell and the uneven movement. Sam seemed to take an inordinate amount of time to sell his birds. He chatted up a large number of families' cooks, whistled while he drove between stops as if he hadn't a care in the world, and spent an unhurried dinner hour among friends from Market Square. Fortunately, Julia had no desire to eat. The proximity of the chickens coupled with her gnawing anxiety killed her appetite. A headache began behind her eyes. The swaying lulled her. She fell asleep sometime during the early afternoon.

"I said you can come out now, miss."

Waking with a start, Julia forgot that she was under a blanket. Everything was very dark. When she pulled it from her face, she found that the daylight had passed, the cart was now stopped on a country road and Sam was grinning at her.

"I reckon you would like to stretch a bit," he observed. He handed her a canteen. "Water, miss. It's cold." He chuckled.

Julia smiled wanly. The bitter wind, unchecked by houses or trees, blew across the barren fields and slapped her in the face. She drank deeply, the water flowing down her parched throat in an icy stream that made her teeth ache. She started to stand up, but Sam shook his head.

''No, miss, not yet. We still have a ways to go and I don't want nobody to see you sitting up in the box with me. You're supposed to disappear, so you have to stay invisible.'' He pointed to the loathsome blanket again.

Julia sighed but made no further protest. She had to trust Sam, just as she trusted Hettie who had arranged her flight. She certainly didn't want to get either of them in trouble, nor did she want to be caught and returned to Prince Street. At least, all the chickens were gone, though their noxious smell remained. Julia lay back down in the bottom of the cart, and once again covered herself with the blanket. This time the wagon took off with more speed. Obviously, the horse knew he was headed for the barn. As she jittered and bounced down Virginia's frozen dirt roads, Julia reviewed the next step of Hettie's plan.

Tonight, she was supposed to stay at an old inn in some village. As the wearisome hours jolted by, she flicked the blanket off her face and drew in deep drafts of the cold night air. Above her, the stars shone like bright diamonds in the black velvet sky. When the everlasting wind chilled her skin, she covered her face once more. Only the thought of seeing Rob again kept her from giving way to despair.

It was not quite how she had envisioned the beginning of her life as an independent woman.

Chapter Eighteen

Thirty-six hours after she had fled from her home, Julia stepped onto the station platform of the Central Railroad Depot in Richmond. Exhaustion blurred her vision so that she did not immediately notice the difference between Alexandria and the Confederate capital. The night before, she had not slept well in the farmer's house at Burke's Station—the promised "inn." The following morning, she boarded a train for Manassas Junction, where she had to bribe the local provost marshal for a pass through the lines. She had told him that she was racing to a family deathbed.

The train out of Manassas was derailed somewhere north of Fredericksburg—an occurrence that was quite common, a fellow passenger assured her, as they picked their way over frozen bracken at the side of the railroad bed. Several hours later, she boarded another train to Rappahannock Station. From there, Julia, and other passengers bound for the Confederacy, climbed into an army ambulance wagon for a trip down country roads to Guinea Station. There, they caught another train, this one headed for Richmond. The journey had utterly drained her.

As Julia mustered her mental and physical resources, she became aware of the city's bustle. A second train screeched into the station, blowing its steam whistle to warn the lines of waiting ambulances and stretcher bearers that another load of Confederate sick and wounded had arrived from far-flung winter encampments.

Men shouted at porters. Porters shouted at each other. Vendors hawked everything from pigs' feet and ginger-bread to used nails. Horses, dogs, children and women added to the hubbub. The sheer wall of noise nearly knocked Julia off her tired feet. Alexandria, though filled with Yankee soldiers, seemed a poky little town in comparison to Richmond—and Julia hadn't even left the depot yet!

Wiping train soot from her face and hugging her carpetbag closer to her body, Julia plunged into the crowd that streamed out toward the street. She had not the slightest idea where she should go. Once on the sidewalk, Julia surveyed the scene with growing dismay. In the fading light of the late afternoon, dray wagons loaded with barrels and boxes, light-sprung buggies, cabs filled with passengers, open carriages, men pushing handcarts, boys running in every direction and dogs racing underfoot vied for space along the cobbled thoroughfare. A living river of people, both black and white and of every age and description, pushed and shoved their way along the sidewalks.

Until now, Julia had thought herself well-acquainted with city living, but this discordant panorama made her feel very sheltered and naive. She had to find a hotel—a nice, respectable one where single ladies could sleep in safety. There must be something like that in Richmond, but where? Just then a distinguished-looking, elderly black man sitting on the driver's box of an enclosed carriage waved at her, and motioned her toward him. Remembering

Hettie's admonition "not to trust nobody in that sinful city," Julia approached with caution.

"Yes?" she asked when she came within hailing distance. "Did you wish to speak to me?"

"Yes'm," he replied, lifting his burnished topper. "Are you looking for the Spotswood Hotel, miss? This here is the hotel's conveyance for ladies and gentlemen of refinement such as yourself," he announced with evident pride.

Julia cast a quick glance inside the carriage. To her relief, she saw that two men and a woman, all fashionably dressed, occupied the two facing seats. There was clearly room enough for one more. One of the men, spying her hesitation, lowered the window.

"We're going to the Spotswood, miss. Please join us." He smiled at her. "I assure you, it is the finest, most elegant hotel in Richmond. General Robert E. Lee himself stayed there once, and so did President and Mrs. Jefferson Davis when they first came to town."

The coachman chuckled in agreement. "That's the gospel truth. It is the best hotel you will find anywhere north of Charleston." He stepped down off the box and held out his hand. "You come along now. I can put your grip on the roof, if you like."

Julia clutched the handles of her bag. "No…thank you. I prefer to hold it."

The coachman opened the door and offered to help her inside. Julia made a split-second decision. Since she had no idea where else to go, she would investigate the Spotswood. If it was not to her liking, she could leave. She gave her hand to the driver who settled her inside the coach. Only when he had closed the door did the faint odor of chicken manure fill the compartment. Julia winced, but said nothing. If she pretended she didn't notice it, perhaps no one else would, either. Lordy, she could just die!

The other woman, seated across from Julia, lifted her handkerchief to her nose and snapped open her fan. Her companion glared at Julia, before turning his gaze to the passersby. A tense silence enveloped the compartment as the coach started up. Julia's seatmate, the man who had encouraged her to join them, continued to smile at her.

"I fear that travel is mighty difficult during these hard times," he finally remarked. "Especially for unaccompanied ladies."

Julia blessed him for his understanding. "Indeed, sir. I am much relieved to finally be here," she replied.

"Do you intend to stay in Richmond for long?" he inquired.

Hettie had also warned Julia against divulging too much personal information to strangers, even if they appeared to be friendly. Julia replied, "I have no idea, sir. It will depend upon my business here." Then she lowered her eyes.

Fortunately, the ride to the promised hotel was short, sparing Julia from further conversation with the gentleman, who threatened to become even more friendly. When the coachman handed her out at the ladies' entrance, she was pleasantly surprised by the grandeur and size of the Spotswood. Rising five stories, the brick edifice took up most of a city block. Its decorative iron facade that arched over the hotel's entryway gleamed despite the dirt and grime of Eighth Street. Warm gaslight streaming from the wide windows beckoned the weary traveler. Tipping the coachman a Federal dime, Julia practically skipped through the double doors into the lobby.

The Spotswood was as packed inside its gilded, plush public rooms as were the sidewalks of Richmond outside the hotel's hospitable walls. Women decked in fashionable—and not so fashionable—day dresses sipped tea and coffee around little marble-topped tables. At one end of the room, a small crowd gathered around someone who played a lively rendition of "The Bonnie Blue Flag" on the piano. The sprightly tune lifted Julia's spirits. She had rarely heard that so-called "Rebel" song in Federal-occupied Alexandria.

When the song ended and the crowd parted to applaud the musician, Julia gasped. The pretty young woman was unashamedly dressed in a smart military jacket with gold braid, a white Garibaldi shirt that Julia had only seen in *Godey's Ladies Book,* and a soft gray wool skirt—that ended just below her knees! Under that she wore a man's blue uniform pants and polished black boots! A smart little black pork pie derby, trimmed with a gold band and ostrich feather, crowned her pert head. Julia had never seen any ensemble so dazzlingly bold and, at the same time, so desirable.

The ringing of desk bells brought Julia back to the reality of her homeless situation. With a shiver of nervous anxiety running down her spine, she approached the polished mahogany desk, and inquired about engaging a room. The sky-high prices quoted by the desk clerk nearly made her swoon.

"Do you accept Federal greenbacks?" she asked hopefully, while under her shawl, she gripped her reticule. Train tickets for the ladies' coaches and the counterfeit travel pass had diminished her funds far more than she had anticipated.

The man behind the desk lifted one dark brow. "Indeed we do, miss. We also accept English sovereigns, French Napoleons, and Mexican doubloons. The Spotswood prides itself in catering to a diverse and international clientele." He wrinkled his nose at her.

Then the clerk scanned the bank of pigeonholes behind him. Very few brass key rings hung there, indicating that the hotel, even in January, was almost filled to capacity. "We are very booked, you know," he began, giving her a sidelong glance.

With a resigned sigh, Julia extracted a five-dollar bill from her hoard. She pushed it across the desk toward him. "Will this help?" she asked, as if she had bribed people all her life.

The man's face broke into a wide grin. "Indeed, indeed, miss," he replied. "We *do* have a room available for that sum, though it is small."

"I'll take it," she breathed, without bothering to ask what was meant by small, or how many nights her five dollars had bought her. Right this minute, all she wanted was to clean herself up, get a decent supper and a good night's sleep, so that she could face the problem of locating Libby Prison in the morning.

Small was no exaggeration. Julia found herself in a tiny garret on the topmost floor. She strongly suspected that, during peacetime, her room and the others like it down the hall had once belonged to the hotel's chambermaids. At least the bed had clean sheets, a small strip of carpet covered the floor, the dresser was dusted, the mirror clean and the washstand's pitcher was filled with fresh water, and an extra filled bucket sat on the floor. Two towels and a tiny chunk of white milled soap completed the furnishings of her new home.

For the first time in two days, Julia stripped off all her clothes, let down her hair and washed herself as best she could in the china basin. She dressed in her only clean underclothes, washed her travel-worn ones and hung them over the back of the upright wooden chair. After brushing her hair two hundred strokes, brushing her teeth and brushing out her second-layer dress, Julia declared herself as ready as she possibly could be to face the "international clientele" of the Spotswood Hotel.

Eight o'clock found her in the dining room where she supped frugally on turtle soup and a plate of roasted beef with lima beans and Irish potatoes. She ate her fill of the hotel's crunchy bread and fresh butter—until she learned that the rolls cost fifty cents apiece and the butter a dollar a pat. Since coffee was three dollars a cup, she settled for tea at two dollars a pot. Fortunately, her Yankee money stretched four times more than the inflated Confederate dollar. Though her sweet tooth craved the delicious-looking cakes and pies, Julia contented herself with some of her dwindling supply of caramels, left over from the Winstead ball. How long ago that seemed! Yet it was less than a month.

While she sipped her hot tea in the ladies' lounge, she listened to the sea of gossip that swept around her. Her waitress had informed her that the Spotswood Hotel was *the* place to hear what all the world was saying. The more Julia could learn of Richmond, the better it would be for her later on when she sought employment and a cheaper place to live.

"Shocking!" gasped a matron in green taffeta. "Painted jezebels sauntering as bold as you please around this lobby. And, my dears, there were some *certain* gentlemen—well known in this city—who were seen in rooms where they ought *not* to have been. Their folly is *not* to be believed!"

The other three women at her table squealed with shocked delight. Julia hoped that she might see one or two of these "jezebels"—at a distance, of course—so that she could describe them to Carolyn. Then she remembered that she would not be seeing Carolyn for a long, long time.

Someone behind her mentioned Libby. Julia stopped

stirring her tea and strained to pick up the conversation without appearing too obvious.

"I find it hard to believe that General John Hunt Morgan wasted some of his precious time in Richmond to visit those horrid Yankees there," continued the woman in a brittle voice.

"I expect he wanted to see if we were treating those men any better than how he was treated in Ohio, before he escaped from their prison. How very clever of him to do that!" remarked the second speaker. "They say that old Abe Lincoln howled like a wild Indian when he heard that piece of derring-do."

The ladies laughed. Then the first speaker continued. "Have either of you ever visited Libby?"

Julia sat up straighter. She wished she had the nerve to join in their conversation, but she had not been introduced.

A chorus of "no's" answered the first speaker. Then a younger woman asked, "Have you?"

The first woman simpered, "Only last week. My cousins were visiting up from the country and they were panting to see a real Yankee in the flesh, so we went."

Julia pushed her chair around a little in order to catch all of the details. She didn't care if they noticed her or not. She had to know the particulars about visiting the prison.

The other two women leaned over their coffee. "Pray do not hold us in suspense a moment longer, Dottie. Were those Yankees just awful?"

Julia's fingers curled round her teacup. How dare these people talk about the Northern prisoners as if the men were some kind of wild animals on exhibition! How would they like it if the Yankee women treated their sons, brothers and husbands in the same demeaning fashion?

Dottie took a sip of coffee to prolong the suspense, then related, "They were the filthiest, smelliest, sorriest bunch of scarecrows that I ever did see. I cannot imagine how the Yankees expect to defeat the South when they look such a fright! We could barely abide being in their presence for more than five minutes.''

Julia bit her lip until it throbbed like her rapid heartbeat. Poor Rob! Was he, too, as dirty, smelly and thin as the woman described? She could hardly imagine it. She had to bring him a basket of comforts tomorrow.

The women at the other table rose like three geese taking flight, and left the lounge. Julia finished her cooling tea while she planned her next day. Before going to the prison, she would buy Rob some food and perhaps socks—would that item be too forward for a lady to give a gentleman? She chided herself. This was wartime and, as she had already noticed in the capital city of the Confederacy, propriety had slipped in the mud.

Julia awoke the following morning with the rattling of sleet and freezing rain against her window pane. Looking out, she saw that Richmond had turned gray and slick overnight. Julia rued that she had not brought her umbrella with her. Nevertheless, she would not cower inside her comfortable hotel when Rob lay so nearby, possibly starving to death.

After a quick breakfast of rolls and expensive coffee, Julia buttoned her cloak, tied on her hat, put on Rob's lovely gloves and prepared to face the day. Stopping to chat with the doorman, she inquired abour directions to the nearest shopping district as well as Libby Prison.

''Don't know what a nice lady like you wants to see those Yankees for,'' the man remarked when she thanked him for his help. ''I hear they are nothing but trash. And…'' Lowering his voice, he whispered in her ear, ''Pardon me for saying so, miss, but everybody in that jail has got cooties, and you don't want to catch them on you, no sir!''

Julia thanked him for his caution, though she did not have the slightest idea what a ''cootie'' was. It sounded nasty.

The sparse stock on the grocer's shelves shocked her. Alexandria's shops and vendors were always well-supplied with every luxury imaginable, thanks to the northern suppliers. For the first time since war had been declared, Julia saw for herself the hardships and privations that so much of the south endured on a daily basis. Richmond painted on a merry face, but the pinched look of the ordinary citizens illustrated the stress of living under the perpetual threat of siege. Many women wore mourning clothes. Most of the men were in uniform. The latest reincarnation of the Confederate National flag hung wet and limp from many flagpoles.

Julia's Yankee money stretched enough to buy a half-dozen apples, a small can of sardines, a packet of salt crackers and a box of soft nougats from Richmond's celebrated Italian confectioner, Mr. Pazzini. At the dry goods store, she added three handkerchiefs and a thick pair of woolen socks to her basket. Recalling the conversation from the previous evening, she purchased a small bar of lye soap and a toothbrush. Watching her fellow shoppers counting out huge quantities of Confederate bills, Julia wondered how anyone could possibly afford to live in Richmond. She didn't allow herself to think what would happen if her funds gave out before her birthday. Once she could draw on her inheritance, all would be well, but for now, she would take each day as it came.

Turning downhill toward the river, Julia made her way to the prison. The neighborhood changed from neat row houses, shops and churches to large gray and brown ware-

Beloved Enemy

houses, interspersed with noisy oyster bars, garish restaurants and tenements that teemed with grubby children and large, frightening dogs. Since the rain had ceased, hopeful lines of washing hung across garbage-strewn alleyways. Rough-looking men, smelling of stale spirits, and women with reddened, chapped faces brushed past her on the tiny bits of broken sidewalk. Julia regretted that she had not hired a cab at the Spotswood, even though it would have cost a fortune. At last, she spied the building, just as the hotel doorman had described it. Outside the long brick warehouse, a faded wooden sign announced Libby & Son, Ship Chandler & Grocer. Dirty whitewash paint covered the brick wall up to the second floor. The sentinels in their gray uniform greatcoats stood out starkly against it.

As Julia drew closer to the entrance on Cary Street, she saw that a dozen or so women paraded back and forth on the sidewalk opposite the prison. Despite the cold, wet weather, they bared their shoulders and breasts that all but fell out of their brightly colored satin bodices. The women shouted rude taunts and bawdy remarks up to the crowded windows of Libby's second and third floors.

"Don't you wish you had some of this sugar, Yankee boy?" called out one soiled dove as she raised her skirts to reveal her lower legs clad in white patterned stockings.

Dozens of disembodied arms stuck out through bars of the open windows above the heads of the grinning sentries. The inmates shouted down some of the foulest words Julia had ever heard. Ducking her head into the folds of her soaked shawl, she crossed the street quickly lest the guards might mistake her for one of the rabble.

At the door, her curiosity got the better of her common sense. She asked the young sentry, "Who are those women?"

He had the grace to blush before answering, "Them?

They's…well, miss, I guess you could call them fancy ladies." He gave her a sidelong look, swallowed hard, then continued. "They're not your kind, miss. You don't want to have anything to do with them. They are…well, um…the sort of lady that a good brother would never introduce to his sister."

Painted jezebels! Aloud, Julia persisted, "But what are they doing *here?* Surely they don't expect to…conduct business with the prisoners."

The sentry's eyebrows went straight up to his hairline. "Service a Yankee?" he sputtered, then turned even redder. "I mean, no, miss. They come around to…um…" At this point, his vocabulary ran out.

"I see," said Julia hurriedly. "I've come to visit the prisoners myself—but purely in Christian charity," she added in a rush, tapping her basket. "Would you be so very kind and tell me with whom I should speak?"

The young guardsman eyed the covered basket. "I'm afraid those Yankees in there won't appreciate anything a fine lady like yourself might do for them. Their souls are far beyond redemption."

Julia bit back her growing impatience. Water from the gutter seeped though the stitching of her walking boots. "I do appreciate your concern," she replied as sweet as sugar, "but there is no harm in trying, is there? The good Lord particularly sought out the worst kinds of sinners for His grace, didn't He?"

The soldier furrowed his brow as he tried to recollect his childhood Bible classes. "I expect so, miss." He opened the door. "You will want to speak with Major Long or Mr. Ross. Good day, miss."

Stepping across the bare wooden threshold, Julia had the uneasy feeling that she had just entered a reasonable facsimile of Dante's Inferno. A potbellied stove set against a brick partition wall hissed as if it were filled with writhing snakes, though it warmed Julia's cold fingers. She removed her gloves, then looked around for someone in charge. A man dressed in a gray sack coat shifted his attention from the papers on his battered desk. Around his waist, he wore two holstered pistols.

"May I be of assistance?" he asked, though none too kindly.

Controlling her jitters, Julia gave him her best smile. "Good morning, sir. My name is Julia Chandler and I have brought a few things for…" She had not given thought how to explain her relationship with Rob until now. "For my cousin. Most regrettable, to be sure, that he turned against his family and went off to fight for the Yankees. It all comes from sending him to one of those schools up there. Turned his head, it did." Taking a page from her mother's repertoire of hysterics, she sniffled a little and wiped her cheeks. "Just about broke his poor mother's heart."

Out of the corner of her eye, Julia saw that her story not only interested the clerk, but also several guards and a little old woman who sat against the far wall on a rough-hewn bench. Gathering more courage from their attention, she continued, "Naturally, the family disowned him on the spot, but I…" She sighed deeply.

"We were playmates so many years ago, and I have always kept a soft spot in my heart for him. When we learned that he was here, I thought it my Christian duty to at least pay him a call. Perhaps he has come to regret his hasty action."

The clerk barely moved a facial muscle. "And the name of this black sheep?"

"Montgomery, Major Robert Montgomery," she said, hoping not to sound too eager. "I do believe he joined a regiment from New York." She gave him another smile. "I would be ever so grateful if you would let me see him—even just for a minute…ahem…so that I can tell his mama that he is safe. She does grieve so for her baby boy."

"Montgomery." The clerk opened a large black ledger, flipped through a few pages, then ran his finger down a column of names. "Robert," he repeated to himself. Then he closed the book with a snap. "Yes, Miss Chandler, your cousin is residing with us. Do you have your pass from the provost marshal?"

A cake of ice hardened in Julia's stomach. Real tears threatened to make their presence known. She had not abandoned her home and security only to be turned away for want of a wretched piece of paper. She allowed her lower lip to quiver, and hoped that this stone-faced man with his little mustache was susceptible to women's tears.

"Oh, dear, no. I had no idea I needed something like that. No one told me. And I have so very little time here in Richmond. Oh, please, kind sir, I mean no harm. I have not come here to abduct my cousin, only to bring him a little hope and cheer—as it is my Christian duty," she added for good measure.

The clerk's stare bored a hole into her soul. She prayed that he wasn't a mind reader. The guards laughed and repeated "kind sir" under their breath to each other. Julia clutched her basket and stared back at him, willing him to give in.

"For heaven's sake, Mr. Ross, just *where* did you hang up your manners today?" snapped the little woman on the bench. She rose and tottered across the room to stand beside Julia. "You ought to be ashamed of yourself for making this poor child cry."

Then, in an undertone that Julia barely heard, she said through stiff lips, "Turn up your waterworks, girl."

Chapter Nineteen

"Montgomery!" shouted the guard over the din on the second floor. "Robert Montgomery! Downstairs! Now!"

Rob looked up from the card game that he was playing with a couple of amiable and talkative Pennsylvanians. He had been in Libby long enough to know it did not bode well for any prisoner to be singled out.

Captain Stu Cramer folded his hand and gave Rob a commiserating look. "What did you do to attract Colonel Turner's personal attention? You haven't been here long enough for him to recognize you on sight."

The third man in their game, Lieutenant Joe Grimwold, smiled. "Maybe Rob is planning an escape, and the colonel wants to have a chat with him about it."

Rob returned the grin, but felt sick inside. He certainly hoped not, though there was precious little he could tell anyone at this point. Whomever was working on the breakout was keeping very closed-mouthed about it.

"Montgomery!" the guard shouted with more impatience. "I ain't got the time to stand here all day yelling for you!"

Rob tossed his cards down on the blanket, then pulled himself to his feet. A brief wave of dizziness caught him.

The sudden privation of decent food had weakened Rob more than he cared to admit. After steadying himself, he picked his way over and around the several hundred men who were packed in the Chickamauga Suite, the long room named for the battle where the majority of the prisoners had been captured the previous September.

The guard pushed him down the first three steps. "I don't cotton to you, Yankee," he informed Rob, giving him another shove in his low back. "I especially don't like you for seducing a fine Southern gal like the one who's waiting for you in the guard room. Now how in the Sam Hill did you accomplish that?" He pushed Rob again, and laughed when the major stumbled down two more steps.

"Don't know either, private," Rob mumbled, while his mind raced. He knew no one here in Richmond, except the name of Elizabeth Van Lew, and she was supposed to be some elderly spinster. Was this summons the Reb's idea of a joke?

His heart nearly stopped when he turned the corner at the bottom of the staircase and saw Julia sitting on a bench. The smile she gave him warmed him more than a bonfire.

"Oh, Rob!" she mouthed, as she rose to meet him.

His brain spun in a kaleidoscope of emotions and desires. He wanted to clutch her so tightly against him that nothing would ever part them again. Standing in the middle of the stark room in her travel-stained cloak, she radiated beauty, like an angel stepped down from a church window. Rebellious tendrils of her cinnamon-flame hair framed her pale face in such an enticing way that he longed to reach out and twine them around his fingers—if only to confirm the reality of this heavenly vision.

Yet Rob held himself in check. His unwashed stench and the itch of a hundred lice bites made him acutely aware of his present condition. How could he possibly touch Julia now? Moreover, his ingrained sense of self-preservation gave him pause. What was Julia doing here in this hell-hole? Wasn't she supposed to be married by now? Where was her husband? Or were the Confederates using her to ferret out the truth of Rob's mission? Had she really betrayed him in her garden and inadvertently played into Lawrence's plan?

To display his true feelings now would be folly, especially when the prison clerk and four of the guards watched him like cats around a wounded mouse. Rob stiffened his features into a mask.

"Good morning, Miss Chandler," he greeted her formally, though his heart hammered in his chest. "I confess, it is a surprise to see you here."

A dart of pain shadowed those luminous green eyes of hers. "Oh, cousin Rob! It has been far, far too long since we last met. Has the army made you grow so cold?" She smiled again, though her lush lips trembled.

"Five minutes, miss," Ross barked from his desk. He glared at Montgomery as if daring him to object.

Rob blinked, trying to focus on Julia's words. Now they were cousins? She stepped toward him. He held up his hand to stop her before a battalion of his vermin could leap on her.

"Don't come any closer, Julia," he cautioned, though his tone was more harsh than he had intended. "I'm not fit for civilized company."

Despite his warning, she drew nearer to him. Her eyes widened when she looked up at him. "You…" she faltered, then began again. "You are much thinner than when I last saw you." She bit her lower lip.

Rob glanced at the nearest guard before he answered. The Reb was close enough to overhear every word, and he made no attempt to hide the fact that he was listening.

Across the room, the civilian clerk, Erasmus Ross, observed them intently with a pocket watch in his hand. Returning to Julia, Rob saw that she fought back tears.

He cleared his throat. "I am afraid, at that time, I was like the biblical fatted calf," he said with more truth than he had intended.

He really wanted to tell her how glad he was to see her. How much he had missed her and how beautiful she looked! He realized, with a start, that this was the first time that they had ever met in daylight.

Julia lowered her voice. "Please believe me, Rob. I had no idea there were any soldiers in our garden that night."

Rob wanted to trust her. He wanted to embrace her, put her head against his chest as he had done in the cold moonlight, and tell her the thousand things that filled his heart. He lifted his good hand to stroke her cheek, saw the grime under his nails and shook his head. He dropped his arm to his side again. The visit was the worst torture the Rebs could have devised—and he doubted they even realized it.

Julia thought she would break in two. How poorly Rob looked and how cold he was to her, as if he blamed her for every minute he had languished inside these filthy, horrid walls! Libby Prison was much worse than she had expected. Rob's coat, with a tear along the shoulder seam, hung loosely from his tall frame. His cheekbones stood out, making his face look like a statue of cold bronze. His dark hair was uncombed and a short, ragged beard covered his once-smooth cheeks. The haunted darkness in his eyes frightened Julia the most. He looked like a dangerous animal that had been kept for too long on a short leash and short rations. He looked as if he could kill with his bare hand.

"Four minutes," snapped the clerk.

Julia jumped at the sound of his grating voice. What could she say in four minutes? She needed hours, days to express all that she wanted to tell Rob, if only he would listen to her. She put her hand on his coat sleeve. He flinched and shook it off.

She moistened her lips. "You once told me that you studied law at Yale. As a lawyer, would you deny a fair hearing to a common criminal? If not, then why do you deny me?" She stepped as close as she dared to him. Her words were only for his ears. "Do you need proof of my fidelity to you? Very well, listen. I have run away from the only home I have ever had. I have left behind me everything that I love—except you."

Rob blinked at her, though he said nothing.

Please, please let him believe her. Julia didn't want to beg him in front of all these strangers, but she would go down on her knees, if that would make him trust her.

"Three minutes." The clerk looked almost gleeful.

Just then, the little woman in black who had helped Julia earlier again rose from the bench. "Mr. Ross!" she snapped. "I do believe that we have heard enough out of your mouth for this day."

"Now, Miss Van Lew, you know I have to keep order here," he shot back, though his tone softened a fraction.

Lizzie Van Lew advanced upon him like a small terrier stalking a large rat. "Exactly so, Mr. Ross, and you do that most admirably. But keeping order does not mean keeping time. We can do that for ourselves."

He bore up under her assault, but looked less forbidding. The four guards backed away. None of them dared to laugh at her. Buoyed by this unexpected intervention, Julia hurried on with her little speech.

"I have brought a few things for you," she whispered, "though I can see that it isn't half as much as you need.

Some apples, sardines, socks—'' She babbled on, afraid if she stopped to take a breath, she would cry on the spot. She held up her little basket to him.

Did Julia just say she loved him?

Words refused to roll off Rob's tongue. She had run away—for him? ''Then you are not married?'' he whispered.

Green fire burned in the depths of her eyes. ''No! I hope I never see Payton again.''

''And you have thrown away your reputation to come here—for me?''

Pink patches stained her white cheeks. ''Yes, and I feel much better for it. Now, please, Rob, take my basket. I'll bring you more next time.''

He placed his hand over hers. ''Thank you, Julia, but I beg you, don't come back. Libby is no place for a lady.''

She gave him a pert smile, one he remembered from the Winsteads' ball. ''I gave up being a lady as my New Year's resolution—''

''Hush!'' Rob interrupted her. He wanted to kiss that smile so badly. ''Don't even tease like that—not here. You may be surrounded by your fellow Confederates, but underneath those gray uniforms, some of these men are the scum of the earth. They would gladly take you at your word.''

''Time's up, Montgomery!'' called Ross.

''No, it isn't,'' countered the remarkable Miss Lizzie. ''Not until I say it's up—unless you want to pay for your own cigars from now on.''

Rob nodded his thanks to her. Then he returned to Julia. She looked as if she had walked every mile to Richmond—for him.

''You have no idea what your visit means to me,'' he began. He had never before felt so helpless in the presence of a female. Some day, he would be able to show Julia how much he appreciated her sacrifice, but not now under the rude gaze of the loutish guards. Not when he was crawling with vermin and dirt. Not when he had nothing to give to her—not even a kiss, though he longed for one of hers. He squeezed her hand.

Julia looked over her shoulder at their audience. She blushed when she returned to him. "Then you *do* believe me, Rob? Every word?"

"Yes," he murmured. Then lowering his head, he kissed her soft hand. It trembled under his lips. He stared with the longing of a thirsty man into the deep green pools of her eyes. "This kiss, if it dared speak, would stretch thy spirits up into the air," he whispered.

"Sweet Shakespeare!" Lowering her lashes, Julia rose up on tiptoe.

Rob shivered. He had to leave her now, before she tried to kiss him. Before he made a fool of himself and cried in front of his enemies. He lifted the basket out of her grasp. "I once told you that 'parting is such sweet sorrow.' That was small talk then. I mean every word of it now."

He turned abruptly and left her. Once back upstairs on his blanket, he closed his eyes, hugged the basket and wept silently.

Lizzie Van Lew waited until Rob's footfalls died away on the stairs before she took command of the guard room once again. Turning to Ross, she said, "There now! Your prisoner is safely back in his den and only six minutes have passed. That wasn't so bad, was it?"

Ross replaced his watch in his waistcoat pocket before he replied in an undertone. "No, Miss Lizzie, but one day you will go too far, and then not even the protection of General Winder will keep you out of trouble."

Lizzie smiled sweetly at him. "I shall see you next week, Mr. Ross, and I won't forget those cigars—or some custard. Is that going too far?"

Ross grinned like a schoolboy. "Miss Lizzie, you are a caution."

She regarded the pretty young girl who still stood rooted in the same spot—staring after the departed man. The more Lizzie studied the girl, the more she concluded that Miss Chandler was straight out of some secluded home deep in the countryside. It was written plain on her face that the child didn't know the first thing about Richmond, and wouldn't last a day without some sort of protection and guidance.

Lizzie picked up her large, now-empty basket, then turned toward Miss Chandler. "Well, young lady, don't dawdle. I have a lot to do today, and I can't waste my time waiting for you to quit your gawking."

The girl snapped back into the present, then looked around to see if Lizzie had spoken to someone else. She blushed in a very becoming way that was not lost on the lusty youngsters who served as prison guards.

"You were addressing me, ma'am?" she asked with the widest green eyes Lizzie had ever seen.

This child was bound for a world of trouble if Lizzie didn't take charge of her immediately. "I did indeed, Miss Chandler. Now come with me. As Mr. Ross so gallantly pointed out earlier, time flies. It's nearly noon and my dinnertime. I detest missing my dinner, and I am sure you do, too. You may carry my basket. Lord knows, this cold wet winter will be the undoing of every bone in my body. Well?"

Julia had no idea why this little birdlike woman had decided to adopt her, but she was very glad that Miss Van

Lew did. Julia had not looked forward to returning to her hotel after such an unnerving visit with Rob. Miss Lizzie spoke of eating dinner as if Julia were invited to share that meal. Blessing her good luck, she smiled and took the basket.

"Much obliged, I am sure," she murmured. "I shall be very glad to accompany you."

The little woman sniffed, then turned on her heel. "Of course you are! Say goodbye to our nice Mr. Ross, and let us be on our way." To the guards, who looked as thunderstruck as Julia felt, she added, "I'll be back in a week or so, boys. I expect you'll be wanting your usual buttermilk and ginger cakes, as well?"

They grinned like four puppies around a puddle of cream. The nearest soldier held the door open for the women. "You be sure to bring Miss Chandler back with you, too."

Julia gulped. It had never occurred to her that she might be in harm's way among Confederate soldiers. It was always the Yankees she had worried about in the past…long ago, in Alexandria.

Miss Lizzie gave the boy a narrow-eyed look of disapproval. "And you mind your manners, Charlie Garland, or I'll be writing a letter to your mother. See if I don't."

He lowered his gaze from Julia, and his neck turned a little red under his collar. "You know I'm just funning, Miss Lizzie."

"Humph!" she replied, as she stomped down the outside steps. "Come along, Miss Chandler. Mind the gutter. And don't you pay any attention to those harlots yonder. What would your mother say if she saw you now? I can't imagine!" She snapped open her green umbrella.

Julia was sure her mother would have fainted quite some time ago.

Chapter Twenty

Clara Chandler took to her bed on the day that Julia ran away. Besides her husband, she allowed only Payton to visit her. He brought a small nosegay of hothouse violets that cost him a fortune in the dead of winter. He considered the price a small one if he could salvage his bleak financial prospects following Julia's rejection of him.

"Oh, my dear, dear boy!" Clara wailed into her handkerchief. "How sweet you are! Violets! I do declare, you are far too good for that ungrateful girl!" Clara had sworn never to mention Julia's name again and, so far, she stuck to her vow.

Payton assumed an expression of noble suffering, though his vanity seethed at Julia's open repudiation of him. "I am so very sorry that you are still unwell, Auntie." He glanced at the bottle of opium drops on the bureau. The level was low, a promising sign that his aunt's mind was befuddled by laudanum fumes.

"I fear that I must return to Belmont," he continued, "but before I go, I wonder if I may have your permission to pay court to your younger daughter, Carolyn?" Carolyn was a hellion, pure and simple, but in five short years, she, too, would inherit a sizable legacy from Grandmother

Lightfoot's estate. By that time, Payton would have molded the chit into a proper lady.

Clara stopped snuffling into her hankie. Sitting up straighter in bed, she gave him a calculating look. "Carolyn?" she mused.

Payton pressed his advantage. "I realize that she is young, Auntie, but she'll be ripe for marriage in another year or so. She's a spirited girl, and I know that she has been difficult for you to manage. As her fiancé, I would be glad to help her learn the etiquette befitting a lady of our social class in Richmond." He shamelessly played upon the two primary concerns of Clara Chandler: Carolyn's outrageous independence and Clara's goal to be aligned with Virginia's first families.

A spark of interest, or cunning, flashed into his aunt's eye. "How kind you are, Payton! So very gracious to even consider engaging yourself to Carolyn after what her wicked sister did to you. Your offer is indeed intriguing, but I must speak to Dr. Chandler about—"

"Clara! We will do no such thing!" Her husband swept into the bedroom. From the stern expression on his uncle's face, Payton suspected that he had heard their whole conversation.

Payton scrambled to save his financial future. "Sir, I had intended to come to you directly to ask for Miss Carolyn's hand. I only wished to see if her mother thought it a worthwhile idea."

The doctor frowned. "Save yourself the trouble, Payton. Carolyn is not yours for the plucking, nor will she be any time in the future." His expression softened a bit when he turned toward his wife, although the resolve in his jawline did not waver. "We have lost one daughter already through this hasty misalliance with Payton, my dear. We shall not make the same mistake a second time."

Clara's face screwed up into immediate tears. Payton had always admired her ability to command her hysterics at will. "Jonah! Whatever will we do about Carolyn? No one will want to marry her after the shameful conduct of…of—"

"Julia?" her husband asked in a sad tone. "I would not worry about that quite yet, Clara. The war will end long before Carolyn is ready to settle down, and I suspect our lives will have a great many changes in the aftermath. We can only hope that Julia will return soon from Richmond, and our family will be reconciled."

Payton quivered like a foxhound on a scent. "You have heard from Julia, sir? She is indeed in Richmond?"

Dr. Chandler sighed. "No letter, if that is what you mean, but I have it on good authority that she followed that Federal officer who is now incarcerated in Libby. I am not surprised. She seemed very much in love with the young man."

"In love with a Yankee?" Clara bleated from the depths of her pillows. "Oh, I could just die!"

Payton ground his teeth behind a thin, plastered smile. He itched to know who had given the doctor this information, but he realized that his uncle would never tell. It did not matter. Julia had made the mistake of fleeing to the city that Payton knew like the back of his hand. Even if she had gone to ground in Richmond, he would find her. Once he had her in hand, he would marry her within twenty-four hours, bound and gagged if necessary. Afterward, it would be a pleasure to make her pay for his humiliation.

To his uncle, he said, "Very well, Doctor, thank you for your hospitality. I will return south in the morning. I have ignored my affairs long enough."

A week from now, he would have Julia under his control. A month from now, he would possess her inheritance and would finally be able to pay off his debts!

Major Scott Claypole folded the secret dispatches that had flowed into Lawrence's office from the various Union commands in the western states—Tennessee, Louisiana, Mississippi, Florida and the Army of the Potomac. Also on his desk lay other secret reports from Pinkerton's agents who worked undercover throughout the Confederacy. Taken altogether, the continuance of the war looked particularly gloomy for the South. The Confederacy's scanty food supplies had been commandeered for the Rebel army by the executive order of President Jefferson Davis. This unpopular move only heightened the dissatisfaction among the civilian population. The desire for peace simmered underground throughout the embattled Confederacy. In addition, Davis planned to conscript seventeen-year-olds to fill the ranks depleted by battle, sickness and desertion. Dixie's land was literally bleeding dry.

Clearly, the Southerners were willing to consider a truce and get on with the business of living—before there would be nothing left to live for. The Union blockade had the Confederacy in a slow stranglehold. The South's fortunes were slipping away as bales of cotton destined for the European market rotted on the wharves. The North could win this war by attrition alone. It would be simply a matter of time before the Rebels sued for peace.

Sitting back in his office chair, Claypole steepled his fingers while he pondered his options. The time had come for him to disengage himself from his Confederate interests as soon as possible. The profits he had made from the black market sales of the U.S. Sanitary Commission's supplies for Union prisoners had come to an end. Like a good poker player, Scott knew when it was time to fold his cards and pocket his winnings. For him, the lucrative game was over.

He consulted his desk calendar. Today was Thursday. Tomorrow, he would take a long weekend furlough, then speed south to Richmond in his guise as a Confederate Brigadier General. He could wrap up his affairs on Sunday, when most of the law-abiding population would be on their knees praying in the city's many churches.

Claypole chuckled to himself as he tied up the reports with red tape. He, too, would be on his knees during his visit to the Southern capital, but it would hardly be in a church. Richmond justifiably enjoyed the reputation of being the ''wickedest city in the world.'' The bordellos reputedly housed more prostitutes than New Orleans and Paris combined. He licked his lips. Since this would be his last time in Richmond until after the war, he would pay farewell visits to all his favorite sporting ladies, especially the ones who inhabited the plush cribs in Locust Alley, a few blocks west of Libby Prison.

Three weeks inside Libby's walls seemed like a lifetime to Rob. How did the veteran inmates stand it? The prisoners fell roughly into three categories: the seriously ill who were housed in two infirmaries on the first floor; the shufflers, by far the majority, whom hunger, cold and a variety of lesser ailments had turned into scarecrows; and the firebrands who often found themselves in solitary confinement in one of the basement's rat-infested cells. As the days rolled by, Rob gave his particular attention to the third group, most of whom lived in the Chickamauga Suite.

Sleeping through part of the day, Rob spent the nighttime hours observing the comings and goings of his fellow prisoners. A remarkable amount of activity took place once the candles were extinguished at seven o'clock. The twin scourges of diarrhea and dysentery forced some of the men to make a continual parade to the slop buckets. Many others couldn't sleep because of the cold winds blowing through the open windows or the lice bites. A secretive few had undisclosed missions in other parts of the old warehouse.

Every evening shortly after the sentry outside called "Eight o'clock and all's well," five men from the Suite disappeared down the stairs to the prisoners' kitchen on the floor below. Yet, Rob could not hear any noise through the floorboards until just after the sentry's call at four in the morning. Then the same five returned to the second floor looking exhausted and smelling strongly of the fetid canal that ran between the prison and the river.

The following night, five different men slipped downstairs after eight and returned at four, again looking haggard. The third night, a different squad of five repeated the same mysterious exit. This time Rob ventured down to the kitchen after them, only to find the room completely empty. Intrigued, he returned upstairs to his bit of floor where he huddled under his thin blanket and mulled over the implications.

On the fourth night, the first group of five again went down the stairs. This time Rob's night vision was good enough to recognize his card-playing friend, Stu Cramer, as one of them. Their leader was A. G. Hamilton.

These must be the men planning to escape that Lawrence told him to find. *They're tunneling, for sure. But where do they intend to come out?*

After they had been gone for an hour, Rob rose and tiptoed around the bodies of the sleeping men. Braving the icy wind, Rob looked out onto Cary Street that ran past

Libby's main entrance. By day, Richmond's prostitutes paraded on the sidewalk across from the prison in their efforts to demoralize the men inside, but at night, the street was quiet.

The moon gave Rob enough light to determine possible escape routes. Just below the window, several sentries marched back and forth, passing each other every few minutes. Across Cary Street and behind the harlots' sidewalk, a wide vacant lot ran the length of the long city block. Every stick and bit of trash on it cast black shadows against the pale white of the frosted ground. An animal, either a cat or rat, scurried across the open area. Even from the distance of his window, Rob could see it clearly. Any tunnel on this side would have to extend over two hundred feet before it could reach the safety of buildings a block away.

Rob slipped into the far room that faced west, overlooking Twentieth Street. More sentinels below the prison and another vacant lot facing Libby. A half dozen tents were pitched on the waste ground. This was home for the prison guards. Rob worked his way back to his room and looked out to see the James River flowing silently past the sleeping city. Between the sentry-guarded warehouse and the river was the half-frozen canal. River's too deep, he concluded, and the ground too wet. The tunnelers would have to dig too far down before going across under the water. The possibility of cave-ins and drowning were too high. That left only the east side of the building.

Once again, there was a vacant lot next to Libby's wall but—Rob craned his neck to see better. Two small office buildings with an enclosed yard between them lay on the far side of the lot. Only fifty or sixty feet separated the prison from the—

"What are you doing, friend?" asked a low voice in his ear. A heavy hand fell on Rob's shoulder.

Rob tensed, but his training kept him from calling out his surprise. Studying Libby's surroundings, he had failed to hear the man come up behind him. "Taking the night air," he replied softly.

"You must need a lot of it," the other observed, not letting go of Rob. "You've been sniffing in all directions."

Though Rob could not see his face, he suspected his interrogator was one of the fifteen men he had watched over the past week. He decided to chance revealing his identity. He prayed that Lawrence's underground network had succeeded in smuggling his recognition password and countersign into the prison.

"I miss seeing the dancing girls at the Canterbury," he said slowly, naming one of Washington's more bawdy music halls.

The other man chuckled in the back of his throat. "And I miss eating oysters at Harvey's saloon," he responded, giving the correct answer. "I surely do, and that's the truth." He released Rob's shoulder.

Rob turned slowly to face the other. The man was shorter and slimmer than he, with bright eyes above a full dark beard.

"Colonel Thomas Rose, at your service, sir," he whispered, "Commander of the 77th Pennsylvania, captured at Chickamauga."

"Major Robert Montgomery, Rhinebeck Legion, New York."

"And wounded at Little Roundtop," Rose added. "Rumors of your exploits have preceded you, Major."

"I see that you have excellent intelligence here," Rob answered, secretly flattered by the tone of respect in Rose's voice.

Rose put his finger to his lips. "Rumor, Major, we get only rumors in here, like knowing about the oysters at Harvey's."

Rob looked around at the hundreds of sleeping prisoners that packed the room, and nodded. Any one of them could be a spy for the Confederates, planted among the Federal officers for the express purpose of ferreting out escape operations.

"Go back to bed, Major," Rose whispered. "We'll speak in the morning over a game of poker. I understand you're very good. It's a fortunate thing Stu Cramer only plays for chicken bones, or he would have lost his shirt to you by now."

Rob grinned in the dark. Here he thought he was the one getting information out of Stu!

The following evening, six men went down to the first-floor kitchen, where Tom Rose gave Rob a tour of their work-in-progress. Once in the kitchen, the men loosened the fire bricks behind one of the cast-iron stoves that used the flue of the warehouse's original open fireplace. A man-sized hole gaped behind the wall, though where it went, Rob could not see.

"It's a leap of faith," Tom assured him, "though not as dire as you might think."

One of the other men produced a small ladder made of rope and wooden rungs. Rose fastened the top of the ladder around the stove's legs, then climbed down into the hole. A few minutes later Rob saw a small glimmer of light at the bottom. Joe Grimwold nudged him.

"You're next. It's in the shape of a backward *S*. Keep your head low. You'll come out inside the fireplace of the old kitchen in the basement. From there, it's five rungs to the floor." He arched one eyebrow. "Step down easy.

There's a lot of furry critters rustling around in the straw down there, and they don't take too kindly to us.''

Though Rob could not grasp the side of the ladder with his right hand, he linked his elbow around each step down in order to balance himself on the flimsy contraption. He marveled that Rose had been able to steal the materials to construct it. Despite Joe's warning, he clipped the top of his head on the *S* bend. When he finally reached the stone floor, he found himself nearly knee-deep in moldering straw. Tom held up a small candle.

"Welcome to Rat Hell, Major," he grinned. "Gateway to Freedomland."

Chapter Twenty-One

A week after she had moved in to live with Lizzie in her palatial mansion on Grace Street, Julia still did not know her eccentric hostess very well. Elizabeth Van Lew, known as Miss Lizzie to her few friends and Crazy Bet to the majority of the citizens of Richmond, was the spinster daughter of an enterprising businessman who had made his fortune in hardware. Since her father's death, Miss Lizzie and her mother were the only full-time residents of the house aside from a number of free black servants. Old Mrs. Van Lew kept to her bed most of the time since she suffered from a number of chronic ailments. However, the household was far from quiet.

Lizzie maintained a voluminous correspondence and her servants were constantly running out the side door on Twenty-fourth Street with messages, letters and copies of the *Richmond Enquirer*. Visitors of the strangest sort presented themselves at the side door all hours of the day and night. A country girl who smoked a pipe came several times with a basket full of eggs. A delivery man, known only as Quaker, from the bakery on North Eighth Street, called almost daily, even though white bread rarely appeared on the Van Lew's table.

Twice since she moved in, Julia had been awakened at night by the heavy tread of a man's feet going upstairs to the third floor. When she asked Lizzie who had arrived during the night, the old woman pretended that she misunderstood the question, and launched into a discussion of the proper feed for hens.

Lizzie spent many of her waking hours in the city, usually dressed in the oddest assortment of clothes. When Julia accompanied her hostess, she noticed that once in public, Lizzie commenced to mumble nursery rhymes aloud, or sing off key, or make the most peculiar conversation with passersby.

Once in a dry goods shop, a woman, dressed respectably in mauve taffeta, took Julia aside and whispered, "You look like a nice girl. What are you doing in company with Crazy Bet? Be careful, young lady. She's a witch!"

Once back at home, Julia related the matron's warning to Lizzie.

Her hostess laughed heartily. "My, my, my, what will they say of me next, I wonder?" Then she gave Julia a shrewd look. "Who do *you* think I am?"

Taken aback by Lizzie's directness, Julia said, "You are my kind benefactress. I don't know what I would have done without you."

Lizzie waved aside the compliment. "Frivle-fravle, my dear, but you didn't answer my question. Do you think I am as mad as the proverbial hatter?" She poured some tea into Julia's cup.

Julia realized that Lizzie would accept nothing but the plain truth, though she might take offense, and toss Julia back into Richmond's crowded streets. She decided to risk it. "I think that you play-act very well, ma'am. At home, you are the most levelheaded person I have ever met, while outside your door, you assume the character of Crazy Bet. I can almost imagine that you enjoy being called a witch.''

Lizzie's smile grew wider. ''You are as sharp as I first thought when I saw you in the guard room.'' She folded her hands in her lap. ''Tell me, my dear, when do you plan to marry that young man of yours?''

Julia nearly spilled her tea onto the carpet. She slowly replaced her cup on the side table while she allowed her heartbeat to return to normal. ''Rob Montgomery is a dear friend, I admit. But I have no intention of marrying him. For all I know, he may be engaged to a girl in New York.''

''Fiddlesticks!'' Lizzie snorted. ''I can tell the real story by the way you two looked at each other.''

Julia lowered her head. Rob had been very cool at their meeting. How could Lizzie possibly see a spark of love in a man who hesitated to even touch Julia? She stroked the back of her hand where his lips had sizzled her skin. No, that wasn't a sign of his love, she told herself. He was merely being gallant, in thanks for the food she had brought him. She refused to examine her own feelings for the Yankee major.

''We have never discussed anything more personal than our childhood pranks,'' she replied. ''We are friends, nothing more.''

Lizzie shook her head. ''Time's a-wastin', child! There's a war going on, if you haven't noticed.''

''But I have,'' Julia blurted out. ''I must confess that Richmond took me by surprise. In Alexandria, we thought all was going well down here, but when I walk about the city, I am alarmed daily by the sights I see, like that woman who was begging for bread with tears running down her cheeks. She was dressed like a lady, but she begged like a…'' Julia bit her lower lip to stanch the pain of that encounter.

Lizzie lifted her eyebrow. "Like a gypsy? Yes, I agree. War is not as glorious or noble as our politicians painted three years ago when they inflamed our young men. War isn't flag-waving or "Dixie"-playing or handsome boys parading down the streets in shiny uniforms. As you have observed, Richmond is sagging at the corners now, but I venture to say that worse times will come before she falls."

Lizzie cocked her head like a small, inquisitive wren eyeing a tasty bread crumb. "Which brings us back to you. Do you love this Robert Montgomery from New York?"

Julia had the uncomfortable feeling that Lizzie could read her heart as easily as a book. "Yes, ma'am, I suppose that I do," she murmured. Her cheeks burned at the admission. "But I've not said a word to him about it. I highly doubt that he feels the same way."

Lizzie chuckled. "Most men don't know what they feel until you hit them over the head with a hammer." She consulted a diamond watch pin that she wore on her bodice. "Nearly noontime. I expect he's worked up an appetite by now. We'll fix you up a basket of dainties to tempt the major. Wilson will accompany you down to Libby and back. I don't want any of those loose women bothering you." She rang a little bell to summon one of her serving men.

Julia uttered a gasp of surprise, followed by excitement. "You want me to go right now?"

"Of course!" Lizzie went over to her desk and scribbled a note in her flurried penmanship. "You have been champing at the bit to see your Rob again, and I expect he's been wondering what happened to you."

"He must think I've gone back home." Julia thought of Carolyn and the cozy room they had shared on Prince Street. "But I can't return now."

Lizzie blotted her note. "Of course you can't. Your reputation is ruined there. You know it, I know it, and I am sure it has dawned on your fine major that you have tossed everything to the winds for him."

She made Julia seem like some flibbertigibbet from a lighthearted novel. "I'll get my hat," Julia said aloud, going into the wide hallway where the marble-topped coat stand held her things. Her fingers shook as she tied the satin ribbons of her dark-green velvet bonnet.

In the parlor, Lizzie instructed Wilson what to pack in the basket, then she came out into the hall just as Julia buttoned up her cloak. She showed her a sealed note addressed only to ER.

"Give this to Mr. Ross," she instructed, stuffing the note into Julia's muff. Then she whispered, "His bark is considerably worse than his bite."

Though Julia said nothing to Lizzie, she had very strong reservations about Mr. Ross. The man looked as though he ate nails for breakfast. Wilson reappeared from the kitchen with a large covered basket. Without further ado, Lizzie shoved them both out the side door.

As Wilson escorted Julia down Church Hill toward the prison, he looked behind them several times. The expression on his face gave her pause. In the week that she had lived with her, Lizzie had warned Julia incessantly that the streets of Richmond were barely safe in the daytime, and never after dark.

"Is someone following us?" she asked him in an undertone when they paused at the corner of Franklin Street.

"I'm not sure, Miss Julia," he rumbled deep in the back of his throat. "But there's been some trashy no-account hanging out across from the house since yesterday afternoon."

"Lizzie has many strange visitors," Julia reminded him,

though his concern chilled her more than the wind off the river.

"Maybe," he muttered, "but I know most of those folk. This one has a mean look about him that I don't like."

"Oh!" Julia burrowed deeper into her cloak's fur collar.

Wilson shot her a grin. "You don't need to worry your head about that man, Miss Julia. That's what I'm here for."

But Julia worried about him all the way to Libby's front door. Once inside the spartan guard room, she had to wait while the prison's adjutant, Major Long, organized a large party of Richmond's ladies and gentlemen who had come to gawk at the prisoners. Mr. Ross sat in the corner at his desk, wearing a thunderous look. After the visitors had been escorted upstairs, Julia stepped forward.

"Oh, you again," he snarled. "Have you come to view the menagerie, too? You have just missed the tour."

Swallowing her ire, Julia handed him the note from Lizzie. With anger and fear tying knots inside her stomach, she watched his face closely while he read it. For the flash of a moment, his expression softened, before he returned to his usual look of sarcasm and disdain. After reading the missive a second time, he wadded it up into a compact ball. Then he ambled over to the small cast-iron stove that attempted to heat the room, and pitched it onto the red coals. He watched in silence while the paper burned to cinders.

Meanwhile, Julia fiddled with the strings of her muff, trying to compose what she would say to Rob. She didn't dare declare her true feelings for him, no matter what Lizzie had suggested. He had never given her any indication that his friendship was more than a passing fancy.

Ross ignored Julia. Instead, he directed his attention to

Wilson who stood against the wall like an ebony statue. "Miss Van Lew wrote that you have something for me."

Without so much as a flicker of an eyelid, the servant nodded slowly, then brought out a bundle of three cigars, wrapped in brown paper, from inside the basket. "Miss Lizzie says that you had better take your time with these, cause good ci-gars are getting mighty scarce nowadays," he remarked, handing the present to Ross.

"She did, did she?" he snarled as he pocketed them. He cast a knowing grin at the sentry who stood near the stairway. "You tell Crazy Bet that I know *exactly* what I will do with my smokes."

This man was insufferable. Without thinking of the consequences, Julia retorted, "Whatever happened to your manners? You should be more grateful for the gift, sir, and more respectful of the giver. Those Havanas came through the blockade, and they cost Miss Van Lew a dollar apiece."

Mr. Ross laughed as if she had just entertained him with a vastly amusing anecdote. "You are a feisty little thing. It's too bad that your…ah…cousin has only got one hand, because I suspect that he'd need two to keep you in line." Before Julia could compose an answer, the clerk glanced at the guard.

"Garland, sashay up those stairs and tell Major Montgomery that he's got a firecracker down here who's ready to explode."

The soldier laughed, then disappeared up the steps. As soon as he was out of sight, Ross leaned over Julia and said in a whisper, "Before you open that pretty mouth again, Miss Chandler, listen very carefully. It appears that I have some business to conduct with the sentry when he returns with your precious Yankee…relative. You will have about five minutes alone with him. I expect you to behave yourself, and not try to smuggle him out of here. It won't work and I'd have to confine the major in solitary—which, I promise you, is most uncomfortable, not to mention rat-infested. Do you understand me?''

Julia looked into the man's eyes. Again, a faint spark of human kindness flashed in them. ''Yes, Mr. Ross, I believe I do.''

Chapter Twenty-Two

"February 6th: Cloudy with some sun, temperatures milder, thank God. Beef—two ounces—for breakfast. Tasted moldy."

Rob dipped his borrowed pen nub into the onion juice that pooled in the bottom of his tin cup. He studied the page that appeared to hold only Shakespeare's Sonnet LXXV. Since the first day of his incarceration in Libby, he had kept a secret diary in the wide margins of the little volume that he had intended for Julia. To idle inspection, the dog-eared sonnet book looked innocent, but around each short poem, Rob penned a running commentary of his imprisonment with an invisible ink that would reveal itself only when the page was heated.

He paused to read the sonnet's opening lines: "So are you to my thoughts as food for life; Or as sweet-season'd showers are to the ground." *And so you are to me, sweet Julia. The memories of your sweet self sustain my soul in this pesthole.* He remembered how they met: he, stone-faced and self-pitying; she, radiant and slightly tipsy from the champagne. He smiled when he recalled her shocking proposition behind the alcove curtains, "Will you have your dastardly way with me?"

Just remembering the scene heated his blood and stirred his manhood. If she made him that same offer now, he might not be the gentleman she thought he was.

His pen dried. Rob dipped it again, then continued to write down the left-hand side of the thick, cream-colored page: "Rumor says that three more of our soldiers incarcerated on Belle Isle died last night from exposure. Have got to find a way to free them, too. Used up the rest of the firewood last night. If the Rebs don't give us more today, we'll have to break up the rest of the benches."

His gaze strayed to the nearest line in the sonnet: "Now counting best to be with you alone." He groaned under his breath.

Why had he acted like such an idiot when Julia came to see him? He should have tossed caution to the wind and taken her in his arms like he wanted to do from the first instant that he saw her in the guard room. He wouldn't make that same mistake twice—that is, if she ever came back. Had she returned to Alexandria, despite her scandalous flight? Or was she still in Richmond?

As soon as he was out of Libby and his mission completed, he would go to her, no matter where she was. Rob did not permit himself to consider marriage an option, since he had long ago given up on that state of happiness. Once with Julia, he would just let fate take its course.

He barely looked up when a group of well-dressed citizens swept by his corner. Most of the women held delicate lace handkerchiefs against their noses in an effort to keep out the odor that wafted up from hundreds of unwashed men.

Rob dipped his pen again. "The tunnel is going well, according to Stu. He is one of the diggers on the third rotation. It is hard to estimate the distance, but Tom Rose thinks we have another seven feet to go before we are under the fence. Meanwhile, the list of escapees has been confirmed. Thirty men will go out the first night. If the tunnel is not discovered, thirty more the second, and thirty more on the third night if luck holds out. Have instructed the first group and part of the second on the route to take and where the food caches can be found. Pray that Lawrence has set them up or the boys will be in trouble on the road.''

Rob regarded the men around him who dozed, whittled bones, read the books and newspapers brought by Miss Lizzie, played chess and cards, and dreamt of food and home. The usual bunch crowded around the open windows over Cary Street to trade ribaldry with the local whores.

''Montgomery!''

Rob pulled himself out of his thoughts. Quick as a cat, he snapped the book shut and stuffed it into his breast pocket, dumped the onion juice between the floorboards and slid the pen under the sack of sawdust that served as his pillow.

''Montgomery! Get your backside here now! You've got a visitor.''

Was it Julia? Hope lifted in his spirit. He pulled himself to his feet, shook his head to clear the dizziness that had become a daily companion, and wiped his hands down his pants. ''Coming,'' he shouted, though his voice sounded more like a croak.

He picked his way toward the stairs amid good-natured guffaws and envious ribbing from his fellow prisoners. Despite the glare from the guard, he stopped at the wash bucket long enough to scrub his hands and face with a sliver of soap. His beard felt thick and coarse to the touch. He couldn't wait to visit his barber in Washington.

''Quit your lollygagging, Yank!'' growled the Reb. ''Nothing is going to make you look or smell any better.

The lady downstairs will have to take you as you are.'' He chortled. ''As if she could take you at all. I'll be glad to take your place.''

Rob balled his good hand into a fist at the gibe. He longed to push this runt down the stairs and pummel him into the ground, but that action would only land Rob in solitary confinement and defeat his sole purpose of being here. Instead, he glared at the youth with hatred in his eye.

''I will remember your face, private. How old are you, anyway?''

The boy swallowed and gripped his rifle. ''Old enough!'' he retorted.

On the fresh side of eighteen, Rob would bet. He said, ''When this war is over, pray that we do not meet again.''

The young soldier momentarily dropped his shield of bravado. Looking away, he muttered, ''We both may be dead before then, Major.''

Rob said nothing further. In a week or two at most, he planned to be back in his cozy room at Ebbitt's Hotel. That should give many a sleepless night to this insolent pup. Brushing off dirt, cobwebs and dust from his frock coat, Rob hurried down the stairs.

When he saw Julia standing in the guard room, he could not hold back the smile from his face. She was an answer to his innermost prayer. He started toward her when Ross intercepted him. Though the clerk was shorter than Rob by a good six inches, he had enough pure spite in him for a man twice his size.

Ross sneered. ''I can't understand why Miss Chandler insists upon returning here to see *you,* Montgomery, but I trust that you will behave. Unfortunately, duty compels me to leave—but only for a minute or two. One slip on your part, one step outside that door yonder, and your life will be forfeit. Do you understand me?'' His dark eyes glinted like daggers.

Rob sucked in his breath. For some unfathomable reason, Ross was giving him a few moments alone with Julia. He would take that gift with no questions asked. Rob nodded. "Perfectly," he snapped.

Then the clerk turned to the guard. "Garland! Come with me. There are discrepancies in the storage shed that I want to discuss with you."

The boy's eyes bugged out. "But, Mr. Ross, sir…the prisoner —''

Ross snapped his fingers as if calling a dog to heel. "There are four men outside this door just waiting to shoot a wandering Yankee." He sent Rob and Julia a pointed look. "I doubt that Major Montgomery would be fool enough to take a walk. Stop sniveling, Garland! I haven't got all day."

With that, Ross all but dragged out the flustered private. Then a tall black man stepped from the shadows. Neither expecting his appearance nor knowing his intentions, Rob shielded Julia. "Who are you? What is your business?" he asked, wondering if the man carried a weapon.

The fellow grinned at him. "No harm, Major Montgomery. Miss Van Lew asked me to give you this, and tell you to make sure that you *read* the good books that she sends to you." He held up the basket.

Rob understood immediately. Lizzie Van Lew smuggled messages folded inside the spines of the novels she sent the prisoners. She already knew about the breakout and her house would be safe for any man too sick to travel. He nodded to Wilson. "Thank Miss Lizzie for us."

The man placed the large basket on the bench, then touched the brim of his brown felt hat. "I'll be right outside, Miss Julia, in case you might need some help." After giving Rob a pointed look, he opened the outer door and left.

Rob experienced a dizzy sensation—alone for the first time in a century, it seemed. He smiled down at Julia, at last alone with the woman he loved. "Julia!" He spoke her name like a prayer to heaven. "You have no idea how glad I am to see you."

For the first time since that fateful night in the garden, a true smile shone through her uncertainty. "Oh, Rob! I was so afraid—" She breathed his name, then checked herself, biting her lower lip in the most provocative way.

He stepped closer to her. "Afraid of me? As you can see, I am kept under lock and key."

She laughed. How good it was to hear her silvery laughter in this dank place! Julia lifted her hand and stroked his cheek above his beard. "I must confess, you do look very fierce."

His skin burned where her warm fingertips touched him. He caught her hand in his and kissed the palm. Sweet clean flesh against his lips that were so chapped from raw windy nights. His senses reeled. "I promise to shave as soon as I can." He interlaced his fingers between hers.

She tilted one slim brow. "Is that truly the very *first* thing you would do, Rob?" She stared at him with an expression of open longing.

He didn't know if she was teasing or chiding him, and he didn't care at this point. They were wasting precious time in trivial banter. He slipped his good arm around her waist. Pulling her against him, he held her tightly. How good she felt! His blood sang in his veins.

"Forgive my appearance, Julia, and forgive me, for I am a starving man," he murmured, his voice husky with desire.

She parted her lips to reply, but Rob swooped down to

capture her mouth with his. Her startled gasp filled him with the sweetness of her breath. Warm chocolate! Frothy, rich cream! Their lips met and matched each other with a desperate savage intensity. Rob lost all sense of time and place. Julia's passionate response finally shattered the hard shell that he had built so carefully around his heart. In the depths of this purgatory, he had found his salvation. He held the only reality of his world within his embrace.

Julia forgot everything she had planned to say to Rob. At their sudden kiss, intense happiness exploded within her, and excitement shot through her veins. In his embrace, she felt as if she were floating off the rough-hewn floorboards of the guard room. She heard no sound but the harsh, uneven rhythm of Rob's breathing, saw nothing but starbursts inside her closed eyelids, felt nothing but some unfathomable ecstasy as his tongue danced within her hot mouth. Her lips burned with his fire.

Trembling, Julia twined her arms around his neck. She couldn't disguise her body's shameless reaction to his passion, nor did she care. The hunger of her desire for fulfillment threatened to overwhelm her.

"Julia, my love," he whispered between his scorching kisses. His lips seared a path from the corner of her mouth, across her cheek, against her earlobe and down her neck to her starched collar. His beard tickled her skin. "Sweet, oh, so sweet."

"Rob," she gasped as his tongue explored her ear. No other words were sufficient for the moment.

He claimed her lips again. Rob's kisses grew more urgent, as if he feared she would dissolve at any moment. Then, like a summer storm passing, he relaxed in her arms. His lips softened then released her mouth to brush a kiss across her forehead. He held her close against him, his uneven breathing fanning her cheek. Despite his thin, disheveled and dirty appearance, Julia had no desire to back out of his embrace. Instead, she savored every moment of their time together. The perplexing Mr. Ross and the guards would return at any minute.

As if he read her thoughts, Rob lifted his head and gazed down at her. "Forgive my lapse in manners, Miss Chandler," he joked with an adorable, lopsided smile. "Your beauty has completely undone me."

Then he grew more serious. "No, it is not merely beauty, but your sweet self, beloved. If I have frightened you, please forgive me."

"I tried to tell you that awful night. I cannot forgive you, when there is nothing to forgive. If there is a fault, then it is mine as much as yours."

A jumble of voices at the top of the stairs warned them that their time alone was nearly gone. Rob kissed her eyes, first one and then the other. "Here are kisses for you to dream on," he murmured.

"And I will dream of you," Julia replied, love spilling from her heart. She ached to hold him close again, but instead she stepped back as the sightseeing Richmonders clattered down the stairs.

Rob coughed, then grinned. "Well, don't dream of me like this or you will suffer a nightmare." Then he shifted to a more serious note as the noisy crowd came nearer. "Quick! Tell me, where are you staying?"

"With Miss Van Lew," she whispered back as several women attired in colorful carriage dresses with wide hoops sailed into the room.

"Another Yankee!" remarked one of the top-hatted men who accompanied them. "I thought I smelled something rank down here."

Rob said nothing, but lifted his chin and squared his

shoulders. His inner strength shone in his flashing dark eyes and in the straight lines of his stance. Every inch of him proclaimed Rob to be a man of character, not a subjugated captive. Julia's pride swelled. The sneering gentleman retreated behind the barricade of gawking women. It amused Julia to see that the ladies recognized Rob's true manliness despite his ragged trappings. One of the younger members of the female party even fluttered behind her handkerchief in her best ballroom style.

The outer door swung open and Wilson stepped inside. "He's a-coming," he announced in general, without seeming the least bit surprised by the sight of the crowded room. Not looking at Julia or Rob, Wilson returned to his spot in the corner where he waited in silence with patient dignity.

The outer door opened once again. Ross, followed by several guards and a Confederate officer, confronted the unusual assortment of people crowding his domain. A fiendish sneer spread across his face.

"Good afternoon again, ladies and gentlemen. I trust that our Northern guests have given you sufficient amusement for the day." He stepped aside and held the door open, allowing the cold wind to blow in.

"Please be so kind as to leave us to our duties now," Ross continued, ushering the crowd out to the muddy street. As one woman passed him, he said in a loud stage whisper. "I do hope that you are not taking too many of our lice with you. We need to keep as many as possible for our prisoners."

He grinned with satisfaction when the women screamed and the men swore. Once the room cleared of the visitors, Ross turned to the officer who had accompanied him. "Sorry about that intrusion, sir. The local population do enjoy their visits here, and General Winder insists that we accommodate them as best we can.''

''No apology necessary,'' said the officer whose back was to Rob and Julia. ''I imagine that you are well compensated for your inconvenience.''

The two men laughed. Beside her, Julia heard Rob suck in his breath. His body grew taut.

''Major Claypole!'' he raged, glaring at the visitor. ''Damn your white-livered soul!''

Chapter Twenty-Three

Sheer, blind panic swept through Scott Claypole at the sound of that all-too-familiar voice. He broke into a cold sweat. He could hear his future crumble down around him like a house of cards. His ears rang as the word "traitor" screamed in his mind.

He was a dead man. Unless—

Ross pounced on the situation like a cat on a mouse. A pensive look rose in his cold eyes, making Claypole uneasy. "Do you have the pleasure of knowing our Major Montgomery, General?" the wily clerk asked.

"General!" Rob exploded. "That weasel is nothing but a lickspittle major in the Federal army."

Ross's lips thinned in an evil smile. "Oh, then you *have* made each other's acquaintance before, I see." He addressed Montgomery. "*General* Clayton here has been the greatest help with our prison facilities. Unfortunately, your Sanitation Commission sends so many boxes of supplies for the prisoners that we cannot possibly store them all," he explained in a soft, singsong voice as if he were speaking to a child.

"Indeed, we were hard pressed to know *what* to do with all those hams, canned peaches, condensed milk, butter, cakes, jams and other assorted luxuries that we consider to be far too rich for our prisoners' diets. Only this morning, we received a thousand perfectly good wool blankets. How can we possibly find room for them in our warehouse? Several years ago, General Clayton presented me with the most marvelous and beneficial plan, whereby these Yankee dainties are sold to our good city's hotels and restaurants—at even more inflated prices than usual. But that is the cost of doing business during wartime, is it not, General?''

While Ross outlined Claypole's lucrative black market operation in excruciating detail, the major tried to formulate a plan. Should he acknowledge his identity or pretend that Montgomery was mistaken?

"General?'' Ross prompted him.

Claypole pivoted slowly around to face his accuser. To his relief, he saw that two guards now restrained Rob. His eyes widened when he spied Miss Chandler standing next to him. The major made a snap decision.

He swept off his gold braided kepi. "Good afternoon, Miss Chandler. I am *most* surprised to see you in this den of iniquity.''

The beauty stepped backward toward the bench. "I do not believe that I know you, sir.'' Her jade eyes turned a deeper shade of green.

"You don't want to,'' Montgomery snarled. "He's the devil himself.''

If looks could kill, Claypole would have been a dead man. Fortunately, Montgomery could do nothing, though his rebuke in front of the delectable Miss Chandler stung Claypole's ego.

Summoning all his arrogance, he said to Ross. "I am surprised to see Major Montgomery in your tender mercies, Erasmus, but I suspect that you do not fully know whom you are harboring. Our good, upright and honest major here is one of the senior operatives in the service of the United States Office of Military Intelligence.'' To Miss Chandler, he added, ''That means spying, my dear. Your sweetheart lies, cheats and steals for a living. I would take anything he says to you with a grain of salt.''

She turned a little pale. ''Oh!'' she murmured.

Montgomery spoke over his shoulder to her, ''Do not believe everything you hear about me, Julia. What is between us is true.''

She said nothing, but looked like a moth mesmerized by a flame. Claypole licked his lips. Perhaps he should offer to console her over a lavish dinner in one of Main Street's restaurants. Miss Chandler looked a little pinched and in need of sustenance—and other delights.

Claypole returned his attention to Montgomery. To save his own life, the major must die. ''You will notice that the Yankee does not deny my accusation, Erasmus. I think that you should confine this prisoner to the solitary cells. Put him on half rations and let him rot there.'' To Rob, he added, ''It is unfortunate that there is no evidence to hang you for spying, Montgomery, but I will look into that matter.''

Montgomery lunged against his guards. ''You will not get away with this, Claypole. I swear that I will bring you down.''

He found the threat laughable. ''That would be amusing to see, Rob, though I will not hold my breath in anticipation.''

Ross narrowed his eyes, then snapped his fingers to the guards. ''Put him in the basement.'' He shook his head at the prisoner. ''Tut, tut, Major, I am most disappointed in you. I thought I told you to behave.''

Montgomery did not look at either man, but at Miss Chandler. "Please believe in me, Julia. I am true to you."

Though she looked near tears, she gave him a tremulous smile. "And I love you, Rob," she whispered.

Her sentiment galled Claypole, and disturbed him as well. He wondered if she knew anything about his true identity, and if she was still loyal to the South. As the guards dragged Montgomery away, Claypole sidled over to her and touched his cap's brim. "I can see that this distasteful affair has been quite a shock for you, Miss Chandler. Allow me to escort you from this place and take you to dinner? A little decent food will help restore your good spirits, I'm sure."

She had the audacity to turn up her nose at him. Then she stepped around him, lifting her hem as if contact with him might foul her. Addressing Ross, she asked, "Please do see that my basket is given to the poor men upstairs? Miss Lizzie would be much annoyed if she thought that you mistreated her little gifts for the prisoners, Mr. Ross."

Once again she detected that strange gleam of kindness in the depths of this hard man's eyes. He nodded. "Please tell Miss Lizzie that I will do all I can for her. Understand me? You *will* tell her that?"

Before Miss Chandler could reply, a large black man pushed himself away from the far wall. "If she forgets, I will," he rumbled. Then he spoke to the lady. "Come along now, Miss Julia. I think you have been here long enough for one day."

She glanced at Scott, then Ross. "I couldn't agree with you more, Wilson," she replied.

Scott had no further chance to press his offer. The big black man whisked her out the door.

"I will inform Colonel Turner of this new twist, General," Ross said, pointing to the closed door that led to the office of Libby's notorious commandant. "I am sure that he will want to express his gratitude to you later this evening at supper. Where are you staying?"

Claypole buttoned his greatcoat, then flicked a bit of dust off the elaborate gold lace that wound up his sleeve. "At the Exchange Hotel. Room 314. Tell Colonel Turner that I will await his company with pleasure." He adjusted his kepi on his head. With his hand on the doorknob, he added, "And mind you, Erasmus, keep that Yankee under close guard. He may be one-armed, but that makes him all the more cunning."

Ross nodded. "Have no worry on that score, General Clayton. I will make Major Montgomery my *special* ward."

Claypole stepped outside where he was greeted with smirks, winks and choice remarks by the *nymphes du monde* across the road. Normally, he would have returned their attentions with pleasure, but today his mind was weighed down with fears for his future.

One particular question nagged at him above all others. What the hell was Montgomery doing in Libby Prison?

When Lizzie Van Lew heard the story of the morning's encounter from Wilson, she put Julia to bed with a hot water bottle and a large bowl of chicken soup. She sat by the girl's bedside while she ate.

"And you are quite certain that your major made no mistake about this general?" she asked, skewering Julia with a penetrating stare.

Julia swallowed a spoonful of the nourishing soup before she replied. "Quite. I could tell Rob was incensed to see him. Called him a traitor."

Lizzie made a note in her small ivory-backed memorandum book. "And you say that Rob called the man by a different name?"

Julia nodded. "I distinctly heard him say Claypole, while Mr. Ross called him General Clayton. I wondered at the difference. I noticed that the general didn't deny anything that Rob said. It was a very heated exchange." She shuddered.

Lizzie jotted down that information. Then she sucked on the end of her pencil while she considered her next step. Of course, she would immediately send Wilson off to the family's farm in Henrico County with an urgent message hidden inside Wilson's boot heel for her "dear uncle," Union General Benjamin Butler. "Uncle" could forward it on to the proper authorities in Military Intelligence.

Whomever this Clayton/Claypole really was, Lizzie smelled him for a rat. If Julia's sweetheart called him a traitor, then he probably was one. In the meantime, she herself would visit Libby before Ross conducted the prisoner roll call at four. For the sake of the upcoming breakout, Montgomery must not languish long in one of those wretched dens.

"Miss Lizzie?" Julia interrupted her thoughts. "What is going on?"

Pulling herself together, she smiled at the girl. "You have had a shock today. Everything will be straightened out eventually—"

Shaking her head, Julia put her soup bowl on the bedside table. "No, I can tell that you are planning to do something. What is it?"

Lizzie eyed her with misgiving. Julia was a bright young thing who had spent a great deal of time investigating the contents of Lizzie's late father's library. Perhaps she was even sharper than her hostess had anticipated. "Whatever do you mean, child?"

Julia enumerated on her fingers as she stared steadily at her hostess. "For one thing, you had Christopher and Wilson tack up dark blankets over the windows in the back parlor—a room that is on the shady side of the house. You write a lot of letters, yet your inkwell is always full. I know that there is a hidden bedroom on the third floor under the eaves."

Lizzie gripped her notebook. "Have you been snooping around my house, young lady?"

"No, ma'am." Julia looked a little hurt by the suggestion. "I heard something crash hard on the floor one morning when you were out. I thought your mother had fallen from her bed, so I rushed upstairs to help her. I saw a little door open at the end of the hall and a man inside. Naturally, I was frightened."

Lizzie could well imagine. "And curious."

Julia nodded slowly. "Exactly. I think I scared that poor young private as much as he scared me. We stared at each other for a breathless moment. He put his finger to his lips and then he…he…" She lowered her head with a shy grin.

"He what?" Lizzie expected all her "midnight visitors" to behave themselves while recuperating in her home. As she recalled, that boy from Ohio had been particularly lively despite his severe case of frostbite. "Just what did my nephew do?"

"Nephew?" Julia laughed. "He *winked* at me before he closed the door." Her expression grew more serious. "And yes, I did notice that he wore a very ragged Federal uniform and that his feet were bandaged. I suspect that you are a Unionist, Miss Lizzie. That's why some of your neighbors call you a witch. And I also think that you do a lot more activities than just send books and cookies to Libby Prison.''

''And will you denounce me to the provost marshal?''

Julia sighed. ''If you had asked me that question a year ago, I would have said yes, but that was before I fled my sheltered life. Now I have seen the face of war for myself, and I hate what it has done to all of us.''

''You met your major from New York,'' Lizzie remarked dryly. ''That would have never happened except for the war.''

Julia smiled with a secret sparkle in her eyes. ''I cannot think of Rob as my enemy, even if he is a spy like that man said he was. To me, Rob has behaved only with gallantry, kindness and a great deal of understanding.'' She giggled. ''Can you keep a secret?''

Lizzie nodded. If Julia only knew the secrets that she kept! ''Of course!''

''The very first time I ever met Rob, I asked him to…to…ruin me.''

Lizzie gaped at the young woman. ''My word! You are full of surprises, Julia. Please tell me *everything*. And afterward, I think I had better tell *you* a few facts about young men.''

Payton Norwood swirled the amber brandy in the bottom of his snifter, then drank it down in one gulp. Thus fortified, he returned to the financial mess in front of him. His string of racehorses were eating their heads off. Their feed bill was two years in arrears and the price of corn and hay had doubled since December. Also, his grocer in Richmond sent a message informing him that there would be no more credit for Belmont until the current debt had been resolved. Payton balled up that obnoxious note and threw it into the low hearth fire that took off the chill of this dreary February day.

His debts could have been resolved by now if he were married to that wayward cousin of his. Cursing Julia under his breath, he poured more of his dwindling stock of brandy. Someone tapped on his study door.

"Who is it?" he growled. If it was that lazy house-keeper of his with yet another complaint, he'd have her whipped.

Barlow stuck his greasy head around the door. Payton motioned him inside. "Did you find her?"

Silas Barlow, a man of low means and no principles, had spent the past few weeks trolling the high spots and foul dens of Richmond in search of Julia. Payton used his services on the occasions when he required nefarious help of one kind or another.

Without offering the man a seat or a drink, he snarled, "Well?"

Barlow sucked on his teeth before replying. "Yep, she's a pretty little thing. She keeps herself to herself and never goes abroad alone."

Payton knew better than to hurry the man. Barlow turned downright nasty when irritated. "So you've seen her? You're sure it's Miss Chandler?"

Barlow sucked some more, then said. "Yep. Found she had checked into the Spotswood couple of weeks ago."

"Spotswood," Payton repeated. Unfortunately, a very public and respectable place. It would be difficult to drag Julia out of there kicking and screaming.

"But she checked out after one night," Barlow drawled.

Payton frowned. "Where did she go from there?" He drummed his fingers on the desktop.

Barlow stared at the brandy decanter. "Talking sure do give a man a thirst," he observed.

Payton swallowed his ire, and poured a small splash into one of his late father's crystal glasses. Without a word, he pushed it across the desk.

Barlow took a long time savoring his liquor. Payton figured he was planning to ask for more money, and tried to calculate how much ready cash he had on hand.

After draining the last drop, Barlow continued. "She dropped out of sight. For a week I couldn't find her. Even paid a visit to Miss Livy's crib on Locust Alley to see if she had taken on a new girl. She had."

Payton sat up in his chair. Julia in a house of prostitution?

"But it weren't her. Nice-looking gal though. Same color of hair, but not her. But Miss Livy did say something about seeing another redhead visiting down at Libby. She and some of her gals go down there to aggravate those incarcerated Yankees."

Payton sat back, slightly disappointed. Libby Prison— he should have thought of that, since that blasted Yankee major was probably kept there. He just didn't expect that Julia would stoop so low as to visit a prison.

"So you saw her at Libby?"

"Nope, but I did some talking with a couple of the sentries and they sure had seen her. They were most impressed by her, though she had only been there twice."

Payton's fingers drummed faster. "So where is she *now?*"

"I'm coming to that part, but another drop of that firewater would sure help with the telling." Barlow's eyes glinted in the firelight, giving him an uncomfortably feral look.

Payton poured a bit more brandy into the emptied glass, then put the decanter down on the floor behind the desk.

"Please go on," he said. He clenched his teeth to keep himself from hurling invective at his minion.

Barlow sniffed the brandy and hummed under his breath. Then he sipped it for an extraordinarily long time, considering the small amount. Finally, he returned the glass to the desk. "She's staying with Crazy Bet."

Payton racked his memory. An eccentric elderly spinster. "What's her real name?"

Barlow scratched his head. "Can't rightly say, but she lives in a big old house up on Grace Street opposite Saint John's Church. You couldn't miss it even at midnight. I'd like my money now, if you please."

"Not yet." Payton pulled at his nose while he mulled over the information. "How many servants live there?"

Barlow shifted his weight. "Don't know exactly. I've seen a couple of men go in and out. Big fellows, look like they know how to handle themselves in a fight. There's a cook, but she never goes past the backyard. Then there are some other folk—not servants. Mostly young men with their hats pulled low. They come and go."

Payton's frown deepened. It sounded as if Julia had located a fortress to hide in. But if he came in the dead of night and caught the household when they were asleep, he could have Julia bundled into a hack before anyone knew what was up. He studied Barlow.

"I have one more little job for you, my friend, and I will pay you double for all your services."

The ruffian grinned, displaying a gap where one of his front teeth had recently been. "You name it, Mr. Norwood. Old Silas Barlow is your man. And let's seal the bargain with the rest of that poteen."

Chapter Twenty-Four

February 9, 1864
Washington, DC

Major Scott Claypole of the United States Army settled back in his chair inside the warren of the Federal War Department with a great sigh of relief. Last night he had burned his Confederate uniform, though with regret. He had enjoyed masquerading as a general in Richmond. However, the problem of Montgomery still worried him. That man enjoyed unusually good health. He might survive a long stretch in solitary confinement, even on the few crumbs Ross would allow him. Claypole needed to devise a secondary plan that would stop Montgomery if he were ever exchanged or escaped. Using a cipher of his own invention, he hastily scribbled an order to the Pinkerton agents stationed in Virginia and the Carolinas.

"Major Robert Montgomery, late of the Rhinebeck Legion, and operative of this office, has been proven to be a traitor to the government of the United States. Disregard all other messages concerning his loyalty. He is currently in Libby Prison posing as a captured Federal officer but may escape by Confederate design. Advise all unit commanders in your territory. Be on the lookout for Montgomery. He is armed and considered to be extremely dangerous. If sighted, shoot to kill. Reward of $5,000 in gold.''

Claypole reread the directive. Then he recalled that Julia Chandler had also been in the guard room when Montgomery denounced him. He didn't expect her to cause him any trouble, yet that niggling possibility pricked him like a thorn in his foot. He added a final postscript following the major's physical description.

"Montgomery may be accompanied by a young woman, Julia Chandler of Alexandria. About twenty years of age, slim, five feet four or five inches tall. Auburn hair and green eyes."

Just thinking about the delectable Miss Chandler made Claypole ache.

"She is unarmed. Apprehend her, and remand her to my custody at once. Signed, Edwin M. Stanton, Secretary of War."

Chuckling, he pushed himself away from his desk, and headed for the telegraph room. Lieutenant Johnson caught him as he reached the door.

"Colonel Lawrence requests your presence in his office, sir."

"Very good, Lieutenant. I will be there momentarily."

Johnson barred the way. "Begging the major's pardon, but the colonel was most insistent. He said *now*." He looked down at the paper in Claypole's hands. "I would be honored to deliver your message, sir."

Claypole's initial irritation changed to pleasure. How ironic that Montgomery's own cousin would send the order for his doom! He handed the paper to him.

"By all means, but make haste, Johnson. Those instructions are most important and need to be implemented at once.''

Flattered to be doing something important, the gullible young man snapped him a quick salute, then dashed down the hall to the telegraph. Humming under his breath, Claypole knocked on Lawrence's door.

"Enter!" the colonel shouted.

Claypole saluted his superior officer. Only after he had come completely into the room did he notice that several officers from the District Provost Marshal were also in attendance.

Lawrence glared at him, looking like a huge walrus in a frock coat. "Major Scott Claypole, you are hereby under arrest for the crime of high treason against the United States." The colonel flushed red in his face. There was no mistaking the well of deep loathing in his eyes. "You will be taken to the Old Capitol Prison at once where you will await your trial."

A drumming filled Claypole's ears. His vision clouded. He gripped the back of the nearest chair as the two provost marshals closed in around him. "Treason?" He gagged with the bile of fear. "There is some mistake."

Rising from his chair, Lawrence waved several reports at him. "I have information from two disparate authorities in Richmond that you have acted as a double agent for the past two years. You will hear the details in court." He turned to the marshals. "Take this piece of filth away."

Who had informed on him? Montgomery was locked deep underground. Julia Chandler? Claypole dug in his heels. "My uncle will be most displeased by your treatment of me. The charges are utterly false."

Balancing his bulk on his knuckles, Lawrence leaned far over his desk. His anger filled the small room. "For your information, I am acting under the *direct order* of your uncle, Secretary Stanton.''

Claypole's eyes rolled back in his head. He sagged in the grip of the marshals. His comfortable future evaporated.

Richmond, Virginia

Once Lizzie had ascertained Julia's true feelings on the subjects of her handsome major and of her political loyalty, the ardent Unionist had no qualms about enlisting her guest into the inner workings of the mansion on Grace Street. Though Julia loved Virginia as much as Lizzie did, the girl's desire for the return of peace now outweighed her allegiance to the Confederacy's ruinous pursuit of the war. Julia Chandler was not a political animal, but a sweet young girl in the first blush of romance. War and love never made good partners.

This morning, Julia helped Lizzie carry up more bedding and blankets to the secret bedroom under the portico's roof. The last message that Lizzie had received from the prison relayed that the tunnel was almost completed. The men's bid for freedom could happen within the next few days. After three weeks of preparations, just about everything was ready to receive those escapees too sick to travel. Though the day was cold, Lizzie blotted perspiration from her brow.

''I am getting too old for these quick runs up and down stairs,'' she remarked to Julia.

The girl laughed. ''You, Lizzie? I think you will outlive us all.''

''Humph!'' Lizzie replied, feeling every day of her forty-five years.

Wilson rapped on the bedroom's small door. ''Miss

Lizzie? You got a note from Mr. John.'' He thrust out a folded letter to her.

''Is that your brother?'' Julia asked. She had heard a number of stories about John Newton Van Lew, who hid from the war on the family's vegetable farm east of Richmond.

''Yes.'' Lizzie pulled down her spectacles from their perch on the top of her head and read her brother's anguished scrawl. ''Damnation!''

Both Wilson and Julia gaped at her. ''John's received notification of conscription,'' she explained, growing red in the face. ''They want him to fight against the Union, for heaven's sake. He's worked himself up into a lather, and wants me out there right away.''

Lizzie shook her head over the note. John always came running to her for help, even as a small boy with skinned knees. She crossed the hall to the third-floor window where she surveyed the panorama of Richmond and the James River below her. The winter sun shone brightly in a clear blue sky, hinting the return of warmer weather soon. Tuesday morning, and nothing unusual to be seen along the riverfront. The clip-clop of a horse and wagon along Grace Street disturbed a few ravens, but all else appeared serene. Lizzie decided that it would be safe to leave Julia for an overnight.

''I shall pack a small bag, Wilson. Tell Christopher to hitch up the horse and I'll be down directly.'' Turning to Julia, she gave her a cheerful smile. ''You'll be just fine here, my dear. Stay indoors and keep Mother entertained. Don't breathe a word about John's latest predicament or she will worry needlessly.''

Julia's voice dropped to a whisper. ''Will he have to go off to war?''

''Hush, child!'' Lizzie scolded with fondness. ''Of

course he won't. I have General John Winder's protection—in writing, no less—and I am sure he will extend that courtesy to John. Heavens! My brother is too old to shoulder a gun. He's likely to blow off a toe or two if he tried to shoot the thing. This is all a tempest in a teapot.''

Julia rubbed her arms. "I do hope so," she murmured.

Lizzie hugged her. "Now put on your best face for Mother, and I'll be back home before you miss me. Wilson and Mary will be here with you as well, so you have nothing to fear. I am afraid that it will be a very quiet, boring day for you.''

Then Lizzie scurried down the hall to fabricate some little story for Mother's ear. No need to upset her—at least, not yet.

Rob awoke from his fitful doze at the sound of a key scraping in the lock of his tiny cell. His stomach growled for food. All he had eaten was some stale corn bread and water. He scrubbed the sleep from his face as the door swung back.

"I do hope you enjoyed your rest, Montgomery," remarked Erasmus Ross in his usual sarcastic tone. "You're going to need it.''

Rob squinted in the dim light provided by a candle lantern hung on the wall outside his cell. "Come to gloat?" he asked the clerk.

Ross rasped a dry laugh. "Haven't the time for that pleasure tonight. Well, don't stare at me like a landed shad. Let's go.''

Rob stumbled to his feet and practically fell out the door. He hated displaying his weakened condition, especially in front of this pitiless man. He blinked several times to adjust his eyes to the flickering light.

"Here," Ross handed Rob his greatcoat and hat from upstairs. "Don't stand there, man. Come on!"

Rob shook his head to clear his fuzzy brain. "Where are you taking me?" he asked warily. "What time is it?" He noticed that the usual sentry was gone from his chair.

Ross strode down the stone passageway. "It's just past seven."

Draping his coat around his shoulders, Rob hurried in Ross's wake. "Morning or evening?" he asked. He could see his breath in the dank basement.

"Evening," Ross barked. "Not up there," he added when Rob paused at the bottom of the stairs that led up to the ground floor. "You're going out a different exit." He chuckled.

Rob's empty stomach knotted up. He was going to be executed in this hole. That's why the guard was gone! He looked around the yawning storage room for something he could use to defend himself.

Ross put his hands on his hips. "Listen, you fool, because I'm only going to say this once. Your friends are breaking out tonight."

Good God! He knew about the tunnel!

Ross continued without a pause. "There's no point in keeping you behind. You'd only cause me more trouble. Yes, I know exactly who you are, Major, and why you're here. You did a good job briefing the men. They're ready. Surprised? A rat can't sneeze in Libby without me knowing it."

He pointed to the thick oak door at the far end of the room. "Through there is Rat Hell. The first group is going out now."

He pointed to the ceiling. "I have allowed the prisoners the privilege of presenting a musical and dance tonight. It has been underway for a quarter of an hour already, and should provide the necessary distraction for your safe get-away. Understand? Now go!''

"Who are you?" Rob asked softly.

"Your bloody guardian angel, and the devil to pay, if you don't get a move on." He started up the stairs, then looked back over his shoulder. "And give Miss Chandler my compliments when next you see her. Fine girl. Too good for you, of course, but marry her, if she'll have you!"

Rob drew himself up. "See you in hell, Ross," he said, giving him the soldier's salute.

Ross returned the honor. "I'll be dancing on the coals." With a silent laugh, he disappeared into the darkness above the stairs.

Rob broke into a wheezing sprint down the passageway, Cautiously, he pulled open the door. Several rats squealed at the intrusion. At the entrance to the tunnel, a dozen pairs of frightened eyes stared at him.

Grinning, Rob held up his hand. "Good evening, gentlemen, I trust I am not too late for the party?"

Payton lounged against the red velvet upholstery of his booth and lit up a smuggled Havana cigar. With a contented sigh, he blew the smoke into the air above his head. Dinner at the Oriental Saloon was always a pleasure. The terrapin soup had been especially good and the baked shad fish was tender and flaky the way he liked it. A juicy slab of beef steak with potatoes, onions, carrots and snaps, all washed down with a bottle of good claret. Now he dawdled over his second glass of French brandy while listening to his dinner companions regale each other with stories of their latest conquests, both financial and feminine.

Payton poked a finger into his waistcoat pocket, extracted his father's gold watch, opened the lid and squinted at the time. At first he thought it read quarter of four. He rubbed his bleary eyes and looked again. Twenty minutes past nine o'clock. Plenty of time. He wanted to wait until Lizzie Van Lew and her household had gone to bed before he banged on their door. He would have the best chance of whisking Julia out of there before that crazy old bat or her servants knew what had happened if he caught them all in bed.

"Champagne!" he called to the waiter.

"What are you celebrating, Norwood?" asked Beau Reynolds, a lifelong chum of Payton's.

"My impending nuptials," Payton replied in a jovial mood.

Beau pretended shocked surprise. "What? I thought the lady had declined your offer."

Even though the quip was said in jest, it still stung Payton like the bite of a mosquito. He covered his embarrassment with a laugh. "Well, it seems that the lady has changed her mind."

Beau held up his flute for the waiter to pour. "Bully for you, Payton! Here's to your future happiness!"

The third member of the party, even more inebriated than the others, waved his flute in the air. "And good luck to the new Mrs. Norwood. God knows she'll need it."

Payton curled his lip, but said nothing. After tonight's work, he would be too rich to care what anyone said to him.

For some unknown reason, sleep eluded Julia. After a day of reading to the elderly Mrs. Van Lew and playing endless games of whist with her, she should be exhausted. Perhaps the emptiness of the big house made her restless. When Saint Paul's distant bells chimed nine o'clock, Julia decided to get up. Wrapped in her dressing gown and slippers, she lit her bedside candle and quietly descended the curving grand staircase. Shadows jumped away from her as she crossed the wide hallway and let herself into the library.

Lizzie's father had left his children with not only a vast wealth of money and bonds, but also books. Julia could have lived happily in his library for years to come. She turned up several of the gas lamps, then ran her fingers along the spines of the books on the nearest shelf. She took down one and thumbed through its slightly musty pages.

It looked interesting. If it wasn't, at least it would put her to sleep. Julia curled herself up in the well-worn leather wing chair, put a knitted afghan over her legs and began to read. Immersed in the machinations of Henry VI's knotty love life, she failed to hear Wilson's rap on the door frame.

"Miss Julia?" he said in a low voice.

Julia jumped. The heavy book fell onto the thick pile carpet. "Wilson! You scared me out of nine lives in one fell swoop. I'm very sorry if I had awakened you."

He shook his head, but did not treat her with his usual smile. "No, miss. I'm wide awake." Then he whispered, "We have visitors at the side door."

"Visitors?" she repeated. Her stomach churned. "Who on earth comes calling at this hour?" *Not with Lizzie gone!*

"It's happened, Miss Julia," Wilson whispered. "The prison breakout. It came sooner than Miss Lizzie expected. There are two men at the door."

His words galvanized her into action. "We must get them inside. It's colder than Russia out there. They'll freeze to death." She scrambled under the chair to locate one of her slippers.

Wilson finally smiled. "Oh, they're inside the door,

miss. In the mudroom. They're a mess and feeling mighty poorly from the look of them.''

Julia turned down the gas lights, grabbed her candle then hurried past him toward the back stairs. She tried to re-member everything that Lizzie had prepared for the escape. ''Is Mary awake?''

Wilson kept up with her. ''Yes, she's cleaning them off now.''

Julia shot him a quizzical look, not quite understanding what he meant. ''We must get their beds warmed. And hot water bottles for their feet. They must be half frozen. And some hot soup. And fresh clothes. Where did Lizzie say she put the clean shirts and underdrawers?''

Before giving Wilson time to answer, she pushed open the swinging door that led through the butler's pantry. In the mudroom, two men, covered from head to toe in dirt and globs of mud, struggled out of their caked boots and socks.

Julia came to a complete standstill. ''Oh, lordy,'' she breathed.

The taller man looked up, and grinned at her; his teeth shone white against the layers of dirt and ragged beard.

''Good evening, Miss Julia. I believe it's ten o'clock. Am I late?''

''Rob!'' In one forward motion, Julia flung herself into his embrace.

Chapter Twenty-Five

With efficiency born of practice, Mary set up a tin bath-tub on a sheet inside the safety of the blacked-out parlor. When clean clothes, hot water, and lye soap had been assembled for Rob and his friend, Stu Cramer, Wilson sent the women out of the room.

"These gentlemen are not going to strip down with you two standing there. Now, shoo!" Wilson flapped his hands as if his wife and Julia were a pair of hens.

Once back in the kitchen, Mary heated up a kettle of soup on the large potbellied stove. Julia nudged the heap of muddy uniforms with the toe of her slipper. "I suppose we should scrape and boil these," she suggested, though it occurred to her that she had not the slightest idea how to boil anything. Hettie had never allowed Julia or Carolyn near her stove.

"Ha!" Mary said out of the side of her mouth. "No use in wasting the time and the water, Miss Julia. Those clothes are fit for nothing but burning." She pulled a pair of poultry shears from one of the kitchen drawers. "You can start with these. Make the pieces small to burn better."

Since she was already covered in grime from Rob's embrace, Julia sat down cross-legged on the tile floor and hacked at the sodden wool pants and coats. The work was considerably harder than snipping embroidery threads or hemming dresses.

"So that's your man, Miss Julia?" Mary asked as she chopped at the clothing with a long kitchen knife.

Julia blushed. "I'm afraid that he doesn't belong to me, but yes, that's Major Montgomery."

"He's fine-looking, even under all that mud. I expect he'll clean up pretty good." She laughed. "And he's yours, that's for sure. Just ripe for the taking. All you have to do is look at his face to see that."

Julia bent her head over her task. "Maybe after the war. We'll see then," she murmured.

Mary tossed a hunk of cloth into the glowing belly of the stove. "I doubt that man is going to wait for peacetime or anything else. You'll see."

The front doorbell chimed. The two women froze. "More escapees?" Julia asked, getting up and brushing off some of the dirt.

Mary shook her head. "Don't you answer it, Miss Julia. Nothing good ever comes in the front door after dark. I'll get Wilson."

Clutching the shears, Julia followed Mary up the back stairs and into the central hall. The front door shuddered under repeated kicks and blows of a cane. The chimes jangled. Wilson, his brown eyes hooded like a hawk, emerged from the parlor, followed by Rob and Stu who were now washed though still unshaven. They were half-dressed in fresh long johns and wrapped in blankets.

"Open it," said Stu, "it must be more of the boys."

Both Rob and Wilson shook their heads. "We were the only two to come here," Rob replied. "Most everyone else was to fan out over Church Hill and head for the Mechanicsville Turnpike. Got to get as many of the men as possible away from the city before dawn.''

''Besides,'' added Wilson, ''people always know to come to the side door. Front door is for Richmond white folks in the daylight. Miss Lizzie never opens the front door after dark, and I'm not going to start now.''

Julia drew closer to Rob. ''But what if it's someone who's been hurt in the escape? Maybe he was shot by a guard and is confused.''

''Not likely,'' Stu spoke up in a voice hoarse from a deep cough. ''Any time the Rebs have discovered an escape, they've rung every bell in the city and called out the hounds. Whips up a real hullabaloo. Listen, the streets are still quiet, except on your doorstep.''

''Open up!'' shouted a man out front. ''Lizzie Van Lew! You have got something that's mine and I've come to get her!''

Julia sagged against Rob. ''Hellfire! It's Payton Norwood! How did he ever find me?''

Rob opened his blanket and wrapped her protectively against him. Though Julia's nerves were stretched to breaking, she still felt a shock of forbidden excitement run though her when his thinly clad thigh pressed against her. His strong body gave her courage, and made her heart skip a beat.

Wilson wrinkled his forehead. ''What's he want with you?''

''My inheritance,'' she whispered, afraid that Payton might hear her voice though the crack under the door. ''He'll get it if he can marry me, but I would rather die first. The varmint's a bully at heart.''

''I can hear that,'' agreed Mary. ''What are we going to do with him? He's bound to wake up the Logans next door, and they won't take too kindly to all that racket.''

Stu coughed into his blanket.

Julia looked at the feverish man. "You two should be in bed before you both catch a worse chill. We've got everything ready upstairs."

Mary took Stu around the waist and guided him toward the staircase. "Now you come along with me and we'll fix you up fine. Major, don't you tarry none. You don't look too good yourself, you know."

Rob held Julia tighter. "Wilson," he whispered. "Blow out the candles. Now, is there a gun in the house?" The man nodded. "Good. Please find it for me. I may be winged on one side, but I used to be able to load and shoot with either hand."

Julia shivered and wrapped her arms around Rob's waist. She looked up at him. "You're going to sh...*shoot* Payton?"

He brushed a quick kiss on the top of her hair. She held him tighter. Her skin prickled with the heat of his body. She wanted to twist herself around him like a vine around a tree trunk.

"He deserves a good round of buckshot," Rob whispered in her ear. His breath warmed and tickled her. "But I don't intend to blow a hole through Miss Lizzie's door. Only if he breaks in. Then it's justifiable."

Wilson returned with an old-fashioned Mississippi percussion-lock rifle and a box of cartridges. "You remember that man I saw hanging around the house the other day, Miss Julia?" he whispered as he handed the ammunition to Rob. "I saw him sneaking across the portico out back. Don't you worry. The door's locked and barred, and I got my cudgel right handy. He won't get in." He glided away down the darkened hall.

Rob passed his blanket to Julia. Then he tore off the top of a cartridge with his teeth, poured the powder and shot down the barrel then wadded the paper down after it with the ramrod. She marveled how dexterous he was with only minimal use of his right hand. Then he pulled a side chair to the center of the hall, and crouched down behind it with the gun barrel resting on the seat.

Just then, old Mrs. Van Lew called from the top of the staircase. "Who's down there?"

"It's Lizzie's mother," Julia whispered to Rob.

He glanced up at the tiny glow of a candle shining over the balustrade. "You'd better go stay with her. Don't worry about Norwood. He won't get by me." He pressed a hard kiss on her lips. "Now hurry!"

Outside, Payton's blows increased in intensity while his language descended in vulgarity. Julia grabbed her candlestick and ran down the hall and up the stairs. Midway, she paused and looked back over her shoulder. The silver spill of the moonlight through the front parlor windows outlined Rob's coiled body. A wave of pride and love washed over Julia. No other woman in history ever had such a gallant, brave chevalier as this man, who guarded her safety with one good hand, an old gun and a world of courage.

She would marry him in half a minute, if he ever asked her.

Mrs. Van Lew called again. Shaking off her romantic fantasy, Julia hurried to the second floor. Lizzie's redoubtable mother had armed herself with her cane and an empty enamel chamber pot. The sight would have been ludicrous if the situation wasn't so fraught with danger. Payton's disturbance could bring the night watchmen, which would be disastrous for the two Yankees in the house.

"It's all right, Mrs. Van Lew," Julia soothed as she helped the old woman back into her bed. "It's some crazy drunk fool who has confused our house with his own, I expect."

The sweet-faced little lady impaled Julia with a piercing look. "If my husband were still alive, he would have shot that man by now so a body could get some rest."

Julia returned a wry smile. "It'll be just fine. Wilson is awake and will take care of him." She thought it prudent not to mention the presence of the escaped prisoners under their roof. She had no idea how much the mother knew of her daughter's secret life as a spy for the Union.

Mrs. Van Lew rearranged her pillows. "A fine time for Lizzie to go off to the farm for some chickens," she huffed, "especially when there's an ornery rooster at the front door."

Julia sat beside the bed and held Mrs. Van Lew's fragile hand. The loud ticking of the mantel clock lulled them both. Julia yawned.

She awoke with a jolt just as the pink of pre-dawn washed over the treetops. Her candle had gutted in its holder, and Mrs. Van Lew snored slightly amid the froth of her lace-edged pillows. Julia rubbed the sleep from her eyes, then glanced at the clock. She had slept for nearly five hours! She pulled on her robe, then tiptoed down to the staircase. Peeking around the curve of the banister, she saw the side chair standing solitary guard in the middle of the downstairs hallway, but Rob was not there. A quick glance at the front door confirmed that Payton had gone without evidence of a forcible entry. Had Rob been arrested by Payton? A cold fear lodged in her stomach.

Wrapping her robe tighter around her, Julia scurried up to the third floor. The secret door at the end of the hall was closed and, to the casual glance, it looked like part of the molding. Holding her breath, Julia opened it slowly on its well-oiled hinges. In the far bed, Stu slept heavily, curled up under several blankets. Julia exhaled with relief when she saw that Rob was in his bed as well, or rather he had fallen across it and his single blanket had slipped half off. The old rifle lay on the floor.

I wonder how long he sat downstairs listening to Payton.

Tenderness engulfed her, especially when she noticed his bare feet hanging over the edge of the mattress. For some inexplicable reason, she found the sight of his toes particularly adorable. She really should get him under the covers before he froze, but Julia had never before been inside a man's bedroom—especially when two scantily-clothed men were also in residence. She rubbed her hands together while she tried to figure out the best way to pull the blankets around him. At that indecisive moment, Rob rolled over.

He squinted at her, then grinned through his scraggly beard. "Evening, Miss Julia. Have you come to have your dastardly way with me?"

Instead of being shocked, she giggled behind her hand. "It's nearly daylight," she whispered with a quick glance at Stu, "and I only wanted to see…that is, to make sure you were all right."

He pulled himself into a sitting position and ran his hand through his hair. Julia picked up the blanket and dropped it lightly over his shoulders. She wanted to touch him, to enfold him in her arms and warm him, yet she held back, suddenly shy. His weight loss in prison accentuated his classic features and, at the same time, revealed the energy and power that lay within him. He was a lone wolf facing the world on his own terms.

Rob's gaze roved over her and his smile broadened. "You are the best sight I have ever seen this early in the morning." The warmth in his liquid-dark eyes beckoned her closer. Julia's question of Payton's whereabouts evaporated.

The silence stretched and encompassed them. He held out his hand to her. Julia placed her fingertips in his palm. His long fingers folded around hers and squeezed with a gentle invitation. Hot blood, as if charged with lightning, surged from her fingers, up her arm and radiated throughout her whole body. Her inner core blazed. Rob bent over and kissed her fingers, one at a time, with agonizing deliberation. Her heartbeat pounded in her temples; her breath almost stopped. Julia felt herself drowning. Leaning toward him, she moistened her lips for his kiss.

Rob raised his head, then he looked over her shoulder and his expression changed into a sheepish grin. "Good morning, Miss Lizzie," he said with the innocent air of a small boy trapped with a warm apple pie. "Welcome home." He released Julia's hand with a squeeze of farewell.

Travel-stained and tired around the eyes, Lizzie folded her arms across her bosom. Julia blushed. How long had she been standing there? Lizzie studied the pair speculatively. "Yes, Wilson told me it was an interesting night."

In the other bed, Stu coughed in his sleep and turned over. Lizzie lowered her voice. "When the two of you are dressed in more respectable attire, come down to the dining room. Mary will have breakfast on the table at eight." Her bright eyes sharpened. "I fear I have dire news that may force a change of plan for both of you." With that warning, she left them.

Rob covered himself with the blanket. "I'm sorry, Julia," he mumbled, looking away. His neck reddened.

Julia swallowed down her acute disappointment. Was he sorry that his seduction had been thwarted, or sorry that he had even thought of it? She tossed her loose hair out of her eyes. "Of course," she murmured. "Please excuse me." She fled the room before he could say anything else.

As she donned her green plaid day dress, Julia chided herself for her lack of discretion. What did Lizzie think of her now? Would she send Julia on her way?

She brushed out her tousled curls. And what did Rob think of her? Would they have really become lovers as Lizzie had so graphically described to Julia? For a well-bred spinster, Lizzie Van Lew knew a great deal about subjects no proper lady ought to know. Staring at her reflection in the looking glass, Julia realized that she would have indeed allowed Rob to seduce her. She chewed on her lower lip. She'd become a hussy like the women outside the prison.

Yet the prospect of giving her virginity to Rob did not shock her, as it once might have. An hour ago, the idea of making love with him had seemed the most wonderful, natural thing to do. Pressing her cool palms against her burning cheeks, Julia wondered how she could possibly sit down opposite him at breakfast as if nothing had happened.

But nothing is exactly what *did* happen, thanks to Lizzie's untimely arrival. With her emotions swimming in confusion, Julia put up her hair in a net and faced the day with the firm resolution not to make a fool of herself again—no matter what.

Lizzie, looking clean and refreshed, gave her attention to her soft-boiled egg when Julia slid into her chair. Rob, across the table, flashed the brief grin of a fellow conspirator. Julia lowered her head; her heart turned over. He had shaved away his dark beard. With the astonishment of sudden discovery, she realized that she had never once seen Rob in the full light of day.

Good gracious, he was very handsome!

When she looked up from her plate, she caught him

staring at her with widened eyes. She instinctively patted her hair, hoping that she met with his approval.

"I'm afraid all we have this morning is corn bread, a bit of bacon, warmed-over peanut soup, soft-boiled eggs—and tea," Lizzie announced with a decided disgust over the tea. She passed Julia a crystal bowl of preserves. "If you slather enough blackberry jam on the bread, it might make up for the lack of butter."

"Thank you," Julia replied in a barely audible voice.

She waited for Lizzie's lecture or for the dire news, but her hostess only said, "Pass the salt, please."

The clink and scrape of silverware against the china plates sounded raucous in Julia's ears. Back at home, Mother had never allowed deadly silences, but had kept the house lively with her histrionics. When Julia stole another quick glance at Rob, she saw him shifting in his chair and fiddling with his fork. His obvious discomfort made Julia feel, perversely, much better.

To break the tension, Julia asked Rob, "What happened to Payton?"

Lizzie replaced her cup in its saucer. "I had wondered that myself."

He dabbed his lips with his napkin, then grinned. "Shortly after Miss Julia went up to stay with your mother," he began, with a pointed reference to Julia's absence from his side, "Mr. Norwood became…um…violently ill. I suspect a surfeit of rich food washed down by too much wine. Then I heard a crash against the door, then silence. Fearing that he might have injured himself, I took the liberty of peeking out. He had merely gone to sleep on the mat." Rob grinned and a devilish look stole into his eyes.

"Since Mr. Norwood has been nothing but a thorn in

Julia's life, I took the opportunity of doing something permanent about him.''

Lizzie adjusted her spectacles on her nose. ''And that was?''

''I hope you do not mind, ma'am, but I helped myself to some of your plain stationery. I sketched out a counterfeit escape map and a list of so-called 'safe houses'. Then I stuffed them into his shoe.''

Lizzie chuckled.

''Naturally, I hoped that the night watch would find him, which they did soon after that. When they discovered the interesting evidence sticking out of Norwood's shoe, they immediately decided to take him to the provost marshal's office. They never bothered knocking on your door. After they left, I went back to my own bed—with Stu,'' he added quickly.

Lizzie's eyes sparkled. ''Once the breakout has been discovered, I suspect that dear Mr. Norwood will soon find himself a resident of Castle Thunder for a while,'' she observed, naming Richmond's infamous lockup for political and civilian prisoners. ''How very clever of you, Major!''

Just then, the bells of Saint Paul's pealed an alarm. The remaining few other churches, which had not yet donated their bells to the cannon foundry, took up the call. Firehouses added to the noise. Julia clenched her napkin in her lap. ''What is it? Are the Yankees attacking the city?''

Lizzie spread more jam on her muffin. ''In the dead of winter? Of course not!'' She smiled at Rob. ''I expect that Colonel Thomas Turner has discovered that some of his guests are missing. This means we will have to act quickly.''

Gasping, Julia glanced at Rob. ''Will the authorities come here?''

Lizzie munched her bread, swallowed then replied. "Of course. I am always on the top of their suspect list—but it will take General Winder some time to organize the dragoons and the city guard before they come round to visit. Captain Cramer will be perfectly safe in his hideaway over the portico. It's *you*, Major, who is in the greater danger."

Chapter Twenty-Six

Lizzie handed Rob a wrinkled broadside. "One of your Pinkerton agents gave me that while I was at the farm. He said that copies had been circulated throughout all the Union lines in Virginia and the Carolinas." She turned to Julia. "I fear your major is a marked man."

Disbelief jolted Rob as he read a detailed description of himself under the inch-high heading: "Traitor!" "Shoot on sight—shoot to kill—$5,000 reward in gold." The black newsprint virtually dripped poison. He swore softly when he saw that Julia was also named and described, and grimaced when he read Stanton's signature. Claypole had done a good job to save his skin. Rob would be shot down by his own side before he even reached Williamsburg. His anger choked his breath.

Julia's eyes reflected her bewilderment. "What is it?" she asked in a frightened voice.

Wordlessly, he handed her the sheet. She moaned when she read it. Rob floundered in a whirlwind of anger and confusion. He had the sensation that the walls of the dining room were closing in on him. His single overriding thought was immediate escape—but where? And what about Julia? The shock had drained the blood from her face.

She raised her head. "How?" she silently mouthed.

Rob gripped the silver knife in his good hand. "Claypole," he growled, wishing he could impale the turncoat. "He's a double agent," he explained to Lizzie. "We saw each other in Libby when he visited, disguised as a Confederate general. Since he knows I will denounce him the minute I return to Washington, he has taken evasive action."

Lizzie regarded him with a steely look. "You realize that you cannot return now, don't you, Rob? With that high a reward, you are a target too good to ignore." She pushed aside her breakfast dishes and placed her elbows on the table. "So the question is, where will you go?"

Rob shook his head slowly. If he stayed in Richmond, he was bound to be recaptured and sent back to Libby. There he would rot until the end of the war, or die of fever and malnutrition. No one in the Office of Military Intelligence would lift a finger to save him now. If he took to the road and headed for New York, how far could he get before someone killed him for the five thousand dollars in gold? Even if he were captured alive, how could he defend himself at his court marshal when the formidable Secretary of War wanted his head on a silver platter?

"You will have to go abroad," said Lizzie. "When the war is over, perhaps cooler heads will listen to reason and it will be safe for you to return."

He gazed across the damask-covered table at the most wonderful woman he had ever known. "Julia?" he asked. "What do *you* want to do?"

"She can remain here with me," Lizzie snapped, watching his reaction closely. "After all, she's not wanted for treason. It's a question of loyalties," she continued. "Now comes the truth of it. Where do yours lie, Major? Julia?"

Julia stretched her hand out to him. "It breaks my heart

to say this, but I will stay here. It's better for Rob that way. They are looking for *two* of us and he can move faster without me.'' Though her bearing was stiff and proud, a glazed look of despair spread across her face.

His soul wrenched in two. ''I want to keep you out of danger,'' he explained in a voice hoarse with emotion he could not name. He laid his hand over hers and stared deeply into those fathomless pools of green.

A little sob escaped Julia's throat. The sound tore at him. How could he abandon her in Richmond? Turn away from the person who had taught him to live again?

''Humph,'' Lizzie snorted, looking from one to the other. ''It's plain to *me* that both of you are afraid to say what you *really* want. Well, my dears, there is no time for sweet speeches and shilly-shallying. It is this simple: if you separate now, you will probably never see each other again. Before this madness is over, it is likely that one of you will die.''

Julia stared at her, openmouthed. Closing his eyes, Rob nodded. He understood exactly what Miss Lizzie meant. He was a live target.

''Harsh words, but that is the way of war,'' Lizzie continued. ''So, make up your minds now, then don't look back. Rob must be at the depot by noon, before Winder's men pay me a call.''

Rob shot her a quizzical look. ''What depot? I can't stay here, I can't go south and I can't go back. How do you propose I leave the country?''

Lizzie's eyes sparkled as if she found perverse pleasure in their predicament. ''On a ship bound to the Bahamas, of course—unless you would prefer to walk to Mexico.''

''A blockade runner!'' Julia exclaimed, comprehension igniting her hope. ''Oh, Rob, you can do it!'' She squeezed his hand.

"Will you come with me?" Their eyes met and held each other. He gripped her tiny hand in his. "I need you, more than you can possibly know. Please?"

Lizzie slammed down her hands on the table. "For heaven's sake, Rob, how can she answer that when she doesn't know what's in your heart? Do you love her or not?"

Julia jumped at the sound, but Rob held steady and never took his eyes from her. "I do, Miss Lizzie," he replied, speaking directly to Julia. "I love you, Julia Chandler, with every fiber of my being. Will you come with me, even though I'm a Yankee?"

Julia held him tighter. Her eyes glazed with tears.

"Well, Julia?" Lizzie rapped on the table with her spoon. "He's asking. Are you taking?"

"Now and forever," she breathed. "I see no enemy here, only the man I love."

Rob wanted to shout, to dance around the table, to give everyone in the house a kiss. He started to rise, but Lizzie thumped the table again. "Not now, Major! You will have time enough to bill and coo on the ship. What we must do now is get the two of you ready."

Julia jumped up from her chair, knocking it over. "I'll pack at once!"

Lizzie held up her hands. "No, I'm afraid you are going to have to travel very lightly—and as a boy." Ignoring their shocked expressions, she hurried on. "The broadside describes a major in the Federal army, accompanied by a young lady with long auburn hair. Even if we disguised Rob as a Confederate, his lame hand would betray his identity. So we will change who you are. Julia will be a young farmboy—and you, Rob, will be his mother." She smiled with triumph.

Rob didn't know whether to laugh or swear. "Miss

Lizzie, how in the hell do you plan to do that? I'm over six feet tall.''

The "old cat" had a plan that she put into action before either of them found their wits to object. Within the next half hour, Mary had cut a foot off Julia's beautiful hair, the shimmering tresses lying in pools around her feet. Instead of her pretty green dress and petticoats, Julia now wore a large red flannel man's shirt stuck into blue wool trousers that had been cut down from a military uniform. Only the suspenders kept Julia's clothes together. A short gray sack coat—another piece of Confederate uniform without the buttons and piping—a battered brown felt hat and a handful of dirt smudged on her face completed Julia's transformation. She wore several pairs of wool socks in order to fit into the walking boots.

Julia studied her new appearance in the mirror, wrinkled her nose and sighed. "Wouldn't old Melinda Winstead laugh herself into a stitch if she could see me now." She gingerly touched her shorn hairline.

Rob snatched a brief kiss before he replied. "I think she would be pea-green, as you Southerners say, since you're the one having all the fun while she sits at home, bored fit to die." When Julia cocked her head at him, he explained. "She told me so herself upon our last meeting."

Now that he had declared his love for her, Rob wanted nothing more than to hold her close and kiss her over and over. However, Lizzie gave him no time. While Rob shaved close to the skin, the surprising lady pulled out of her clothes chest the most outlandish garb he had ever seen.

"You'll be a chinquapin woman," she explained, shaking out a large pair of buckskin trousers. "I must admit those farmwives dress more practically than we town ladies do. You step into these and this—'' She handed him an oversized dress made of faded yellow-and-red calico.

Rob lifted an eyebrow as he held up the garment against his long body. The hem came down just below his knees. He hoped the buckskins fit. Lizzie tossed him a knitted brown shawl and a dirty white apron. She pronounced his own shoes "good enough."

"You can put a few personal odds and ends in this basket, but be sure to keep it covered so your fellow travelers don't see your razor," she rattled on. "And shave often!"

"Wilson will cut you a walking stick you can use to hunch over. Limp a little. Keep your head down and don't talk. Your New York accent will be a dead giveaway. Let Julia do all your talking for you." Lizzie shot him a wicked grin. "After all, she *is* the man of the family."

Rob exploded with indignation when Lizzie handed him a wide-brimmed calico sunbonnet. "You cannot expect me to wear *that!*"

Stu, who observed the proceedings, laughed so hard he had to grasp the doorjamb. "Hell's bells, Rob, you sure look a pretty picture."

Rob bared his teeth. "You will *never* tell a living soul about this."

Lizzie put her hands on her hips. "I expect that Captain Cramer will dine out on this story alone for years to come. Don't argue, Rob, there's no time." She consulted her watchpin. "You finish putting yourself together while I get some papers you will need. Come along, Captain. You should know by now that ladies like to dress in private."

Stu laughed all the way out the door and down the hall.

Alone with his new identity, Rob realized exactly how Julia must feel without her long hair. At least, she looked adorable, though he would never dare tell her. But what was she going to think of him?

He tried on the bonnet and had to admit that it hid his masculine haircut and features well enough. Then he pulled it off. He was not wearing that thing any longer than he had to.

When Julia saw him come down the stairs, it took every ounce of willpower to keep her face straight. Only the thought of what lay ahead of them sobered her. They were not off to a costume party, but fleeing for their lives—and their future together. Rob had said he loved her, but nothing about marriage. But she couldn't worry about that now. Just take one day at a time.

Lizzie met them at the bottom of the staircase with a packet wrapped in a piece of oilskin. "Do not lose this. In it are two documents signed by the British Consul here attesting to the fact that Mrs. Sarah Broadfoot and her son, Sam, are under the protection of Her Royal Majesty's government."

"How did you get them?" Rob asked, examining the papers. "The signature looks real and so does the stamp."

"Of course it's real!" Lizzie huffed. "Mr. Crindland, the consul, is very fond of fried chicken and I make extra sure that he always has fresh chickens to dine on. I never know just when I might need some help from the British. Now pay attention. Here are your travel passes for Wilmington from the provost marshal. General Winder is a delightful old gentleman and has been my guest here on many occasions," she added.

Julia stuffed the passes in her shirt pocket. This adventure was really going to happen. Her heart pounded.

Lizzie's instructions flowed faster. "A packet of Confederate money—it's all I can spare so use it wisely. Julia, you have your greenbacks? Good. Finally, a note for the harbormaster at Wilmington. He'll get you on board the next runner out. You'll have to pay him extra, of course. After that, everything will be in God's hands.''

Julia glanced at Rob. He gave her a smile of encouragement.

Lizzie stood on tiptoe and kissed Rob on the cheek. ''Good luck and take good care of Julia, or I'll find you later and have your hide.''

He hugged her. ''Yes, ma'am,'' he replied in falsetto, though his eyes remained serious.

When Lizzie turned to her, Julia felt her tears welling up. Putting her arms around the older woman, she whispered, ''I can never fully repay you for all your kindness. As soon as I can get my legacy, I'll send you some money. Thank you so very much for everything.''

Lizzie hugged her, then gave her a shake. ''Keep your money. You are going to need every penny for your new life. You be good and take care of that man. Keep him out of trouble,'' she replied briskly.

After a round of goodbyes with Stu, Mary, Wilson and Christopher, Lizzie announced that it was time to stop the caterwauling and be off.

Her last-minute instructions flew faster than a hailstorm. ''Put on that bonnet right now, Rob. Look old. Julia, rub the dirt around your cheeks. You are a little streaky. You will catch your train at the Richmond and Petersburg depot on Byrd Street.'' She pointed out the general direction. ''Wilson will follow behind you at a distance to see you safe to the station. Don't look around for him. Remember, you are from the country and are new to Richmond. Don't get friendly with strangers.''

Julia puffed out her cheeks with a couple of deep

breaths. The first step out the door would be the hardest. The palms of her hands sweated.

Lizzie opened the side door. "Stay out of the dragoons' way. I imagine they are scouring the city now, looking for escaped prisoners. If you see any of your friends, Rob, don't signal to them. You don't know them."

Still spewing advice and directions, she followed them out as far as the back gate. "You've got food in your basket, but don't gobble it all at once. It has to last, maybe until Nassau. God bless both of you—and Rob, be sure and *marry that girl!*" She slammed the gate behind them.

Julia's cheeks burned. She didn't dare look at Rob, but her pulse throbbed with pent-up anticipation. She waited for him to say something—to ask her to marry him. They walked for several blocks in heart-stopping silence. Beside her, Rob stared straight ahead and hunched over his walking stick until they arrived at a busy intersection. Then he slipped his hand—his wounded one, sheathed in a black knit fingerless glove—through the crook of her elbow as naturally as an elderly woman would take the arm of a strong boy.

"Here's my hand, my little darling," he crackled in his falsetto, "Help this great fool across the street." He peeked around the brim of his bonnet. "Will you also take my hand and walk down the aisle with me in a church in Nassau?" he continued in a hoarse whisper. "And will you help me down the road for the rest of our lives?"

Julia's heart soared right up to her throat. "Are you asking me to *marry* you?"

"Reckon so," he cackled like an ancient crone.

Julia touched the brim of her hat with trembling fingers. "Then I would be honored, sir," she whispered as they turned down Eighth Street toward the depot.

Rob squeezed her arm. "Good. I look forward to my loving little wife having her dastardly way with me." He winked.

Epilogue

January 1866
Alexandria, Virginia

"Papa!" Carolyn dashed up the stairs to her father's study. Without bothering to knock, she burst into the room. Dr. Chandler looked up from his newspaper. He had aged a great deal since last April when Clara had died of an apoplectic fit following the news of General Lee's surrender at Appomattox Court House. Carolyn hoped that the letter in her hand would bring him much-needed cheer.

"It's from Julia!" She sat down on the footstool at his feet. "She's in the Bahama Islands! Oh, Papa! She's not dead—she's married! And a mother!"

"Lord have mercy!" Hettie laughed from the doorway.

A smile tweaked the corners of Jonah's tired mouth. "It's really Julia?" he asked, as if he had just awakened from a long nap. "Our Julia?" He had not said her name aloud in a long time. He rubbed his eyes. "Please read it for me, Carolyn. My eyes are a little sore."

71 Carolyn grinned at him. "It says, 'Dear Papa, Mother—' Oh! Julia doesn't know."

Hettie came into the room and stood near the doctor's chair. "How could she? Go on, child, read the good news," she prompted.

Carolyn nodded. "It says, 'Please forgive me for not writing to you sooner, but there was little chance of an assured mail delivery to you until now. I have had many adventures since I last saw you. Carolyn would just itch to know of them all.' Oh! She's said that just to tease me!"

Carolyn made a face as if her sister were standing in front of her. Then she continued, "'As Carolyn knows, I went to Richmond to find Major Montgomery. We left the city in February 1864, and were lucky enough to catch a blockade runner out of Wilmington, North Carolina.' Great balls of fire!" Carolyn whistled through her teeth.

Jonah leaned over. "Did you say Julia sailed on a blockade runner? But that was highly dangerous. I had no idea she was so brave."

Carolyn nodded. "It's not fair, Papa! Julia's had all the fun." After a stern look from Hettie, she picked up the narrative. "'To make a long story short—' Oh, Julia, I could just spit! You should have told it all, not just dangle it out there like catnip!"

Hettie smiled. "Maybe paper's scarce down there. So, what does she say about the islands? Do they really have palm trees there like I've seen in *Harper's Magazine?*"

Carolyn ran her finger along the lines to find her place. "'Rob and I were married on March 13, 1864, in a lovely church in Nassau Town. It's made out of coral blocks and is shaded by beautiful palm trees.'"

"There!" Hettie beamed. "I knew it! Palm trees for sure."

"Married." The doctor sat back in his chair. "Married in a proper church, too! Thank the good Lord for that!"

"I always thought that Major Montgomery was a proper gentleman," Hettie observed. "Go on, Miss Carolyn."

"'For reasons I will explain later, Rob and I were unable to return immediately to the United States. However, we *do* plan to come back in the spring!' Oh, Papa! Julia's coming home!"

Jonah looked up to Hettie. "I think a little sherry would be in order for all of us after Carolyn finishes the letter. Go on, my dear."

Carolyn could barely sit still. "'In the meantime, Rob has found employment as a lawyer and business here has been lively. I teach classes at a little school here for the English children. We live in a little pink house on the hillside overlooking the harbor.' A *pink* house! How delicious!" Carolyn smacked her lips. "Could you ever imagine such a thing?"

"And about the baby?" Hettie prompted.

"Oh, yes!" Carolyn skimmed through the letter. "Ah! 'Our little girl—' Oh, there's another girl in the family! '—was born on the 29th of July 1865. She is quite healthy, Papa, so you don't have to worry on that account. She has her father's dark hair, but my green eyes. She is just like you, Carolyn, always getting into mischief.' Good for her!" Carolyn cheered.

"Does this sweet child have a name?" Hettie inquired. A fond expression creased her dark face.

Carolyn giggled. "Oh, I'm sorry. I must have skipped that part. Here it is! 'We have named her Elizabeth Ross Montgomery.'"

Carolyn looked up at her father. "Papa, do we know anybody named Elizabeth or Ross?"

* * * * *

Author Note

One hundred and nine Union officers escaped from Libby Prison on that frosty night of February 9-10, 1864, making it the largest American POW breakout in military history. It was also the most successful. Two escapees drowned while trying to swim the swollen streams, forty-eight were recaptured, but fifty-nine men made it to freedom. Among the recaptured prisoners returned to Libby was "tunnel king" Colonel Thomas E. Rose of the 77th Pennsylvania Infantry. Rose immediately began plans for another escape, but his Confederate warders had had enough of his ingenuity. On April 30, 1864, he was exchanged for a Confederate colonel at City Point, Virginia.

While there is no record of a character like Robert Montgomery in Libby, the prisoners did have inside help in the person of the enigmatic Erasmus W. Ross, who was the civilian clerk under British protection. Very little is known about this man as he died soon after the end of the Civil War in the fire that destroyed the famous Spotswood Hotel in 1870. While Ross was remembered by the majority of the prisoners as an evil-tempered man, there are a few recorded incidents where he helped some of the prisoners to escape. Some scholars believe that Ross was a

Union spy in very deep cover who worked with Elizabeth Van Lew.

Miss Lizzie Van Lew was probably the most successful female undercover agent for the Union during the war. Her mansion on Grace Street really did have a secret room over the portico, and she was privy to the breakout plans. Also, she happened to be in the country with her brother on February 9th. After the war, Lizzie remained in Richmond where she was reviled by the population as a traitor to the Confederacy. When she died in 1900, at the advanced age of eighty-one, she was buried in an unmarked grave in Shockhoe Cemetery at the far northern edge of Richmond. When some of the Union veterans of Libby heard about Lizzie's death, they sent down a large granite boulder from Massachusetts with a bronze plaque inscribed with her name, dates and the old soldiers' fond sentiments. Her home was deliberately torn down during the 1920s, and today an elementary school occupies the site.

Libby Prison was also taken apart, not for demolition, but for exhibition at the Columbian Exposition at Chicago in 1892. The prison warehouse stayed in Chicago for several years after the Exposition, then it was disassembled once again and went on national tour. The train carrying the pieces was derailed in Indiana where an enterprising farmer bought the bricks and lumber, and used them to build a barn. In the 1960s, the barn was torn down during the Civil War Centennial, and the pieces dispersed. Occasionally parts of the old Libby Prison turn up at Civil War Collectors' Fairs and in antique barns.

Finally, I am deeply grateful to Carol Bessette, a Certified Master Tour Guide of Washington, D.C., for providing books, maps and a great perspective of Washington and Alexandria, Virginia, in 1864.

FALL IN LOVE WITH
FOUR HANDSOME HEROES
FROM HARLEQUIN HISTORICALS.

On sale May 2004

THE ENGAGEMENT
by Kate Bridges

Inspector Zack Bullock
North-West Mounted Police officer

HIGH COUNTRY HERO
by Lynna Banning

Cordell Lawson
Bounty hunter, loner

On sale June 2004

THE UNEXPECTED WIFE
by Mary Burton

Matthias Barrington
Widowed ranch owner

THE COURTING OF WIDOW SHAW
by Charlene Sands

Steven Harding
Nevada rancher

Visit us at www.eHarlequin.com

HARLEQUIN HISTORICALS®

HHWEST31

FALL IN LOVE
ALL OVER AGAIN
WITH
HARLEQUIN HISTORICALS

On Sale March 2004

THE NORMAN'S BRIDE
by Terri Brisbin

A mysterious mercenary saves the life of a beautiful young woman. When she cannot remember her past, is a future together possible?

RAKE'S REWARD
by Joanna Maitland

A spinster hires on as a wealthy dowager's companion but never imagines she'll be required to wager her virtue to a roguish gambler!

On Sale April 2004

WAYWARD WIDOW
by Nicola Cornick

An honorable man falls in love with a scandalous widow. Will he lure her from her wicked ways—straight into his heart?

NOT QUITE A LADY
by Margo Maguire

A beautiful innkeeper bewitches a man who doesn't believe in her special powers. Can she convince him that their love is magical?

Visit us at www.eHarlequin.com

HARLEQUIN HISTORICALS®

Savor these stirring tales of romance with Harlequin Historicals

On sale May 2004

THE LAST CHAMPION by Deborah Hale

Once betrothed, then torn apart by civil war, will Dominie de Montford put aside her pride and seek out Armand Flambard's help to save her estate from a vicious outlaw baron?

THE DUKE'S MISTRESS by Ann Elizabeth Cree

Years ago Lady Isabelle Milborne had participated in her late husband's wager, which had ruined Justin, the Duke of Westmore. And now the duke will stop at nothing to see justice served.

On sale June 2004

THE COUNTESS BRIDE by Terri Brisbin

A young count must marry a highborn lady in order to inherit his lands. But a poor young woman with a mysterious past is the only one he truly desires....

A POOR RELATION by Joanna Maitland

Desperate to avoid fortune hunters, Miss Isabella Winstanley poses as a penniless chaperone. But will she allow herself to be ensnared by the dashing Baron Amburley?

COMING NEXT MONTH FROM

HARLEQUIN HISTORICALS®

- **THE LAST CHAMPION**
  by **Deborah Hale,** author of BEAUTY AND THE BARON
  Though once betrothed, Armand Flambard and
  Dominie De Montford were now on opposite sides of the
  civil war raging in England. But when Dominie found herself
  in dire straits, Armand was the only man who could help her.
  Would they be able to put aside the pain of the past and find
  a love worth waiting for?
    HH #703 ISBN# 29303-8 $5.25 U.S./$6.25 CAN.

- **THE ENGAGEMENT**
  by **Kate Bridges,** author of THE SURGEON
  After his brother jilted Dr. Virginia Waters at the altar, mounted
  police officer Zack Bullock did the decent thing and offered a marriage of convenience…but then broke off the engagement when vil-
  lains threatened Virginia's life. And to make matters worse, Zack's
  commanding officer ordered him to act as the tempestuous beauty's
  bodyguard.…
    HH #704 ISBN# 29304-6 $5.25 U.S./$6.25 CAN.

- **THE DUKE'S MISTRESS**
  by **Ann Elizabeth Cree,** author of MY LADY'S PRISONER
  Three years ago Lady Isabelle Milborne had participated in
  a wager that had ruined Justin, the Duke of Westmore. Now Justin
  would stop at nothing to see justice served, but would he be content
  to have Belle as his mistress for just the Season, or would he need
  her in his life forever?
    HH #705 ISBN# 29305-4 $5.25 U.S./$6.25 CAN.

- **HIGH COUNTRY HERO**
  by **Lynna Banning,** author of THE SCOUT
  Bounty hunter Cordell Lawson needed a doctor to treat a wounded
  person stranded in an isolated cabin, and Sage Martin West was
  his only hope. As Sage and Cordell traveled to the victim, their
  attraction was nearly impossible to deny. Could the impulsive bounty
  hunter and the sensible, cautious doctor overcome their differences
  and find a lasting love?
    HH #706 ISBN# 29306-2 $5.25 U.S./$6.25 CAN.

KEEP AN EYE OUT FOR ALL FOUR
OF THESE TERRIFIC NEW TITLES

HHCNM04